FOREVER OD

Dean Koon
Pennsylvania.
one bestseller
and their dog

ALSO BY DEAN KOONTZ

The Taking
Odd Thomas
The Face
By the Light of the Moon
One Door Away From Heaven
From the Corner of His Eye
False Memory
Seize the Night
Fear Nothing
Mr. Murder
Dragon Tears
Hideaway
Cold Fire
The Bad Place
Midnight
Lightning
Watchers
Strangers
Twilight Eyes
Darkfall
Phantoms
Whispers
The Mask
The Vision
The Face of Fear
Night Chills
Shattered
The Voice of the Night
The Servants of Twilight
The House of Thunder
The Key to Midnight
The Eyes of Darkness
Shadowfires
Winter Moon
The Door to December
Dark Rivers of the Heart
Icebound
Strange Highways
Intensity
Sole Survivor
Ticktock
The Funhouse
Demon Seed
Life Expectancy

For automatic updates on Dean Koontz visit HarperCollins.co.uk and register for AuthorTracker

DEAN KOONTZ

Forever Odd

HarperCollins*Publishers*

HarperCollins*Publishers*
77–85 Fulham Palace Road,
Hammersmith, London W6 8JB

www.harpercollins.co.uk

This paperback edition 2006
1

First published in Great Britain by
HarperCollins*Publishers* 2005

A catalogue record for this book is available
from the British Library

ISBN 978–0–00–786629–8

Set in Meridien by
Palimpsest Book Production Limited,
Grangemouth, Stirlingshire

Printed and bound in Great Britain by
Clays Ltd, St Ives plc

This book is for Trixie, though she will never read it. On the most difficult days at the keyboard, when I despaired, she could always make me laugh. The words *good dog* are inadequate in her case. She is a good heart and a kind soul, and an angel on four feet.

Unearned suffering is redemptive.

—Martin Luther King Jr.

Look at those hands, Oh God, those hands toiled to raise me.

—Elvis Presley at his mother's casket

1

WAKING, I HEARD A WARM WIND STRUMMING the loose screen at the open window, and I thought *Stormy,* but it was not.

The desert air smelled faintly of roses, which were not in bloom, and of dust, which in the Mojave flourishes twelve months of the year.

Precipitation falls on the town of Pico Mundo only during our brief winter. This mild February night was not, however, sweetened by the scent of rain.

I hoped to hear the fading rumble of thunder. If a peal had awakened me, it must have been thunder in a dream.

Holding my breath, I lay listening to the silence, and felt the silence listening to me.

The nightstand clock painted glowing numbers on the gloom—2:41 A.M.

For a moment I considered remaining in bed. But these days I do not sleep as well as I did when

I was young. I am twenty-one and much older than when I was twenty.

Certain that I had company, expecting to find two Elvises watching over me, one with a cocky smile and one with sad concern, I sat up and switched on the lamp.

A single Elvis stood in a corner: a life-size cardboard figure that had been part of a theater-lobby display for *Blue Hawaii.* In a Hawaiian shirt and a lei, he looked self-confident and happy.

Back in 1961, he'd had much to be happy about. *Blue Hawaii* was a hit film, and the album went to number one. He had six gold records that year, including "Can't Help Falling in Love," and he was falling in love with Priscilla Beaulieu.

Less happily, at the insistence of his manager, Tom Parker, he had turned down the lead in *West Side Story* in favor of mediocre movie fare like *Follow That Dream.* Gladys Presley, his beloved mother, had been dead three years, and still he felt the loss of her, acutely. Only twenty-six, he'd begun to have weight problems.

Cardboard Elvis smiles eternally, forever young, incapable of error or regret, untouched by grief, a stranger to despair.

I envy him. There is no cardboard replica of me as I once was and as I can never be again.

The lamplight revealed another presence, as patient as he was desperate. Evidently he had been watching me sleep, waiting for me to wake.

I said, "Hello, Dr. Jessup."

Dr. Wilbur Jessup was incapable of a response. Anguish flooded his face. His eyes were desolate pools; all hope had drowned in those lonely depths.

"I'm sorry to see you here," I said.

He made fists of his hands, not with the intention of striking anything, but as an expression of frustration. He pressed his fists to his chest.

Dr. Jessup had never previously visited my apartment; and I knew in my heart that he no longer belonged in Pico Mundo. But I clung to denial, and I spoke to him again as I got out of bed.

"Did I leave the door unlocked?"

He shook his head. Tears blurred his eyes, but he did not wail or even whimper.

Fetching a pair of jeans from the closet, slipping into them, I said, "I've been forgetful lately."

He opened his fists and stared at his palms. His hands trembled. He buried his face in them.

"There's so much I'd like to forget," I continued as I pulled on socks and shoes, "but only the small stuff slips my mind—like where I left the keys, whether I locked the door, that I'm out of milk. . . ."

Dr. Jessup, a radiologist at County General Hospital, was a gentle man, and quiet, although he had never before been *this* quiet.

Because I had not worn a T-shirt to bed, I plucked a white one from a drawer.

I have a few black T-shirts, but mostly white. In addition to a selection of blue jeans, I have two pair of white chinos.

This apartment provides only a small closet. Half of it is empty. So are the bottom drawers of my dresser.

I do not own a suit. Or a tie. Or shoes that need to be shined.

For cool weather, I own two crew-neck sweaters.

Once I bought a sweater vest. Temporary insanity. Realizing that I had introduced an unthinkable level of complexity to my wardrobe, I returned it to the store the next day.

My four-hundred-pound friend and mentor, P. Oswald Boone, has warned me that my sartorial style represents a serious threat to the apparel industry.

I've noted more than once that the articles in Ozzie's wardrobe are of such enormous dimensions that he keeps in business those fabric mills I might otherwise put in jeopardy.

Barefoot, Dr. Jessup wore cotton pajamas. They were wrinkled from the rigors of restless sleep.

"Sir, I wish you'd say something," I told him. "I really wish you would."

Instead of obliging me, the radiologist lowered his hands from his face, turned, and walked out of the bedroom.

I glanced at the wall above the bed. Framed behind glass is a card from a carnival fortune-telling machine. It promises YOU ARE DESTINED TO BE TOGETHER FOREVER.

Each morning, I begin my day by reading those seven words. Each night, I read them again, sometimes more than once, before sleep, if sleep will come to me.

I am sustained by the certainty that life has meaning. As does death.

From a nightstand, I retrieved my cell phone. The first number on speed dial is the office of Wyatt Porter, chief of the Pico Mundo Police Department. The second is his home number. The third is his cell phone.

More likely than not, I would be calling Chief Porter, one place or another, before dawn.

In the living room, I turned on a light and discovered that Dr. Jessup had been standing in the dark, among the thrift-shop treasures with which the place is furnished.

When I went to the front door and opened it, he did not follow. Although he had sought my assistance, he couldn't find the courage for what lay ahead.

In the rubescent light from an old bronze lamp with a beaded shade, the eclectic decor—Stickley-style armchairs, plump Victorian footstools, Maxfield Parrish prints, carnival-glass vases—evidently appealed to him.

"No offense," I said, "but you don't belong here, sir."

Dr. Jessup silently regarded me with what might have been supplication.

"This place is filled to the brim with the past. There's room for Elvis and me, and memories, but not for anyone new."

I stepped into the public hall and pulled the door shut.

My apartment is one of two on the first floor of a converted Victorian house. Once a rambling single-family home, the place still offers considerable charm.

For years I lived in one rented room above a garage. My bed had been just a few steps from my refrigerator. Life was simpler then, and the future clear.

I traded that place for this not because I needed more space, but because my heart is here now, and forever.

The front door of the house featured an oval of leaded glass. The night beyond looked sharply beveled and organized into a pattern that anyone could understand.

When I stepped onto the porch, this night proved to be like all others: deep, mysterious, trembling with the potential for chaos.

From porch steps to flagstone path, to public sidewalk, I looked around for Dr. Jessup but didn't see him.

In the high desert, which rises far east beyond Pico Mundo, winter can be chilly, while our low-desert nights remain mild even in February. The curbside Indian laurels sighed and whispered in the balmy wind, and moths soared to street lamps.

The surrounding houses were as quiet as their windows were dark. No dogs barked. No owls hooted.

No pedestrians were out, no traffic on the streets. The town looked as if the Rapture had occurred, as if only I had been left behind to endure the reign of Hell on Earth.

By the time I reached the corner, Dr. Jessup rejoined me. His pajamas and the lateness of the hour suggested that he had come to my apartment from his home on Jacaranda Way, five blocks north in a better neighborhood than mine. Now he led me in that direction.

He could fly, but he plodded. I ran, drawing ahead of him.

Although I dreaded what I would find no less than he might have dreaded revealing it to me, I wanted to get to it quickly. As far as I knew, a life might still be in jeopardy.

Halfway there, I realized that I could have taken the Chevy. For most of my driving life, having no car of my own, I borrowed from friends as needed. The previous autumn, I had inherited a 1980 Chevrolet Camaro Berlinetta Coupe.

Often I still act as though I have no wheels.

Owning a few thousand pounds of vehicle oppresses me when I think about it too much. Because I try not to think about it, I sometimes forget I have it.

Under the cratered face of the blind moon, I ran.

On Jacaranda Way, the Jessup residence is a white-brick Georgian with elegant ornamentation. It is flanked by a delightful American Victorian with so many decorative moldings that it resembles a wedding cake, and by a house that is baroque in all the wrong ways.

None of these architectural styles seems right for the desert, shaded by palm trees, brightened by climbing bougainvillea. Our town was founded in 1900 by newcomers from the East Coast, who fled the harsh winters but brought with them cold-climate architecture and attitude.

Terri Stambaugh, my friend and employer, owner of the Pico Mundo Grille, tells me that this displaced architecture is better than the dreary acres of stucco and graveled roofs in many California desert towns.

I assume that she is right. I have seldom crossed the city line of Pico Mundo and have never been beyond the boundaries of Maravilla County.

My life is too full to allow either a jaunt or a journey. I don't even watch the Travel Channel.

The joys of life can be found anywhere. Far places only offer exotic ways to suffer.

Besides, the world beyond Pico Mundo is haunted by strangers, and I find it difficult enough to cope with the dead who, in life, were known to me.

Upstairs and down, soft lamplight shone at some windows of the Jessup residence. Most panes were dark.

By the time I reached the foot of the front-porch steps, Dr. Wilbur Jessup waited there.

The wind stirred his hair and ruffled his pajamas, although why he should be subject to the wind, I do not know. The moonlight found him, too, and shadow.

The grieving radiologist needed comforting before he could summon sufficient strength to lead me into his house, where he himself no doubt lay dead, and perhaps another.

I embraced him. Only a spirit, he was invisible to everyone but me, yet he felt warm and solid.

Perhaps I see the dead affected by the weather of this world, and see them touched by light and shadow, and find them as warm as the living, not because this is the way they are but because this is the way I want them to be. Perhaps by this device, I mean to deny the power of death.

My supernatural gift might reside not in my mind but instead in my heart. The heart is an artist that paints over what profoundly disturbs it, leaving on the canvas a less dark, less sharp version of the truth.

Dr. Jessup had no substance, but he leaned heavily upon me, a weight. He shook with the sobs that he could not voice.

The dead don't talk. Perhaps they know things about death that the living are not permitted to learn from them.

In this moment, my ability to speak gave me no advantage. Words would not soothe him.

Nothing but justice could relieve his anguish. Perhaps not even justice.

When he'd been alive, he had known me as Odd Thomas, a local character. I am regarded by some people—wrongly—as a hero, as an eccentric by nearly everyone.

Odd is not a nickname; it's my legal handle.

The story of my name is interesting, I suppose, but I've told it before. What it boils down to is that my parents are dysfunctional. Big-time.

I believe that in life Dr. Jessup had found me intriguing, amusing, puzzling. I think he had liked me.

Only in death did he know me for what I am: a companion to the lingering dead.

I see them and wish I did not. I cherish life too much to turn the dead away, however, for they deserve my compassion by virtue of having suffered this world.

When Dr. Jessup stepped back from me, he had changed. His wounds were now manifest.

He had been hit in the face with a blunt object,

maybe a length of pipe or a hammer. Repeatedly. His skull was broken, his features distorted.

Torn, cracked, splintered, his hands suggested that he had desperately tried to defend himself—or that he had come to the aid of someone. The only person living with him was his son, Danny.

My pity was quickly exceeded by a kind of righteous rage, which is a dangerous emotion, clouding judgment, precluding caution.

In this condition, which I do not seek, which frightens me, which comes over me as though I have been possessed, I can't turn away from what must be done. I plunge.

My friends, those few who know my secrets, think my compulsion has a divine inspiration. Maybe it's just temporary insanity.

Step to step, ascending, then crossing the porch, I considered phoning Chief Wyatt Porter. I worried, however, that Danny might perish while I placed the call and waited for the authorities.

The front door stood ajar.

I glanced back and saw that Dr. Jessup preferred to haunt the yard instead of the house. He lingered in the grass.

His wounds had vanished. He appeared as he had appeared before Death had found him—and he looked scared.

Until they move on from this world, even the dead can know fear. You would think they have nothing to lose, but sometimes they are wretched with anxiety, not about what might lie Beyond, but about those whom they have left behind.

I pushed the door inward. It moved as smoothly, as silently as the mechanism of a well-crafted, spring-loaded trap.

2

FROSTED FLAME-SHAPED BULBS IN SILVER-plated sconces revealed white paneled doors, all closed, along a hallway, and stairs rising into darkness.

Honed instead of polished, the marble floor of the foyer was cloud-white, looked cloud-soft. The ruby, teal, and sapphire Persian rug seemed to float like a magic taxi waiting for a passenger with a taste for adventure.

I crossed the threshold, and the cloud floor supported me. The rug idled underfoot.

In such a situation, closed doors usually draw me. Over the years, I have a few times endured a dream in which, during a search, I open a white paneled door and am skewered through the throat by something sharp, cold, and as thick as an iron fence stave.

Always, I wake before I die, gagging as if still impaled. After that, I am usually up for the day, no matter how early the hour.

My dreams aren't reliably prophetic. I have never, for instance, ridden bareback on an elephant, naked, while having sexual relations with Jennifer Aniston.

Seven years have passed since I had that memorable night fantasy as a boy of fourteen. After so much time, I no longer have any expectation that the Aniston dream will prove predictive.

I'm pretty sure the scenario with the white paneled door will come to pass. I can't say whether I will be merely wounded, disabled for life, or killed.

You might think that when presented with white paneled doors, I would avoid them. And so I would . . . if I had not learned that fate cannot be sidestepped or outrun. The price I paid for that lesson has left my heart an almost empty purse, with just two coins or three clinking at the bottom.

I prefer to kick open each door and confront what waits rather than to turn away—and thereafter be required to remain alert, at all times, for the creak of the turning knob, for the quiet rasp of hinges behind my back.

On this occasion, the doors did not attract me. Intuition led me to the stairs, and swiftly up.

The dark second-floor hallway was brightened only by the pale outfall of light from two rooms.

I've had no dreams about open doors. I went

to the first of these two without hesitation, and stepped into a bedroom.

The blood of violence daunts even those with much experience of it. The splash, the spray, the drip and drizzle create infinite Rorschach patterns in every one of which the observer reads the same meaning: the fragility of his existence, the truth of his mortality.

A desperation of crimson hand prints on a wall were the victim's sign language: *Spare me, help me, remember me, avenge me.*

On the floor, near the foot of the bed, lay the body of Dr. Wilbur Jessup, savagely battered.

Even for one who *knows* that the body is but the vessel and that the spirit is the essence, a brutalized cadaver depresses, offends.

This world, which has the potential to be Eden, is instead the hell before Hell. In our arrogance, we have made it so.

The door to the adjacent bathroom stood half open. I nudged it with one foot.

Although blood-dimmed by a drenched shade, the bedroom lamplight reached into the bathroom to reveal no surprises.

Aware that this was a crime scene, I touched nothing. I stepped cautiously, with respect for evidence.

Some wish to believe that greed is the root of murder, but greed seldom motivates a killer. Most homicide has the same dreary cause: The bloody-minded murder those whom they envy, and for what they covet.

That is not merely a central tragedy of human existence: It is also the political history of the world.

Common sense, not psychic power, told me that in this case, the killer coveted the happy marriage that, until recently, Dr. Jessup had enjoyed. Fourteen years previously, the radiologist had wed Carol Makepeace. They had been perfect for each other.

Carol came into their marriage with a seven-year-old son, Danny. Dr. Jessup adopted him.

Danny had been a friend of mine since we were six, when we had discovered a mutual interest in Monster Gum trading cards. I traded him a Martian brain-eating centipede for a Venusian methane slime beast, which bonded us on first encounter and ensured a lifelong brotherly affection.

We've also been drawn close by the fact that we are different, each in his way, from other people. I see the lingering dead, and Danny has osteogenesis imperfecta, also called brittle bones.

Our lives have been defined—and deformed—by our afflictions. My deformations are primarily social; his are largely physical.

A year ago, Carol had died of cancer. Now Dr. Jessup was gone, too, and Danny was alone.

I left the master bedroom and hurried quietly

along the hallway toward the back of the house. Passing two closed rooms, heading toward the open door that was the second source of light, I worried about leaving unsearched spaces behind me.

After once having made the mistake of watching television news, I had worried for a while about an asteroid hitting the earth and wiping out human civilization. The anchorwoman had said it was not merely possible but probable. At the end of the report, she smiled.

I worried about that asteroid until I realized I couldn't do anything to stop it. I am not Superman. I am a short-order cook on a leave of absence from his grill and griddle.

For a longer while, I worried about the TV news lady. What kind of person can deliver such terrifying news—and then smile?

If I ever did open a white paneled door and get skewered through the throat, the iron pike—or whatever—would probably be wielded by that anchorwoman.

I reached the next open door, stepped into the light, crossed the threshold. No victim, no killer.

The things we worry about the most are never the things that bite us. The sharpest teeth always take their nip of us when we are looking the other way.

Unquestionably, this was Danny's room. On the wall behind the disheveled bed hung a poster of John Merrick, the real-life Elephant Man.

Danny had a sense of humor about the deformities—mostly of the limbs—with which his condition had left him. He looked nothing like Merrick, but the Elephant Man was his hero.

They exhibited him as a freak, Danny once explained. *Women fainted at the sight of him, children wept, tough men flinched. He was loathed and reviled. Yet a century later a movie was based on his life, and we know his name. Who knows the name of the bastard who owned him and put him on exhibit, or the names of those who fainted or wept, or flinched? They're dust, and he's immortal. Besides, when he went out in public, that hooded cloak he wore was way cool.*

On other walls were four posters of ageless sex goddess Demi Moore, who was currently more ravishing than ever in a series of Versace ads.

Twenty-one years old, two inches short of the five feet that he claimed, twisted by the abnormal bone growth that sometimes had occurred during the healing of his frequent fractures, Danny lived small but dreamed big.

No one stabbed me when I stepped into the hall once more. I wasn't expecting anyone to stab me, but that's when it's likely to happen.

If Mojave wind still whipped the night, I couldn't hear it inside this thick-walled Georgian structure, which seemed tomblike in its stillness, in its conditioned chill, with a faint scent of blood on the cool air.

I dared not any longer delay calling Chief Porter. Standing in the upstairs hall, I pressed 2 on my cell-phone keypad and speed-dialed his home.

When he answered on the second ring, he sounded awake.

Alert for the approach of a mad anchorwoman or worse, I spoke softly: "Sir, I'm sorry if I woke you."

"Wasn't asleep. I've been sitting here with Louis L'Amour."

"The writer? I thought he was dead, sir."

"About as dead as Dickens. Tell me you're just lonesome, son, and not in trouble again."

"I didn't *ask* for trouble, sir. But you better come to Dr. Jessup's house."

"I'm hoping it's a simple burglary."

"Murder," I said. "Wilbur Jessup on the floor of his bedroom. It's a bad one."

"Where's Danny?"

"I'm thinking kidnapped."

"Simon," he said.

Simon Makepeace—Carol's first husband, Danny's father—had been released from prison four months ago, after serving sixteen years for manslaughter.

"Better come with some force," I said. "And quiet."

"Someone still there?"

"I get the feeling."

"You hold back, Odd."

"You know I can't."

"I don't understand your compulsion."

"Neither do I, sir."

I pressed END and pocketed the cell phone.

3

ASSUMING THAT DANNY MUST BE STILL nearby and under duress, and that he was most likely on the ground floor, I headed toward the front stairs. Before I began to descend, I found myself turning and retracing the route that I'd just followed.

I expected that I would return to the two closed doors on the right side of the hall, between the master bedroom and Danny's room, and that I would discover what lay behind them. As before, however, I wasn't drawn to them.

On the left side were three other closed doors. None of those had an attraction for me, either.

In addition to the ability to see ghosts, a gift I'd happily trade for piano artistry or a talent for flower arranging, I've been given what I call psychic magnetism.

When someone isn't where I expect to find him, I can go for a walk or ride my bicycle, or cruise in a car, keeping his name or face in my mind, turning randomly from one street to another; and sometimes in minutes, sometimes in an hour, I encounter the one I'm seeking. It's like setting a pair of those Scottie-dog magnets on a table and watching them slide inexorably toward each other.

The key word is *sometimes.*

On occasion, my psychic magnetism functions like the finest Cartier watch. At other times, it's like an egg timer bought at a cheap discount store's going-out-of-business sale; you set it for poached, and it gives you hard-boiled.

The unreliability of this gift is not proof that God is either cruel or indifferent, though it might be one proof among many that He has a sense of humor.

The fault lies with me. I can't stay sufficiently relaxed to let the gift work. I get distracted: in this case, by the possibility that Simon Makepeace, in willful disregard of his surname, would throw open a door, leap into the hallway, and bludgeon me to death.

I continued through the lamplight that spilled from Danny's room, where Demi Moore still looked luminous and the Elephant Man still looked pachydermous. I paused in the gloom at an intersection with a second, shorter hallway.

This was a big house. It had been built in 1910

by an immigrant from Philadelphia, who had made a fortune in either cream cheese or gelignite. I can never remember which.

Gelignite is a high explosive consisting of a gelatinized mass of nitroglycerin with cellulose nitrate added. In the first decade of the previous century, they called it gelatin dynamite, and it was quite the rage in those circles where they took a special interest in blowing up things.

Cream cheese is cream cheese. It's delicious in a wide variety of dishes, but it rarely explodes.

I would like to have a firmer grasp of local history, but I've never been able to devote as much time to the study of it as I have wished. Dead people keep distracting me.

Now I turned left into the secondary hallway, which was black but not pitch. At the end, pale radiance revealed the open door at the head of the back stairs.

The stairwell light itself wasn't on. The glow rose from below.

In addition to rooms and closets on both sides, which I had no impulse to search, I passed an elevator. This hydraulic-ram lift had been installed prior to Wilbur and Carol's wedding, before Danny—then a child of seven—had moved into the house.

If you are afflicted with osteogenesis imperfecta, you can occasionally break a bone with remarkably little effort. When six, Danny had fractured his right wrist while snap-dealing a game of Old Maid.

Stairs, therefore, pose an especially grave risk. As a child, at least, if he had fallen down a flight of stairs, he would most likely have died from severe skull fractures.

Although I had no fear of falling, the back stairs spooked me. They were spiral and enclosed, so it wasn't possible to see more than a few steps ahead.

Intuition told me someone waited down there.

As an alternative to the stairs, the elevator would be too noisy. Alerted, Simon Makepeace would be waiting when I arrived below.

I could not retreat. I was compelled to go down—and quickly—into the back rooms of the lower floor.

Before I quite realized what I was doing, I pushed the elevator-call button. I snatched my finger back as though I'd pricked it on a needle.

The doors did not at once slide open. The elevator was on the lower floor.

As the motor hummed to life, as the hydraulic mechanism sighed, as the cab rose through the shaft with a faint swish, I realized that I had a plan. Good for me.

In truth, the word *plan* was too grandiose. What I had was more of a trick, a diversion.

The elevator arrived with a *bink* so loud in the

silent house that I twitched, though I had expected that sound. When the doors slid open, I tensed, but no one lunged out at me.

I leaned into the cab and pushed the button to send it back to the ground floor.

Even as the doors rolled shut, I hurried to the staircase and rushed blindly down. The value of the diversion would diminish to zero when the cab arrived below, for then Simon would discover that I wasn't, after all, on board.

The claustrophobia-inducing stairs led into a mud room off the kitchen. Although a stone-floored mud room might have been essential in Philadelphia, with that city's dependably rainy springs and its snowy winters, a residence in the sun-seared Mojave needed it no more than it needed a snowshoe rack.

At least it wasn't a storeroom full of gelignite.

From the mud room, one door led to the garage, another to the backyard. A third served the kitchen.

The house had not originally been designed to have an elevator. The remodel contractor had been forced to situate it, not ideally, in a corner of the large kitchen.

No sooner had I arrived in the mud room, dizzy from negotiating the tight curve of the spiral staircase, than a *bink* announced the arrival of the cab on the ground floor.

I snatched up a broom, as though I might be

able to sweep a murderous psychopath off his feet. At best, surprising him by jamming the bristles into his face might damage his eyes and startle him off balance.

The broom wasn't as comforting as a flamethrower would have been, but it was better than a mop and certainly more threatening than a feather duster.

Positioning myself by the door to the kitchen, I prepared to take Simon off his feet when he burst into the mud room in search of me. He didn't burst.

After what seemed to be enough time to paint the gray walls a more cheerful color, but what was in reality maybe fifteen seconds, I glanced at the door to the garage. Then at the door to the backyard.

I wondered if Simon Makepeace had already forced Danny out of the house. They might be in the garage, Simon behind the wheel of Dr. Jessup's car, Danny bound and helpless in the backseat.

Or maybe they were headed across the yard, toward the gate in the fence. Simon might have a vehicle of his own in the alleyway behind the property.

I felt inclined, instead, to push through the swinging door and step into the kitchen.

Only the under-the-cabinet lights were on, illuminating the countertops around the perimeter of the room. Nevertheless, I could see that I was alone.

Regardless of what I could see, I sensed a presence. Someone could have been crouched, hiding on the farther side of the large center work island.

Fierce with broom, gripping it like a cudgel, I cautiously circled the room. The gleaming mahogany floor pealed soft squeaks off my rubber-soled shoes.

When I had rounded three-quarters of the island, I heard the elevator doors roll open behind me.

I spun around to discover not Simon, but a stranger. He'd been waiting for the elevator, and when I hadn't been in it, as he had expected, he'd realized that it was a ruse. He'd been quick-witted, hiding in the cab immediately before I entered from the mud room.

He was sinuous and full of coiled power. His green gaze shone bright with terrible knowledge; these were the eyes of one who knew the many ways out of the Garden. His scaly lips formed the curve of a perfect lie: a smile in which malice tried to pass as friendly intent, in which amusement was in fact dripping venom.

Before I could think of a serpent metaphor to describe his nose, the snaky bastard struck. He squeezed the trigger of a Taser, firing two darts that, trailing thin wires, pierced my T-shirt and delivered a disabling shock.

I fell like a high-flying witch suddenly deprived of her magic: hard, and with a useless broom.

4

WHEN YOU TAKE MAYBE FIFTY THOUSAND volts from a Taser, some time has to pass before you feel like dancing.

On the floor, doing a broken-cockroach imitation, twitching violently, robbed of basic motor control, I tried to scream but wheezed instead.

A flash of pain and then a persistent hot pulse traced every nerve pathway in my body with such authority that I could see them in my mind's eye as clearly as highways on a road map.

I cursed my attacker, but the invective issued as a whimper. I sounded like an anxious gerbil.

He loomed over me, and I expected to be stomped. He was a guy who would enjoy stomping. If he wasn't wearing hobnail boots, that was only because they were at the cobbler's shop for the addition of toe spikes.

My arms flopped, my hands spasmed. I couldn't cover my face.

He spoke, but his words meant nothing, sounded like the sputter and crackle of short-circuiting wires.

When he picked up the broom, I knew from the way he held it that he intended to drive the blunt metal handle into my face repeatedly, until the Elephant Man, compared to me, would look like a *GQ* model.

He raised that witchy weapon high. Before he slammed it into my face, however, he turned abruptly away, looking toward the front of the house.

Evidently he heard something that changed his priorities, for he threw the broom aside. He split through the mud room and no doubt left the house by the back door.

A persistent buzzing in my ears prevented me from hearing what my assailant had heard, but I assumed that Chief Porter had arrived with deputies. I had told him that Dr. Jessup lay dead in the master bedroom on the second floor; but he would order a by-the-book search of the entire house.

I was anxious not to be found there.

In the Pico Mundo Police Department, only the chief knows about my gifts. If I am ever again the first on the scene of a crime, a lot of deputies will wonder about me more than they do already.

The likelihood was small to nonexistent that

any of them would leap to the conclusion that sometimes the dead come to me for justice. Still, I didn't want to take any chances.

My life is already *muy* strange and so complex that I keep a grip on sanity only by maintaining a minimalist lifestyle. I don't travel. I walk almost everywhere. I don't party. I don't follow the news or fashion. I have no interest in politics. I don't plan for the future. My only job has been as a short-order cook, since I left home at sixteen. Recently I took a leave of absence from that position because even the challenge of making sufficiently fluffy pancakes and BLTs with the proper crunch seemed too taxing on top of all my other problems.

If the world knew what I am, what I can see and do, thousands would be at my door tomorrow. The grieving. The remorseful. The suspicious. The hopeful. The faithful. The skeptics.

They would want me to be a medium between them and their lost loved ones, would insist that I play detective in every unsolved murder case. Some would wish to venerate me, and others would seek to prove that I was a fraud.

I don't know how I could turn away the bereft, the hopeful. In the event that I learned to do so, I'm not sure I'd like the person I would have become.

Yet if I could turn no one away, they would wear me down with their love and their hate.

They would grind me on their wheels of need until I had been reduced to dust.

Now, afraid of being found in Dr. Jessup's house, I flopped, twitched, and scrabbled across the floor. No longer in severe pain, I was not yet fully in control of myself, either.

As if I were Jack in the giant's kitchen, the knob on the pantry door appeared to be twenty feet above me. With rubbery legs and arms still spastic, I don't know how I reached it, but I did.

I've a long list of things I don't know how I've done, but I've done them. In the end, it's always about perseverance.

Once in the pantry, I pulled the door shut behind me. This close dark space reeked of pungent chemical scents the likes of which I had never before smelled.

The taste of scorched aluminum made me half nauseous. I'd never previously tasted scorched aluminum; so I don't know how I recognized it, but I felt sure that's what it was.

Inside my skull, a Frankenstein laboratory of arcing electrical currents snapped and sizzled. Overloaded resistors hummed.

Most likely my senses of smell and taste weren't reliable. The Taser had temporarily scrambled them.

Detecting a wetness on my chin, I assumed blood. After further consideration, I realized I was drooling.

During a thorough search of the house, the pantry would not be overlooked. I'd only gained a minute or two in which to warn Chief Porter.

Never before had the function of a simple pants pocket proved too complicated for me to understand. You put things in, you take things out.

Now for the longest time, I couldn't get my hand into my jeans pocket; someone seemed to have sewn it shut. Once I finally got my hand in, I couldn't get it back out. At last I extracted my hand from the clutching pocket, but discovered that I'd failed to bring my cell phone with it.

Just when the bizarre chemical odors began to resolve into the familiar scents of potatoes and onions, I regained possession of the phone and flipped it open. Still drooling but with pride, I pressed and held 3, speed-dialing the chief's mobile number.

If he was personally engaged in the search of the house, he most likely wouldn't stop to answer his cell phone.

"I assume that's you," Wyatt Porter said.

"Sir, yes, right here."

"You sound funny."

"Don't feel funny. Feel Tasered."

"Say what?"

"Say Tasered. Bad guy buzzed me."

"Where are you?"

"Hiding in the pantry."

"Not good."

"It's better than explaining myself."

The chief is protective of me. He's as concerned as I am that I avoid the misery of public exposure.

"This is a terrible scene here," he said.

"Yes, sir."

"Terrible. Dr. Jessup was a good man. You just wait there."

"Sir, Simon might be moving Danny out of town right now."

"I've got both highways blocked."

There were only two ways out of Pico Mundo—three, if you counted death.

"Sir, what if someone opens the pantry door?"

"Try to look like canned goods."

He hung up, and I switched off my phone.

I sat there in the dark awhile, trying not to think, but that never works. Danny came into my mind. He might not be dead yet, but wherever he was, he was not anywhere good.

As had been true of his mother, he lived with an affliction that gravely endangered him. Danny had brittle bones; his mother had been pretty.

Simon Makepeace most likely wouldn't have been obsessed with Carol if she had been ugly or even plain. He wouldn't have killed a man over her, for sure. Counting Dr. Jessup, two men.

I had been alone in the pantry up to this point.

Although the door didn't open, I suddenly had company.

A hand clasped my shoulder, but that didn't startle me. I knew my visitor had to be Dr. Jessup, dead and restless.

5

DR. JESSUP HAD BEEN NO DANGER TO ME when he was alive, nor was he a threat now.

Occasionally, a poltergeist—which is a ghost who can energize his anger—is able to do damage, but they're usually just frustrated, not genuinely malicious. They feel they have unfinished business in this world, and they are people for whom death has not diminished the stubbornness that characterized them in life.

The spirits of thoroughly evil people do not hang around for extended periods of time, wreaking havoc and murdering the living. That's pure Hollywood.

The spirits of evil people usually leave quickly, as though they have an appointment, upon death, with someone whom they dare not keep waiting.

Dr. Jessup had probably passed through the pantry door as easily as rain through smoke. Even walls were no barrier to him anymore.

When he took his hand off my shoulder, I assumed that he would settle on the floor, cross-legged Indian style, as I was sitting, and evidently he did. He faced me in the dark, which I knew when he reached out and gripped my hands.

If he couldn't have his life back, he wanted reassurance. He did not have to speak to convey to me what he needed.

"I'll do my best for Danny," I said too softly to be heard beyond the pantry.

I did not intend my words to be taken as a guarantee. I haven't earned that level of confidence from anyone.

"The hard truth is," I continued, "my best might not be good enough. It hasn't always been enough before."

His grip on my hands tightened.

My regard for him was such that I wanted to encourage him to let go of this world and accept the grace that death offered him.

"Sir, everyone knows you were a good husband to Carol. But they might not realize just how very good a father you were to Danny."

The longer a liberated spirit lingers, the more likely he will get stuck here.

"You were so kind to take on a seven-year-old with such medical problems. And you always made him feel that you were proud of him, proud of how he suffered without complaint, his courage."

By virtue of the way that he had lived, Dr. Jessup had no reason to fear moving on. Remaining here, on the other hand—a mute observer incapable of affecting events—guaranteed his misery.

"He loves you, Dr. Jessup. He thinks of you as his real father, his only father."

I was thankful for the absolute darkness and for his ghostly silence. By now I should be somewhat armored against the grief of others and against the piercing regret of those who meet untimely deaths and must leave without goodbyes, yet year by year I become more vulnerable to both.

"You know how Danny is," I continued. "A tough little customer. Always the wisecrack. But I know what he really feels. And surely you know what you meant to Carol. She seemed to *shine* with love for you."

For a while I matched his silence. If you push them too hard, they clutch up, even panic.

In that condition, they can no longer see the way from here to there, the bridge, the door, whatever it is.

I gave him time to absorb what I'd said. Then: "You've done so much of what you were put here to do, and you did it well, you got it right. That's all we can expect—the chance to get it right."

After another mutual silence, he let go of my hands.

Just as I lost touch with Dr. Jessup, the pantry door opened. Kitchen light dissolved the darkness, and Chief Wyatt Porter loomed over me.

He is big, round-shouldered, with a long face. People who can't read the chief's true nature in his eyes might think he's steeped in sadness.

As I got to my feet, I realized that the residual effects of the Taser had not entirely worn off. Phantom electrical sounds sizzled inside my head again.

Dr. Jessup had departed. Maybe he had gone on to the next world. Maybe he had returned to haunting the front yard.

"How do you feel?" the chief asked, stepping back from the pantry.

"Fried."

"Tasers don't do real harm."

"You smell burnt hair?"

"No. Was it Makepeace?"

"Not him," I said, moving into the kitchen. "Some snaky guy. You find Danny?"

"He's not here."

"I didn't think so."

"The way's clear. Go to the alley."

"I'll go to the alley," I said.

"Wait at the tree of death."

"I'll wait at the tree of death."

"Son, are you all right?"

"My tongue itches."

"You can scratch it while you wait for me."

"Thank you, sir."

"Odd?"

"Sir?"

"Go."

6

THE TREE OF DEATH STANDS ACROSS THE alley and down the block from the Jessup place, in the backyard of the Ying residence.

In the summer and autumn, the thirty-five-foot brugmansia is festooned with pendant yellow trumpet flowers. At times, more than a hundred blooms, perhaps two hundred, each ten to twelve inches long, depend from its branches.

Mr. Ying enjoys lecturing on the deadly nature of the lovely brugmansia. Every part of the tree—roots, wood, bark, leaves, calyxes, flowers—is toxic.

One shred of its foliage will induce bleeding from the nose, bleeding from the ears, bleeding from the eyes, and explosive terminal diarrhea. Within a minute, your teeth will fall out, your tongue will turn black, and your brain will begin to liquefy.

Perhaps that is an exaggeration. When Mr. Ying

first told me about the tree, I was a boy of eight, and that is the impression I got from his disquisition on brugmansia poisoning.

Why Mr. Ying—and his wife as well—should take such pride in having planted and grown the tree of death, I do not know.

Ernie and Pooka Ying are Asian Americans, but there's nothing in the least Fu Manchu about them. They're too amiable to devote any time whatsoever to evil scientific experiments in a vast secret laboratory carved out of the bedrock deep beneath their house.

Even if they have developed the capability to destroy the world, I for one cannot picture anyone named Pooka pulling the GO lever on a doomsday machine.

The Yings attend Mass at St. Bartholomew's. He's a member of the Knights of Columbus. She donates ten hours each week to the church thrift shop.

The Yings go to the movies a lot, and Ernie is notoriously sentimental, weeping during the death scenes, the love scenes, the patriotic scenes. He once even wept when Bruce Willis was unexpectedly shot in the arm.

Yet year after year, through three decades of marriage, while they adopted and raised two orphans, they diligently fertilized the tree of death, watered it, pruned it, sprayed it to ward off spider mite and whitefly. They replaced their back porch with a much larger redwood deck, which they furnished to provide numerous viewpoints where they can sit together at breakfast or during a warm desert evening, admiring this magnificent lethal work of nature.

Wishing to avoid being seen by the authorities who would be going to and coming from the Jessup house during the remaining hours of the night, I stepped through the gate in the picket fence at the back of the Ying property. Because taking a seat on the deck without invitation seemed to be ill-mannered, I sat in the yard, under the brugmansia.

The eight-year-old in me wondered if the grass could have absorbed poison from the tree. If sufficiently potent, the toxin might pass through the seat of my jeans.

My cell phone rang.

"Hello?"

A woman said, "Hi."

"Who's this?"

"Me."

"I think you have the wrong number."

"You do?"

"Yes, I think so."

"I'm disappointed," she said.

"It happens."

"You know the first rule?"

"Like I said—"

"You come alone," she interjected.

"—you've got a wrong number."

"I'm *so* disappointed in you."

"In me?" I asked.

"Very much so."

"For being a wrong number?"

"This is pathetic," she said, and terminated the call.

The woman's caller ID was blocked. No number had appeared on my screen.

The telecom revolution does not always facilitate communication.

I stared at the phone, waiting for her to misdial again, but it didn't ring. I flipped it shut.

The wind seemed to have swirled down a drain in the floor of the desert.

Beyond the motionless limbs of the brugmansia, which were leafy but flowerless until late spring, in the high vault of the night, the stars were sterling-bright, the moon a tarnished silver.

When I checked my wristwatch, I was surprised to see 3:17 A.M. Only thirty-six minutes had passed since I had awakened to find Dr. Jessup in my bedroom.

I had lost all awareness of the hour and had assumed that dawn must be drawing near. Fifty thousand volts might have messed with my watch, but it had messed more effectively with my sense of time.

If the tree branches had not embraced so much of the sky, I would have tried to find Cassiopeia, a constellation with special meaning for me. In classic mythology, Cassiopeia was the mother of Andromeda.

Another Cassiopeia, this one no myth, was the mother of a daughter whom she named Bronwen. And Bronwen is the finest person I have ever known, or ever will.

When the constellation of Cassiopeia is in this hemisphere and I am able to identify it, I feel less alone.

This isn't a reasoned response to a configuration of stars, but the heart cannot flourish on logic alone. Unreason is an essential medicine as long as you do not overdose.

In the alley, a police car pulled up at the gate. The headlights were doused.

I rose from the yard under the tree of death, and if my buttocks had been poisoned, at least they hadn't yet fallen off.

When I got into the front passenger's seat and pulled the door shut, Chief Porter said, "How's your tongue?"

"Sir?"

"Still itch?"

"Oh. No. It stopped. I hadn't noticed."

"This would work better if you took the wheel, wouldn't it?"

"Yeah. But that would be hard to explain, this being a police car and me being just a fry cook."

As we drifted along the alleyway, the chief

switched on the headlights and said, "What if I cruise where I want, and when you feel I should turn left or right, you tell me."

"Let's try it." Because he had switched off the police radio, I said, "Won't they be wanting to reach you?"

"Back there at the Jessup house? That's all aftermath. The science boys are better at that than I am. Tell me about the guy with the Taser."

"Mean green eyes. Lean and quick. Snaky."

"Are you focusing on him now?"

"No. I only got a glimpse of him before he zapped me. For this to work, I've got to have a better mental picture—or a name."

"Simon?"

"We don't know for certain that Simon's involved."

"I'd bet my eyes against a dollar that he is," Chief Porter said. "The killer beat on Wilbur Jessup long after he was dead. This was a *passionate* homicide. But he didn't come alone. He's got a kill buddy, maybe someone he met in prison."

"Just the same, I'll try for Danny."

We drove a couple of blocks in silence.

The windows were down. The air looked clear yet carried the silica scent of the Mojave vastness by which our town is embraced. Scatterings of crisp leaves, shed by Indian laurels, crunched under the tires.

Pico Mundo appeared to have been evacuated.

The chief glanced sideways at me a couple times, then said, "You ever going back to work at the Grille?"

"Yes, sir. Sooner or later."

"Sooner would be better. Folks miss your home fries."

"Poke makes good ones," I said, referring to Poke Barnett, the other short-order cook at the Pico Mundo Grille.

"They're not so bad you have to choke them down," he admitted, "but they're not in the same league with yours. Or his pancakes."

"Nobody can match the fluff factor in my pancakes," I agreed.

"Is it some culinary secret?"

"No, sir. It's a born instinct."

"A gift for pancakes."

"Yes, sir, it seems to be."

"You feel magnetized yet or whatever it is you feel?"

"No, not yet. And it would be better if we don't talk about it, just let it happen."

Chief Porter sighed. "I don't know when I'm ever going to get used to this psychic stuff."

"I never have," I said. "Don't expect I ever will."

Strung between the boles of two palm trees in front of the Pico Mundo High School, a large banner declared GO, MONSTERS!

When I attended PMHS, the sports teams were

called the Braves. Each cheerleader wore a headband with a feather. Subsequently, this was deemed an insult to local Indian tribes, though none of the Indians ever complained.

School administrators engineered the replacement of *Braves* with *Gila Monsters*. The reptile was said to be an ideal choice because it symbolized the endangered environment of the Mojave.

In football, basketball, baseball, track, and swimming, the Monsters haven't equaled the winning record of the Braves. Most people blame it on the coaches.

I used to believe that all educated people knew an asteroid might one day strike the earth, destroying human civilization. But perhaps a lot of them haven't heard about it yet.

As though reading my mind, Chief Porter said, "Could've been worse. The Mojave yellow-banded stink bug is an endangered species. They could've called the team *Stink Bugs*."

"Left," I suggested, and he turned at the next intersection.

"I figured if Simon was ever coming back here," Chief Porter said, "he would've done it four months ago, when he was released from Folsom. We ran special patrols in the Jessup neighborhood during October and November."

"Danny said they were taking precautions at the house. Better door locks. An upgraded security system."

"So Simon was smart enough to wait. Gradually everyone let down their guard. Fact is, though, when the cancer took Carol, I didn't expect Simon would come back to Pico Mundo."

Seventeen years previously, jealous to the point of obsession, Simon Makepeace had become convinced that his young wife had been having an affair. He'd been wrong.

Certain that assignations had occurred in his own home, when he had been at work, Simon tried to coax the name of any male visitor from his then four-year-old son. Because there had been no visitor to identify, Danny had not been able to oblige. So Simon picked up the boy by the shoulders and tried to *shake* the name out of him.

Danny's brittle bones snapped. He suffered fractures of two ribs, the left clavicle, the right humerus, the left humerus, the right radius, the right ulna, three metacarpals in his right hand.

When he couldn't shake a name out of his son, Simon threw the boy down in disgust, breaking his right femur, his right tibia, and every tarsal in his right foot.

Carol had been grocery shopping at the time. Returning home, she found Danny alone, unconscious, bleeding, a shattered humerus protruding through the flesh of his right arm.

Aware that charges of child abuse would be filed against him, Simon had fled. He understood that his freedom might be measured in hours.

With less to lose and therefore with less to constrain him, he set out to take vengeance on the man whom he most suspected of being his wife's lover. Because no lover existed, he merely perpetrated a second act of mindless violence.

Lewis Hallman, whom Carol had dated a few times before her marriage, was Simon's prime suspect. Driving his Ford Explorer, he stalked Hallman until he caught him on foot, then ran him down and killed him.

In court, he claimed that his intention had been to frighten Lewis, not to murder him. This assertion seemed to be contradicted by the fact that after running down his victim, Simon had turned and driven over him a second time.

He expressed remorse. And self-loathing. He wept. He offered no defense except emotional immaturity. More than once, sitting at the defendant's table, he prayed.

The prosecution failed to get him on second-degree murder. He was convicted of manslaughter.

If that particular jury could be reconstituted and polled, no doubt it would unanimously support the change from *Braves* to *Gila Monsters*.

"Turn right at the next corner," I advised the chief.

As the consequence of a conviction for assault involving a violent altercation in prison, Simon Makepeace had served his full sentence for manslaughter and a shorter term for the second offense. He had not been paroled; therefore, on release, he had been free to consort with whomever he wished and to go wherever he wanted.

If he had returned to Pico Mundo, he was now holding his son captive.

In letters he had written from prison, Simon had judged Carol's divorce and second marriage to be infidelity and betrayal. Men with his psychological profile frequently concluded that if they couldn't have the women they wanted, then no one would have them.

Cancer had taken Carol from Wilbur Jessup and from Simon; but Simon might still have felt a need to punish the man who had taken his role as her lover.

Wherever Danny might be, he was in a desperate place.

Although neither as psychologically nor as physically vulnerable as he had been seventeen years ago, Danny was no match for Simon Makepeace. He could not protect himself.

"Let's drive through Camp's End," I suggested.

Camp's End is a ragged, burnt-out neighborhood where bright dreams go to die and dark dreams are too often born. Other trouble had more than once led me to those streets.

As the chief accelerated and drove with greater purpose, I said, "If it's Simon, he won't put up with Danny very long. I'm surprised he didn't kill him at the house, when he killed Dr. Jessup."

"Why do you say that?"

"Simon never quite believed he could have produced a son with a birth defect. The osteogenesis imperfecta suggested to him that Carol had cheated on him."

"So every time he looks at Danny . . ." The chief didn't need to finish the thought. "The boy's a wise-ass, but I've always liked him."

Descending toward the west, the moon had yellowed. Soon it might be orange, a jack-o'-lantern out of season.

7

EVEN STREET LAMPS WITH TIME-OCHERED glass, even moonlight failed to smooth a layer of romance over the crumbling stucco, the warped clapboard, and the peeling paint of the houses in Camp's End. A porch roof swagged. A zigzag of tape bandaged a wound in window glass.

While I waited for inspiration, Chief Porter cruised the streets as if conducting a standard patrol.

"Since you've not been working at the Grille, how do you fill the hours these days?"

"I read quite a bit."

"Books are a blessing."

"And I think a lot more than I used to."

"I wouldn't recommend thinking too much."

"I don't carry it so far as brooding."

"Even pondering is sometimes too far."

Next door to an unweeded lawn lay a dead lawn, which itself lay next door to a lawn in which grass had long ago been replaced by pea gravel.

Skilled landscapers had rarely touched the trees in this neighborhood. What had not been permanently misshapen by bad pruning had instead been allowed to grow unchecked.

"I wish I could believe in reincarnation," I said.

"Not me. Once down the track is enough of a test. Pass me or fail me, Dear Lord, but don't make me go through high school again."

I said, "If there's something we want so bad in this life but we can't have it, maybe we could get it the next time around."

"Or maybe not getting it, accepting less without bitterness, and being grateful for what we have is a part of what we're here to learn."

"You once told me that we're here to eat all the good Mexican food we can," I reminded him, "and when we've had our fill, it's time to move on."

"I don't recollect being taught that in Sunday school," Chief Porter said. "So it's possible I'd consumed two or three bottles of Negra Modelo before that theological insight occurred to me."

"It would be hard to accept a life here in Camp's End without some bitterness," I said.

Pico Mundo is a prosperous town. But no degree of prosperity can be sufficient to eliminate all misfortune, and sloth is impervious to opportunity.

Where an owner showed pride in his home, the fresh paint, the upright picket fence, the well-barbered shrubs only emphasized the debris, decay, and dilapidation that characterized the surrounding properties. Each island of order did not offer hope of a community-wide transformation, but instead seemed to be a dike that could not long hold back an inevitably rising tide of chaos.

These mean streets made me uneasy, but though we cruised them for some time, I didn't feel that we were close to Danny and Simon.

At my suggestion, we headed for a more welcoming neighborhood, and the chief said, "There's worse lives than those in Camp's End. Some are even content here. Probably some Camp Enders could teach us a thing or two about happiness."

"I'm happy," I assured him.

For a block or so, he didn't say anything. Then: "You're at peace, son. There's a big difference."

"Which would be what?"

"If you're still, and if you don't hope too much, peace will come to you. It's a grace. But you have to *choose* happiness."

"It's that easy, is it? Just choose?"

"Making the decision to choose isn't always easy."

I said, "This sounds like you've been thinking too much."

"We sometimes take refuge in misery, a strange kind of comfort."

Although he paused, I said nothing.

He continued: "But no matter what happens in life, happiness is there for us, waiting to be embraced."

"Sir, did this come to you after three bottles of Negra Modelo, or was it four?"

"It must have been three. I never drink as many as four."

By the time we were circling through the heart of town, I had decided that for whatever reason, psychic magnetism wasn't working. Maybe I needed to be driving. Maybe the shock from the Taser had temporarily shorted my psychic circuits.

Or maybe Danny was already dead, and subconsciously I resisted being drawn to him, only to find him brutalized.

At my request, at 4:04 A.M. according to the Bank of America clock, Chief Porter pulled to the curb to let me out at the north side of Memorial Park, around which the streets define a town square.

"Looks like I'm not going to be any help with this one," I said.

In the past, I've had reason to suspect that when a situation involves people especially close to me, about whom I have the most intense personal feelings, my gifts do not serve me as well as they do when there is even a slight degree of emotional detachment. Maybe feelings interfere with psychic function, as also might a migraine headache or drunkenness.

Danny Jessup was as close to me as a brother could have been. I loved him.

Assuming that my paranormal talents have a higher source than genetic mutation, perhaps the explanation for uneven function is more profound. This limitation might be for the purpose of preventing the exploitation of these talents toward selfish ends; but morc likely, fallibility is meant to keep me humble.

If humility is the lesson, I have learned it well. More than a few days have dawned in which an awareness of my limitations filled me with a gentle resignation that, till afternoon or even twilight, kept me in bed as effectively as would have shackles and hundred-pound lead weights.

As I opened the car door, Chief Porter said, "You sure you don't want me to drive you home?"

"No, thank you, sir. I'm awake, fully charged, and hungry. I'm going to be the first through the door for breakfast at the Grille."

"They don't open till six."

I got out, bent down, looked in at him. "I'll sit in the park and feed the pigeons for a while."

"We don't have pigeons."

"Then I'll feed the pterodactyls."

"What you're gonna do is sit in the park and think."

"No, sir, I promise I won't."

I closed the door. The patrol car pulled away from the curb.

After watching the chief drive out of sight, I entered the park, sat on a bench, and broke my promise.

8

AROUND THE TOWN SQUARE, CAST-IRON lampposts, painted black, were crowned with three globes each.

At the center of Memorial Park, a handsome bronze statue of three soldiers—dating from World War II—was usually illuminated, but at the moment it stood in darkness. The spotlight had probably been vandalized.

Recently a small but determined group of citizens had been demanding that the statue be replaced, on the grounds that it was militaristic. They wanted Memorial Park to memorialize a man of peace.

The suggestions for the subject of the new memorial ranged from Gandhi to Woodrow Wilson, to Yasir Arafat.

Someone had proposed that a statue of Gandhi should be modeled after Ben Kingsley, who had played the great man in the movie. Then perhaps the actor could be induced to be present at the unveiling.

This had led Terri Stambaugh, my friend and the owner of the Grille, to suggest that a statue of Gandhi should be modeled after Brad Pitt in the hope that *he* would then attend the ceremony, which would be a big deal by Pico Mundo standards.

At the same town meeting, Ozzie Boone had offered himself as the subject of the memorial. "Men of my formidable diameter are never sent to war," he said, "and if everyone were as fat as I am, there could be no armies."

Some had taken this as mockery, but others had found merit in the idea.

Perhaps someday the current statue will be replaced by one of a very fat Gandhi modeled after Johnny Depp, but for the moment, the soldiers remain. In darkness.

Old jacarandas, drenched with purple flowers come spring, line the main streets downtown, but Memorial Park boasts magnificent phoenix palms; under the fronds of one, I settled on a bench, facing the street. The nearest street lamp was not near, and the tree shaded me from the increasingly ruddy moonlight.

Although I sat in gloom, Elvis found me. He materialized in the act of sitting beside me.

He was dressed in an army uniform dating from the late 1950s. I can't say with any authority whether it was actually a uniform from his service in the military or if it might have been a costume that he wore in *G.I. Blues*, which had been filmed, edited, and released within five months of his leaving the army in 1960.

All the other lingering dead of my acquaintance appear in the clothes in which they died. Only Elvis manifests in whatever wardrobe he fancies at the moment.

Perhaps he meant to express solidarity with those who wished to preserve the statue of the soldiers. Or he just thought he looked cool in army khaki, which he did.

Few people have lived so publicly that their lives can reliably be chronicled day by day. Elvis is one of those.

Because even his mundane activities have been so thoroughly documented, we can be all but certain that he never visited Pico Mundo while alive. He never passed through on a train, never dated a girl from here, and had no other connection whatsoever with our town.

Why he should choose to haunt this well-fried corner of the Mojave instead of Graceland, where he died, I did not know. I had asked him, but the rule of silence among the dead was one that he would not break.

Occasionally, usually on an evening when we sit in my living room and listen to his best music, which we do a lot lately, I try to engage him in conversation. I've suggested that he use a form of sign language to reply: thumbs-up for *yes*, thumbs-down for *no*. . . .

He just looks at me with those heavy-lidded, half-bruised eyes, even bluer than they appear in his movies, and keeps his secrets to himself. Often he'll smile and wink. Or give me a playful punch on the arm. Or pat my knee.

He's an affable apparition.

Here on the park bench, he raised his eyebrows and shook his head as if to say that my propensity for getting in trouble never ceased to amaze him.

I used to think that he was reluctant to leave this world because people here had been so good to him, had loved him in such numbers. Even though he had lost his way badly as a performer and had become addicted to numerous prescription medications, he had been at the height of his fame when he died, and only forty-two.

Lately, I've evolved another theory. When I have the nerve, I'll propose it to him.

If I've got it right, I think he'll weep when he hears it. He sometimes does weep.

Now the King of Rock 'n' Roll leaned forward on the bench, peered west, and cocked his head as if listening.

I heard nothing but the faint thrum of wings as bats fished the air above for moths.

Still gazing along the empty street, Elvis raised

both hands palms-up and made come-to-me gestures, as though inviting someone to join us.

From a distance, I heard an engine, a vehicle larger than a car, approaching.

Elvis winked at me, as if to say that I was engaged in psychic magnetism even if I didn't realize it. Instead of cruising in search, perhaps I had settled where I knew—somehow—that my quarry would cruise to me.

Two blocks away, a dusty white-paneled Ford van turned the corner. It came toward us slowly, as if the driver might be looking for something.

Elvis put a hand on my arm, warning me to remain seated in the shrouding shadows of the phoenix palm.

Light from a street lamp washed the windshield, sluiced through the interior of the van as it passed us. Behind the wheel was the snaky man who had Tasered me.

Without realizing that I moved, I had sprung to my feet in surprise.

My movement didn't catch the driver's attention. He drove past and turned left at the corner.

I ran into the street, leaving Sergeant Presley on the bench and the bats to their airborne feast.

9

THE VAN SWUNG OUT OF SIGHT AT THE corner, and I ran in its windless wake, not because I am brave, which I am not, neither because I am addicted to danger, which I also am not, but because inaction is not the mother of redemption.

When I reached the cross street, I saw the Ford disappearing into an alley half a block away. I had lost ground. I sprinted.

When I reached the mouth of the alley, the way ahead lay dark, the street brighter behind me, with the consequence that I stood as silhouetted as a pistol-range target, but it wasn't a trap. No one shot at me.

Before I arrived, the van had turned left and vanished into an intersecting passage. I knew where it had gone only because the wall of the corner building blushed with the backwash of taillights.

Racing after that fading red trace, certain that I was gaining now because they had to slow to take the tight turn, I fumbled the cell phone from my pocket.

When I arrived where alley met alley, the van had vanished, also every glimmer and glow of it. Surprised, I looked up, half expecting to see it levitating into the desert sky.

I speed-dialed Chief Porter's mobile number—and discovered that no charge was left in the battery. I hadn't plugged it in overnight.

Dumpsters in starlight, hulking and odorous, bracketed back entrances to restaurants and shops. Most of the wire-caged security lamps, managed by timers, had switched off in this last hour before dawn.

Some of the two- and three-story buildings featured roll-up doors. Behind most would be small receiving rooms for deliveries of merchandise and supplies; only a few might be garages, but I had no way to determine which they were.

Pocketing the useless phone, I hurried forward a few steps. Then I halted: unsettled, uncertain.

Holding my breath, I listened. I heard only my storming heart, the thunder of my blood, no engine either idling or receding, no doors opening or closing, no voices.

I had been running. I couldn't hold my breath for long. The echo of my exhalation traveled the narrow throat of the alleyway.

At the nearest of the big doors, I put my right ear to the corrugated steel. The space beyond seemed to be as soundless as a vacuum.

Crossing and recrossing the alley, from roll-up to roll-up, I heard no clue, saw no evidence, but felt hope ticking away.

I thought of the snake man driving. Danny must have been in back, with Simon.

Again I was running. Out of the alley, into the next street, right to the intersection, left onto Palomino Avenue, before I fully understood that I had given myself to psychic magnetism once more, or rather that it had seized me.

As reliably as a homing pigeon returns to its dovecote, a dray horse to its stable, a bee to its hive, I sought not home and hearth, but trouble. I left Palomino Avenue for another alley, and surprised three cats into hissing flight.

The boom of a gun startled me more than I had frightened the cats. I almost tucked and rolled, but instead dodged between two Dumpsters, my back to a brick wall.

Echoes of echoes deceived the ear, concealed the source. The report had been loud, most likely a shotgun blast. But I couldn't determine the point of origin.

I had no weapon at hand. A dead cell phone isn't much of a blunt instrument.

In my strange and dangerous life, I have only once resorted to a gun. I shot a man with it. He had been killing people with a gun of his own.

Shooting him dead saved lives. I have no intellectual or moral argument with the use of firearms any more than I do with the use of spoons or socket wrenches.

My problem with guns is emotional. They fascinate my mother. In my childhood, she made much grim use of a pistol, as I have recounted in a previous manuscript.

I cannot easily separate the rightful use of a gun from the sick purpose to which she put hers. In my hand, a firearm feels as if it has a life of its own, a cold and squamous kind of life, and also a wicked intent too slippery to control.

One day my aversion to firearms might be the death of me. But I've never been under the illusion that I will live forever. If not a gun, a germ will get me, a poison or a pickax.

After huddling between the Dumpsters for a minute, perhaps two, I came to the conclusion that the shotgun blast had not been meant for me. If I'd been seen and marked for death, the shooter would have approached without delay, pumping another round into the chamber and then into me.

Above some of these downtown businesses were apartments. Lights had bloomed in a few of them, the shotgun having made moot the later settings of alarm clocks.

On the move again, I found myself drawn to

the next intersection of alleyways, then left without hesitation. Less than half a block ahead stood the white van, this side of the kitchen entrance to the Blue Moon Cafe.

Beside the Blue Moon is a parking lot that runs through to the main street. The van appeared to have been abandoned at the rear of this lot, nose out toward the alleyway.

Both front doors stood open, spilling light, no one visible beyond the windshield. As I drew cautiously closer, I heard the engine idling.

This suggested that they had fled in haste. Or intended to return for a quick getaway.

The Blue Moon doesn't serve breakfast, only lunch and dinner. Kitchen workers do not begin to arrive until a couple hours after dawn. The cafe should have been locked. I doubted that Simon had shot his way inside to raid the restaurant refrigerators.

There are easier ways to get a cold chicken leg, though maybe none quicker.

I couldn't imagine where they had gone—or why they abandoned the van if in fact they were not returning.

From one of the second-floor lighted apartment windows, an elderly woman in a blue robe gazed down. She appeared less alarmed than curious.

I eased to the passenger's side of the vehicle, slowly circled toward the rear.

At the back, the pair of doors on the cargo hold also stood open. Interior light revealed no one inside.

Sirens rose in the night, approaching.

I wondered who had fired the shotgun, at whom, and why.

As deformed and vulnerable as he is, Danny couldn't have wrested the weapon away from his tormentors. Even if he had tried to use the shotgun, the recoil would have broken his shoulder, if not also one of his arms.

Turning in a circle, mystified, I wondered what had happened to my friend with brittle bones.

10

P. OSWALD BOONE, FOUR-HUNDRED-POUND culinary black belt in white silk pajamas, whom I'd recently awakened, moved with the grace and swiftness of a dojo master as he whipped up breakfast in the kitchen of his Craftsman-style house.

At times his weight scares me, and I worry about his suffering heart. But when he's cooking, he seems weightless, floating, like those gravity-defying warriors in *Crouching Tiger, Hidden Dragon*—though he didn't actually bound over the center island.

Watching him that February morning, I considered that if he had spent his life killing himself with food, it might also be true that without the solace and refuge of food, he would have been dead long ago. Every life is complicated, every mind a kingdom of unmapped mysteries, and Ozzie's more than most.

Although he never speaks of how or what or

why, I know that his childhood was difficult, that his parents broke his heart. Books and excess poundage are his insulation against pain.

He is a writer, with two successful series of mystery novels and numerous nonfiction books to his credit. He is so productive that the day may come when one copy of each of his books, stacked on a scale, will surpass his body weight.

Because he had assured me that writing would prove to be psychic chemotherapy effective against psychological tumors, I had written my true story of loss and perseverance—and had put it in a drawer, at peace if not happy. To his dismay, I had told him that I was done with writing.

I believed it, too. Now here I am again, putting words to paper, serving as my own psychological oncologist.

Perhaps in time I will follow Ozzie's every example, and weigh four hundred pounds. I won't be able to run with ghosts and slip down dark alleyways in quite the swift and stealthy fashion that I do now; but perhaps children will be amused by my hippopotamic heroics, and no one will disagree that bringing laughter to children in a dark world is admirable.

While Ozzie cooked, I told him about Dr. Jessup and all that had occurred since the dead radiologist had come to me in the middle of the night. Although as I recounted events I worried about Danny, I worried as well about Terrible Chester.

Terrible Chester, the cat about which every dog has nightmares, allows Ozzie to live with him. Ozzie cherishes this feline no less than he loves food and books.

Although Terrible Chester has never clawed me with the ferocity of which I believe he is capable, he *has* more than once urinated on my shoes. Ozzie says this is an expression of affection. This theory holds that the cat is marking me with his scent to identify me as an approved member of his family.

I have noticed that when Terrible Chester wishes to express his affection for Ozzie, he does so by cuddling and purring.

Since Ozzie opened the front door to me, as we passed through the house, and during the time that I sat in the kitchen, I had not seen Terrible Chester. This made me nervous. My shoes were new.

He is a big cat, so fearless and self-impressed that he disdains sneaking. He doesn't creep into a room, but always makes an entrance. Although he expects to be the center of attention, he projects an air of indifference—even contempt—that makes it clear he wishes for the most part to be adored from a distance.

Although he does not sneak, he can appear at your shoes suddenly and by surprise. The first indication of trouble can be a briefly mystifying warm dampness of the toes.

Until Ozzie and I moved to the back porch to take our breakfast al fresco, I kept my feet off the floor, on a chair rung.

The porch overlooks a lawn and a half-acre woodlet of laurels, podocarpus, and graceful California peppers. In the golden morning sunshine, songbirds trilled and death seemed like a myth.

Had the table not been a sturdy redwood model, it would have groaned under the plates of lobster omelets, bowls of potatoes au gratin, stacks of toast, bagels, Danish, cinnamon rolls, pitchers of orange juice and milk, pots of coffee and cocoa. . . .

"'What is food to one is to others bitter poison,'" Ozzie quoted happily, toasting me with a raised forkful of omelet.

"Shakespeare?" I asked.

"Lucretius, who wrote before the birth of Christ. Lad, I promise you this—I shall never be one of these health wimps who views a pint of heavy cream with the same horror that saner men reserve for atomic weapons."

"Sir, those of us who care about you would suggest that vanilla *soy milk* isn't the abomination you say it is."

"I do not permit blasphemy, the F-word, or obscenities such as soy milk at my table. Consider yourself chastised."

"I stopped in Gelato Italiano the other day.

They now have some flavors with half the fat."

He said, "The horses stabled at our local racetrack produce tons of manure each week, and I don't stock my freezer with that, either. So where does Wyatt Porter think Danny might be?"

"Most likely Simon earlier stashed a second set of wheels in the lot beside the Blue Moon, in case things went bad at the Jessup house and someone saw him leaving there in the van."

"But no one saw the van at the Jessup house, so it wasn't a hot vehicle."

"No."

"Yet he switched at the Blue Moon anyway."

"Yes."

"Does that make sense to you?"

"It makes more sense than anything else."

"For sixteen years, he remained obsessed with Carol, so obsessed that he wanted Dr. Jessup dead for having married her."

"So it seems."

"What does he want with Danny?"

"I don't know."

"Simon doesn't seem like the type who'd yearn for an emotionally satisfying father-son relationship."

"It doesn't fit the profile," I agreed.

"How's your omelet?"

"Fantastic, sir."

"There's cream in it, and butter."

"Yes, sir."

"Also parsley. I'm not opposed to a portion of green vegetables now and then. Roadblocks won't be effective if Simon's second vehicle has four-wheel drive and he goes overland."

"The sheriff's department is assisting with aerial patrols."

"Do you have any sense whether Danny's still in Pico Mundo?"

"I get this strange feeling."

"Strange—how?"

"A wrongness."

"A wrongness?"

"Yes."

"Ah, everything's crystal-clear now."

"Sorry. I don't know. I can't be specific."

"He isn't . . . dead?"

I shook my head. "I don't think it's that simple."

"More orange juice? It's fresh-squeezed."

As he poured, I said, "Sir, I've been wondering—where's Terrible Chester?"

"Watching you," he said, and pointed.

When I turned in my chair, I saw the cat ten feet behind me and above, perched on an exposed ceiling truss that supported the porch roof.

He is reddish-orange with black markings. His eyes are as green as emeralds fired by sunlight.

Ordinarily, Terrible Chester favors me—or anyone—with only a casual glance, as if human beings bore him beyond tolerance. With his eyes and attitude, he can express a dismissive judgment of humanity, a contempt, that even a minimalist writer like Cormac McCarthy would need twenty pages to convey.

Never previously had I been an object of intense interest to Chester. Now he held my gaze, did not look away, did not blink, and seemed to find me to be as fascinating as a three-headed extraterrestrial.

Although he didn't appear to be poised to pounce, I did not feel comfortable turning my back on this formidable cat; however, I felt less comfortable engaging in a staring match with him. He would *not* look away from me.

When I faced the table again, Ozzie was taking the liberty of spooning another serving of potatoes onto my plate.

I said, "He's never stared at me like that before."

"He was staring at you much the same way the entire time we were in the kitchen."

"I didn't see him in the kitchen."

"When you weren't looking, he crept into the room, pawed open a cabinet door, and hid under the sink."

"He must've been quick."

"Oh, Odd, he was a prince of cats, lightning-quick and quiet. I was so proud of him. Once inside the cabinet, he held the door ajar with his body and watched you from concealment."

"Why didn't you say something?"

"Because I wanted to see what he would do next."

"Most likely it involves shoes and urine."

"I don't think so," Ozzie said. "This is all new."

"Is he still up there on the beam?"

"Yes."

"And still watching me?"

"Intently. Would you like a Danish?"

"I've sort of lost my appetite."

"Don't be silly, lad. Because of Chester?"

"He has something to do with it. I'm remembering once before when he was this intense."

"Refresh my memory."

I couldn't prevent my voice from thickening. "August . . . and all of that."

Ozzie stabbed the air with a fork: "Oh. You mean, the ghost."

The previous August, I had discovered that, like me, Terrible Chester can see those troubled souls who linger this side of death. He had regarded that spirit no less intently than he now studied me.

"You aren't dead," Ozzie assured me. "You're as solid as this redwood table, though not as solid as me."

"Maybe Chester knows something I don't."

"Dear Odd, because you're such a naive young man in some ways, I'm sure there's a great deal he knows that you don't. What did you have in mind?"

"Like that my time's soon up."

"I'm sure it's something less apocalyptic."

"Such as?"

"Are you carrying any dead mice in your pockets?"

"Just a dead cell phone."

Ozzie studied me solemnly. He was genuinely concerned. At the same time, he is too good a friend ever to coddle me.

"Well," he said, "if your time is soon up, all the more reason to have a Danish. The one with pineapple and cheese would be the perfect thing with which to end a last meal."

11

WHEN I SUGGESTED THAT I HELP CLEAN OFF the table and wash the dishes before going, Little Ozzie—who is actually fifty pounds heavier than his father, Big Ozzie—dismissed the suggestion by gesturing emphatically with a slice of buttered toast.

"We've only been sitting here forty minutes. I'm never at the morning table less than an hour and a half. I do some of my finest plotting over breakfast coffee and raisin brioche."

"You should write a series set in the culinary world."

"Already, bookstore shelves overflow with mysteries about chefs who are detectives, food critics who are detectives. . . ."

One of Ozzie's series features a hugely obese detective with a slim sexy wife who adores him. Ozzie has never married.

His other series is about a likable female detective with lots of neuroses—and bulimia. Ozzie is about as likely to develop bulimia himself as he is likely to change his wardrobe entirely to spandex.

"I've considered," he said, "starting a series about a detective who is a pet communicator."

"One of those people who claims to be able to talk to animals?"

"Yes, but he would be the real thing."

"So animals would help him solve crimes?" I asked.

"They would, yes, but they'd also complicate his cases. Dogs would almost always tell him the truth, but birds would often lie, and guinea pigs would be earnest but prone to exaggeration."

"I feel for the guy already."

In silence, Ozzie spread lemon marmalade on brioche, while I picked at the pineapple-cheese Danish with a fork.

I needed to leave. I needed to *do* something. Sitting still another moment seemed intolerable.

I nibbled some Danish.

We seldom sit in silence. He's never at a loss for words; I can usually find a few of my own.

After a minute or two, I realized that Ozzie was staring at me no less intently than was Terrible Chester.

I had attributed this lull in the conversation to his need to chew. Now I realized this could not be the case.

Brioche is made with eggs, yeast, and butter.

It melts in your mouth with very little chewing.

Ozzie had fallen silent because he was brooding. And he was brooding about me.

"What?" I asked.

"You didn't come here for breakfast," he said. "Certainly not for *this much* breakfast."

"And you didn't come here to tell me about Wilbur Jessup, or about Danny."

"Well, yes, that is why I came, sir."

"Then you've told me, and you obviously don't want that Danish, so I suppose you'll be going now."

"Yes, sir," I said, "I should be going," but I didn't get up from my chair.

Pouring a fragrant Colombian blend from a thermos shaped like a coffeepot, Ozzie did not once shift his eyes from me.

"I've never known you to be deceitful with anyone, Odd."

"I assure you I can dissemble with the best of them, sir."

"No, you can't. You're a poster boy for sincerity. You have all the guile of a lamb."

I looked away from him—and discovered that Terrible Chester had descended from the roof beams. The cat sat on the top porch step, still staring intently at me.

"But more amazing still," Ozzie continued, "I've seldom known you to indulge in *self*-deceit."

"When will I be canonized, sir?"

"Smart-mouthing your elders will forever keep you out of the company of saints."

"Darn. I was looking forward to having a halo. It would make such a convenient reading lamp."

"As for self-deceit, most people find it as essential for survival as air. You rarely indulge in it. Yet you insist you came here just to tell me about Wilbur and Danny."

"Have I been insisting?"

"Not with conviction."

"Why do *you* think I came here?" I asked.

"You've always mistaken my absolute self-assurance for profound thought," he said without hesitation, "so when you're looking for deep insight, you seek an audience with me."

"You mean all the profound insights you've given me over the years were actually shallow?"

"Of course they were, dear Odd. Like you, I'm only human, even if I have eleven fingers."

He does have eleven, six on his left hand. He says one in ninety thousand babies is born with this affliction. Surgeons routinely amputate the unneeded digit.

For some reason that Ozzie has never shared with me, his parents refused permission for the surgery. He was the fascination of other children: the eleven-fingered boy; eventually, the eleven-fingered fat boy; and then the eleven-fingered fat boy with the withering wit.

"As shallow as my insights might have been," he said, "they were sincerely offered."

"That's some comfort, I guess."

"Anyway, you came here today with a burning philosophical question that's troubling you, but it troubles you so much you don't want to ask, after all."

"No, that isn't it," I said.

I looked at the congealing remains of my lobster omelet. At Terrible Chester. At the lawn. At the small woods so green in the morning sun.

Ozzie's moon-round face could be smug and loving at the same time. His eyes twinkled with an expectation of being proved right.

At last I said, "You know Ernie and Pooka Ying."

"Lovely people."

"The tree in their backyard . . ."

"The brugmansia. It's a magnificent specimen."

"Everything about it is deadly, every root and leaf."

Ozzie smiled as Buddha would have smiled if Buddha had written mystery novels and had relished exotic methods of murder. He nodded approvingly. "Exquisitely poisonous, yes."

"Why would nice people like Ernie and Pooka want to grow such a deadly tree?"

"For one thing, because it's beautiful, especially when it's in flower."

"The flowers are toxic, too."

After popping a final morsel of marmaladed

brioche into his mouth and savoring it, Ozzie licked his lips and said, "One of those enormous blooms contains sufficient poison, if properly extracted, to kill perhaps a third of the people in Pico Mundo."

"It seems reckless, even perverse, to spend so much time and effort nurturing such a deadly thing."

"Does Ernie Ying strike you as a reckless and perverse man?"

"Just the opposite."

"Ah, then Pooka must be the monster. Her self-deprecating manner must disguise a heart of the most malevolent intention."

"Sometimes," I said, "it seems to me that a friend might not take such pleasure in making fun of me as you do."

"Dear Odd, if one's friends do not openly laugh at him, they are not in fact his friends. How else would one learn to avoid saying those things that would elicit laughter from strangers? The mockery of friends is affectionate, and inoculates against foolishness."

"That sure sounds profound," I said.

"Medium shallow," he assured me. "May I educate you, lad?"

"You can try."

"There's nothing reckless about growing the brugmansia. Equally poisonous plants are everywhere in Pico Mundo."

I was dubious. "Everywhere?"

"You're so busy with the supernatural world that you know too little about the natural."

"I don't get much time to go bowling, either."

"Those flowering oleander hedges all over town? *Oleander* in Sanskrit means 'horse killer.' Every part of the plant is deadly."

"I like the variety with red flowers."

"If you burn it, the smoke is poisonous," Ozzie said. "If bees spend too much time with oleander, the honey will kill you. Azaleas are equally fatal."

"Everybody plants azaleas."

"Oleander will kill you quickly. Azaleas, ingested, take a few hours. Vomiting, paralysis, seizures, coma, death. Then there's savin, henbane, foxglove, jimsonweed . . . all here in Pico Mundo."

"And we call her *Mother* Nature."

"There's nothing fatherly about time and what it does to us, either," Ozzie said.

"But, sir, Ernie and Pooka Ying *know* the brugmansia is deadly. In fact, its deadliness is why they planted and nurtured it."

"Think of it as a Zen thing."

"I would—if I knew what that meant."

"Ernie and Pooka seek to understand death and to master their fear of it by domesticating it in the form of the brugmansia."

"That sounds medium shallow."

"No. That's actually profound."

Although I didn't want the Danish, I picked it up and took a huge bite. I poured coffee into a mug, to have something that I could hold.

I couldn't sit there any longer doing nothing. I felt that if my hands weren't busy, I'd start tearing at things.

"Why," I wondered, "do people tolerate murder?"

"Last time I looked, it was against the law."

"Simon Makepeace killed once. And they let him out."

"The law isn't perfect."

"You should've seen Dr. Jessup's body."

"Not necessary. I have a novelist's imagination."

As my hands had gotten busy with Danish I didn't want and with coffee I didn't drink, Ozzie's hands had gone still. They were folded on the table in front of him.

"Sir, I often think about all those people, shot. . . ."

He did not ask to whom I was referring. He knew that I meant the forty-one shot at the mall the previous August, the nineteen dead.

I said, "Haven't watched or read the news in a long time. But people talk about what's happening in the world, so I hear things."

"Just remember, the news isn't life. Reporters have a saying—'If it bleeds, it leads.' Violence sells, so violence gets reported."

"But why does bad news sell so much better than good?"

He sighed and leaned back in his chair, which creaked. "We're getting close now."

"Close to what?"

"To the question that brought you here."

"That burning philosophical thing? No, sir, there isn't one. I'm just . . . rambling."

"Ramble for me, then."

"What's wrong with people?"

"Which people?"

"Humanity, I mean. What's wrong with humanity?"

"That was a very short ramble indeed."

"Sir?"

"Your lips should feel scorched. The burning question just fell from them. It's quite a puzzler to put to another mortal."

"Yes, sir. But I'll be happy even with one of your standard shallow answers."

"The correct question has three equal parts. What's wrong with humanity? Then . . . what's wrong with nature, with its poison plants, predatory animals, earthquakes, and floods? And last . . . what's wrong with cosmic time, as we know it, which steals everything from us?"

Ozzie may assert that I mistake his absolute self-confidence for profundity; but I do not. He *is* truly wise. Evidently, however, life has taught him that the wise make targets of themselves.

A lesser mind might try to hide its brilliance behind a mask of stupidity. He chooses, instead, to conceal his true wisdom under a flamboyant pretense of erudition that he is pleased to let people think is the best of him.

"Those three questions," he said, "have the same answer."

"I'm listening."

"It's no good if I just give it to you. You'll resist it—and waste years of your life looking for an answer that pleases you more. When you arrive at it on your own, however, you'll be convinced by it."

"That's all you have to say?"

He smiled and shrugged.

"I come here with a burning philosophical question, and all I get is breakfast?"

"You got quite a lot of breakfast," he said. "I will tell you this much—you already know the answer and always have. You don't have to discover it so much as *recognize* it."

I shook my head. "Sometimes, you're a frustrating man."

"Yes, but I'm always gloriously fat and fun to look at."

"You can be as mystical as a damn . . ." Terrible Chester still sat on the top porch step, riveted by me. ". . . as mystical as a damn cat."

"I'll take that as a compliment."

"It wasn't meant as one." I pushed my chair

away from the table. "I'd better go."

As usual when I leave, he insisted on struggling to his feet. I am always concerned that the effort to get up will spike his blood pressure into the stroke zone and fell him on the spot.

He hugged me, and I hugged him, which we always do on parting, as if we do not expect to see each other again.

I wonder if sometimes the distribution of souls gets screwed up, and the wrong spirit ends up in the wrong baby. I suppose this is blasphemous. But then, with my smart mouth, I've already blown any chance of sainthood.

Surely, with his kind heart, Ozzie was meant for slim good health and ten fingers. And my life would make more sense if I had been his son instead of the offspring of the troubled parents who had failed me.

When the hug was done, he said, "What now?"

"I don't know. I never do. It comes to me."

Chester did not pee on my shoes.

I walked to the end of the deep yard, through the woodlet, and left by the gate in the back fence.

12

NOT ENTIRELY TO MY SURPRISE, AGAIN THE Blue Moon Cafe.

The cloak of night had dressed the alleyway with some romance, but daylight had stripped it of the pretense of beauty. This was not a realm of filth and vermin; it was merely gray, grim, drab, and unwelcoming.

All but universally, human architecture values front elevations over back entrances, public spaces over private. For the most part, this is a consequence of limited resources, budgets.

Danny Jessup says that this aspect of architecture is also a reflection of human nature, that most people care more about their appearance than they do about the condition of their souls.

Although I'm not as cynical as Danny, and although I don't think the analogy between back doors and souls is well drawn, I'll admit to seeing some truth in what he says.

What I could not see, here in the pale-lemon morning light, was any clue that might lead me a single step closer to him or to his psychotic father.

The police had done their work and gone. The Ford van had been hauled away.

I hadn't come here with the expectation that I would find a clue overlooked by the authorities and, shifting into Sherlock, would track down the bad guys in a rush of deductive reasoning.

I returned because this was where my sixth sense had failed me. I hoped to find it again, as though it were a spool of ribbon that I'd dropped and that had rolled out of sight. If I could locate the loose end of the ribbon, I could follow it to the spool.

Opposite the kitchen entrance of the cafe was the second-floor window from which the elderly woman in the blue robe had watched as I had approached the van only hours ago. The drapes were shut.

Briefly I considered having a word with her. But she had already been interviewed by the police. They are far more skilled than I am at teasing valuable observations from witnesses.

I walked slowly north to the end of the block. Then I turned and walked south, past the Blue Moon.

Trucks were angled between the Dumpsters; early deliveries were being received, inspected, inventoried. Shopkeepers, almost an hour ahead of their employees, were busy at the rear entrances of their establishments.

Death came, Death went, but commerce flowed eternal.

A few people noticed me. I knew none of them well, some of them not at all.

The character of their recognition was uncomfortably familiar to me. They knew me as the hero, as the guy who stopped the lunatic who had shot all those people the previous August.

Forty-one were shot. Some were crippled for life, disfigured. Nineteen died.

I might have prevented all of it. *Then* I might have been a hero.

Chief Porter says hundreds would have perished if I hadn't acted when I did, how I did. But the potential victims, those spared, do not seem real to me.

Only the dead seem real.

None of them have lingered. They all moved on.

But too many nights I see them in my dreams. They appear as they were in life, and as they might have been if they had survived.

On those nights, I wake with a sense of loss so terrible that I would prefer not ever to wake again. But I do wake, and I go on, for that is what the daughter of Cassiopeia, one of the nineteen, would want me to do, would *expect* me to do.

I have a destiny that I must earn. I live to earn it, and then to die.

The only benefit of being tagged a hero is that you are regarded by most people with some degree of awe and that, by playing to this awe, by wearing a somber expression and avoiding eye contact, you can almost always ensure that your privacy will be respected.

Wandering the alleyway, occasionally observed but undisturbed, I came to a narrow undeveloped lot. A chain-link fence restricted access.

I tried the gate. Locked.

A sign declared MARAVILLA COUNTY FLOOD-CONTROL PROJECT, and in red letters warned AUTHORIZED PERSONNEL ONLY.

Here I discovered the unspooled ribbon of my sixth sense. Touching the chain-link gate, I felt certain that Danny had gone this way.

A lock would be no impediment to a determined fugitive like Simon Makepeace, whose criminal skills had been enhanced by years of prison learning.

Beyond the fence, in the center of the lot, stood a ten-foot-square slump-stone building with a concrete barrel-tile roof. The two plank doors on the front of this structure were no doubt also locked, but the hardware looked ancient.

If Danny had been forced through this gate and through those doors, as I sensed he had been,

Simon had not chosen this route on impulse. This had been part of his plan.

Or perhaps he had intended to retreat here only if things went badly at Dr. Jessup's place. Because of my timely arrival at the radiologist's house and because of Chief Porter's decision to block both highways, they had come here.

After parking in the Blue Moon lot, Simon had not put Danny in another vehicle. They had instead gone through this gate, through those doors, and down into a world below Pico Mundo, a world that I knew existed but that I had never visited.

My first impulse was to reach Chief Porter and to share what I intuited.

Turning away from the fence, I felt restrained by a subsequent intuition: Danny's situation was so tenuous that a traditional search party, pursuing them into the depths, would likely be the death of him.

Furthermore, I sensed that while his situation might be grave, he was not in *imminent* danger. In this particular chase, speed wasn't as important as stealth, and the pursuit would be successful only if I remained acutely observant of every detail the trail provided.

I had no way of knowing any of this to be true. I *felt* it in a half-assed precognitive way that is far more than a hunch but far short of an unequivocal vision.

Why I see the dead but cannot hear from them, why I can seek with psychic magnetism and sometimes find, but only sometimes, why I sense the looming threat but not its details, I do not know. Perhaps nothing in this broken world can be pure or of a piece, unfractured. Or perhaps I haven't learned to harness all the power I possess.

One of my most bitter regrets from the previous August is that in the rush and tumble of events, I had at times relied on reason when gut feelings would have served me better.

Daily I walk a high wire, always in danger of losing my balance. The essence of my life is supernatural, which I must respect if I am to make the best use of my gift. Yet I live in the rational world and am subject to its laws. The temptation is to be guided entirely by impulses of an otherworldly origin—but in *this* world a long fall will always end in a hard impact.

I survive by finding the sweet spot between reason and unreason, between the rational and the irrational. In the past, my tendency has been to err on the side of logic, at the expense of faith—faith in myself and in the Source of my gift.

If I failed Danny, as I believed that I had failed others the previous August, I would surely come to despise myself. In failure, I would resent having been given the gift that defines me. If my destiny can be fulfilled only through the use of my sixth sense, too great a loss of self-respect and self-confidence would lead me to another fate different from the one that I desire, making a lie of the fortune-machine card that is framed above my bed.

This time I would choose to err on the side of illogic. I had to trust intuition, and plunge as I had never plunged before, with blind faith.

I would not call Chief Porter. If my heart said I alone must go after Danny, I would obey my heart.

13

AT MY APARTMENT, I STUFFED A SMALL BACK-pack with items I might need, including two flashlights and a package of spare batteries.

In the bedroom, I stood at the foot of the bed, silently reading the framed card on the wall: YOU ARE DESTINED TO BE TOGETHER FOREVER.

I wanted to pry out the backing and remove the card from the frame, to take it with me. I would feel safer with it, protected.

This was a variety of irrational thought that could never serve me well. A card dispensed by a machine in a carnival arcade is not the equivalent of a fragment of the true cross.

Another and even less rational thought tormented me. In pursuit of Danny and his father, I might die, and having crossed the sea of death, arriving on the shore of the next world, I would want to have the card to present to whatever Presence met me there.

This, I would say, *is the promise I was made. She came here ahead of me, and now you must take me to her.*

In truth, although the circumstances in which we had gotten this fortune from the machine had seemed extraordinary and meaningful, no miracle had been involved. The promise was not of divine origin; it was one that she and I had made to each other, with mutual trust in the mercy of God to grant us the grace of eternity together.

If a Presence meets me on the farther shore, I cannot prove a divine contract merely with a card from a fortune-telling machine. If the afterlife I envision is different from the one Heaven has planned for me, I can't invoke the threat of litigation and demand the name of a good attorney.

Conversely, if this grace should be granted and the promise of the card fulfilled, the Presence who meets me on that distant shore will be Bronwen Llewellyn herself, my Stormy.

The proper place for the card was in the frame. There it would be safe and could continue to inspire me if I returned from this expedition alive.

When I went into the kitchen to call Terri Stambaugh at the Pico Mundo Grille, Elvis was sitting at the table, weeping.

I hate seeing him like this. The King of Rock 'n' Roll should never cry.

He shouldn't pick his nose, either, but occasionally he does. I am sure this is a joke. A ghost has no need to pick its nose. Sometimes he pretends to find a nugget and to flick it at me, then grins boyishly.

Lately, he'd been reliably cheerful. But he suffered sudden mood swings.

Dead more than twenty-seven years, with no purpose in this world but unable to move on, as lonely as only the lingering dead can be, he had reason to wallow in melancholy. The cause of his distress, however, appeared to be the salt and pepper shakers on the table.

Terri, as devoted a Presley fan and authority as anyone alive, had given me the two ceramic Elvises, each four inches high, which dated to 1962. The one dressed in white dispensed salt from his guitar; the one in black gave pepper from his pompadour.

Elvis looked at me, pointed at the salt shaker, at the pepper, then at himself.

"What's wrong?" I asked, though I knew that he would not answer.

He turned his face to the ceiling, as though to Heaven, with an expression of abject misery, sobbing silently.

The salt and pepper shakers had stood on the table since the day after Christmas. He had previously been amused by them.

I doubted that he had been moved to despair by the long-delayed realization that his image had been exploited to sell cheap, cheesy merchandise.

Of the hundreds if not thousands of Elvis items that had been marketed over the years, scores were tackier than these ceramic collectibles, and he had not disapproved of licensing them.

Tears streamed down his cheeks, dripped off his jaw line, off his chin, but vanished before they spattered the table.

Unable to comfort or even understand Elvis, eager to get back to the Blue Moon alleyway, I used the kitchen phone to call the Grille, where they were in the breakfast rush.

I apologized for my bad timing, and Terri said at once, "Have you heard about the Jessups?"

"Been there," I said.

"You're in it, then?"

"To the neck. Listen, I've got to see you."

"Come now."

"Not in the Grille. All the old gang will want to chat. I'd like to see them, but I'm in a hurry."

"Upstairs," she said.

"I'm on my way."

When I hung up the phone, Elvis gestured to get my attention. He pointed at the salt shaker, pointed at the pepper shaker, formed a V with the forefinger and middle finger of his right hand, and blinked at me tearfully, expectantly.

This appeared to be an unprecedented attempt at communication.

"Victory?" I asked, reading the usual meaning in that hand sign.

He shook his head and thrust the V at me, as though urging me to reconsider my translation.

"Two?" I said.

He nodded vigorously. He pointed at the salt shaker, then at the pepper shaker. He held up two fingers.

"Two Elvises," I said.

This statement reduced him to a mess of shuddering emotion. He huddled, head bowed, face in his hands, shaking.

I rested my right hand on his shoulder. He felt as solid to me as every spirit does.

"I'm sorry, sir. I don't know what's upsetting you, or what I should do."

He had nothing more to convey to me either by expression or by gesture. He had retreated into his grief, and for the time being he was as lost to me as he was lost to the rest of the living world.

Although I regretted leaving him in that bleak condition, my obligation to the living is greater than to the dead.

14

TERRI STAMBAUGH OPERATED THE PICO Mundo Grille with her husband, Kelsey, until he died of cancer. Now she runs the place herself. For almost ten years, she has lived alone above the restaurant, in an apartment approached by stairs from the alleyway.

Since she lost Kelsey, when she was only thirty-two, the man in her life has been Elvis. Not his ghost, but the history and the myth of him.

She has every song the King ever recorded, and she has acquired encyclopedic knowledge of his life. Terri's interest in all things Presley preceded my revelation to her that his spirit inexplicably haunts our obscure town.

Perhaps as a defense against giving herself to another living man after Kelsey, to whom she has pledged her heart far beyond the requirement of their wedding vows, Terri loves Elvis. She loves not just his music and his fame, not merely the *idea* of him; she loves Elvis the man.

Although his virtues were many, they were outnumbered by his faults, frailties, and shortcomings. She knows that he was self-centered, especially after the early death of his beloved mother, that he found it difficult to trust anyone, that in some ways he remained an adolescent all his life. She knows how, in his later years, he escaped into addictions that spawned in him a meanness and a paranoia that were against his nature.

She is aware of all this and loves him nonetheless. She loves him for his struggle to achieve, for the passion that he brought to his music, for his devotion to his mother.

She loves him for his uncommon generosity even if there were times when he dangled it like a lure or wielded it like a club. She loves him for his faith, although he so often failed to follow its instructions.

She loves him because in his later years he remained humble enough to recognize how little of his promise he had fulfilled, because he knew regret and remorse. He never found the courage for true contrition, though he yearned to achieve it and the rebirth that would have followed it.

Loving is as essential to Terri Stambaugh as constant swimming is essential to the shark. This is an infelicitous analogy, but an accurate one. If a shark stops moving, it drowns; for survival, it requires uninterrupted movement. Terri must love or die.

Her friends know she would sacrifice herself for them, so deeply does she commit. She loves not just a burnished memory of her husband but loves who he truly was, the rough edges and the smooth. Likewise, she loves the potentiality *and* the reality of each friend.

I climbed the stairs, pressed the bell, and when she opened the door, she said at once, as she drew me across the threshold, "What can I do, Oddie, what do you need, what are you getting yourself into this time?"

When I was sixteen and desperate to escape from the psychotic kingdom that was my mother's home, Terri gave me a job, a chance, a life. She is still giving. She is my boss, my friend, the sister I never had.

After we embraced, we sat cater-corner at the kitchen table, holding hands on the red-and-white-checkered oilcloth. Her hands are strong and worn by work, and beautiful.

Elvis's "Good Luck Charm" was on her music system. Her speakers are never sullied by the songs of other singers.

When I told her where I believed Danny had been taken and that intuition insisted I go after him alone, her hand tightened on mine. "Why would Simon take him down there?"

"Maybe he saw the roadblock and turned around. Maybe he had a police-band radio and heard about it that way. The flood tunnels are another route out of town, under the roadblocks."

"But on foot."

"Wherever he surfaces with Danny, he can steal a car."

"Then he's already done that, hasn't he? If he took Danny down there hours ago, at least four hours ago, he's long gone."

"Maybe. But I don't think so."

Terri frowned. "If he's still in the flood tunnels, he took Danny there for some other reason, not to get him out of town."

Her instincts do not have the supernatural edge that mine do, but they are sharp enough to serve her well.

"I told Ozzie—there's something wrong with this."

"Wrong with what?"

"All this. Dr. Jessup's murder and all the rest. A *wrongness*. I can feel it, but I can't define it."

Terri is one of the handful of people who know about my gift. She understands that I am compelled to use it; she would not attempt to argue me out of action. But she wishes that this yoke would be lifted from me.

So do I.

As "Good Luck Charm" gave way to "Puppet

on a String," I put my cell phone on the table, told her that I had forgotten to plug it in the previous night, and asked to borrow hers while she recharged mine.

She opened her purse, fished out the phone. "It's not cell, it's satellite. But will it work down there, underground?"

"I don't know. Maybe not. But it'll probably work wherever I am when I come up again. Thanks, Terri."

I tested the volume of the ringer, dialed it down a little.

"And when mine is recharged," I said, "if you get any peculiar calls on it . . . give out the number of your phone, so they can try to reach me."

"Peculiar—how?"

I'd had time to mull over the call that I received while sitting under the poisonous brugmansia. Maybe the caller had dialed a wrong number. Maybe not.

"If it's a woman with a smoky voice, cryptic, won't give her name—I want to talk to her."

She raised her eyebrows. "What's that about?"

"I don't know," I said honestly. "Probably nothing."

As I tucked her phone into a zippered pocket on my backpack, she said, "Are you coming back to work, Oddie?"

"Soon maybe. Not this week."

"We got you a new spatula. Wide blade, microbeveled front edge. Your name's inlaid in the handle."

"That's cool."

"Entirely cool. The handle's red. Your name's in white, and it's in the same lettering as the original Coca-Cola logo."

"I miss frying," I said. "I love the griddle."

The staff of the diner had been my family for more than four years. I still felt close to them.

When I saw them these days, however, two things precluded the easy camaraderie we had enjoyed in the past: the reality of my grief, and their insistence on my heroism.

"Gotta go," I said, getting to my feet and shouldering the backpack once more.

Perhaps to detain me, she said, "So . . . has Elvis been around lately?"

"Just left him crying in my kitchen."

"Crying again? What about?"

I recounted the episode with the salt and pepper shakers. "He actually made an effort to help me understand, which is something new, but I didn't get it."

"Maybe I do," she said, as she opened the door for me. "You know he was an identical twin."

"I knew that, yeah, but I forgot."

"Jesse Garon Presley was stillborn at four o'clock in the morning, and Elvis Aaron Presley came into the world thirty-five minutes later."

"I half remember you telling me about that. Jesse was buried in a cardboard box."

"That's all the family could afford. He was laid to rest in Priceville Cemetery, northeast of Tupelo."

"How's that for fate?" I said. "Identical twins—they're going to look exactly alike, sound alike, and probably have exactly the same talent. But one becomes the biggest star in music history, and the other is buried as a baby in a cardboard box."

"It haunted him all his life," Terri said. "People say that he often talked to Jesse late at night. He felt like half of himself was missing."

"He sort of lived that way, too—like half of him was missing."

"He sort of did," she agreed.

Because I knew what that felt like, I said, "I've suddenly got more sympathy for the guy."

We hugged, and she said, "We need you here, Oddie."

"I need me here," I agreed. "You're everything a friend should be, Terri, and nothing that one shouldn't."

"When would it be a good idea for me to start worrying?"

"Judging by the look on your face," I said, "you already have."

"I don't like you going down there in the tunnels. It feels like you're burying yourself alive."

"I'm not claustrophobic," I assured her as I

stepped out of the kitchen, onto the exterior landing.

"That's not what I meant. I'm giving you six hours, then I'm calling Wyatt Porter."

"I'd rather you wouldn't do that, Terri. I'm as sure as I've ever been about anything—I've got to do this alone."

"Are you really? Or is this . . . something else?"

"What else would it be?"

Clearly, she had a specific fear, but she didn't want to put it into words. Instead of answering me, or even searching my eyes for an answer, she scanned the sky.

Dirty clouds were scudding in from the north-northeast. They looked like scrub rags that had swabbed a filthy floor.

I said, "There's more to this than Simon's jealousies and obsessions. A weirdness, I don't know what, but a SWAT team isn't going to bring Danny out of there alive. Because of my gift, I'm his best chance."

I kissed her on the forehead, turned, and started down the steps toward the alley.

"Is Danny dead already?" she asked.

"No. Like I said, I'm being drawn to him."

"Is that true?"

Surprised, I halted, turned. "He's alive, Terri."

"If Kelsey and I had been blessed with a child, he could've been as old as you."

I smiled. "You're sweet."

She sighed. "All right. Eight hours. Not a minute more. You might be a clairvoyant or a medium, or whatever it is you are, but I've got women's intuition, by God, and that counts for something, too."

No sixth sense was required for me to understand that it would be pointless to try to negotiate her up from eight hours to ten.

"Eight hours," I agreed. "I'll call you before then."

After I had started down the open stairs again, she said, "Oddie, the main reason you came here really *was* to borrow my phone—wasn't it?"

When I stopped and looked up again, I saw that she had come off the landing, onto the first step.

She said, "I guess for my own peace of mind, I've got to lay it out there. . . . You didn't come here to say good-bye, did you?"

"No."

"True?"

"True."

"Swear to God."

I raised my right hand as though I were an Eagle Scout making a solemn pledge.

Still dubious, she said, "It would be shitty of you to go out of my life with a lie."

"I wouldn't do that to you. Besides, I can't get where I want to go by conscious or unconscious suicide. I've got my strange little life to lead.

Leading it the best I can—that's how I buy the ticket to where I want to be. You know what I mean?"

"Yeah." Terri settled down on the top step. "I'll sit here and watch you go. It feels like bad luck to turn my back on you just now."

"Are you okay?"

"Go. If he's alive, go to him."

I turned away from her and descended the stairs once more.

"Don't look back," she said. "That's bad luck, too."

I reached the bottom of the stairs and followed the alleyway to the street. I didn't look back, but I could hear her softly crying.

15

I DID NOT SCOUT FOR OBSERVERS, DID NOT loiter in the hope that an ideal opportunity would arise, but walked directly to the nine-foot chain-link barrier and scaled it. I dropped onto the property of the Maravilla County Flood-Control Project less than ten seconds after reaching the alley side of the fence.

Few people expect bold trespassing in daylight. If anyone saw me scale the fence, he would most likely assume that I was one of the authorized personnel referenced on the gate sign and that I had lost my key.

Clean-cut young men, neatly barbered and beardless, are not readily suspected of nefarious activity. I am not only barbered and beardless but have no tattoos, no earring, no eyebrow ring, no nose ring, no lip ring, and have not subjected my tongue to a piercing.

Consequently, the most that anyone might

suspect about me is that I am a time-traveler from some distant future in which the oppressive cultural norms of the 1950s have been imposed once more on the populace by a totalitarian government.

The slump-stone utility building featured screened ventilation cutouts under the eaves. They were not large enough to admit even a trim young man with a low-profile haircut.

Earlier in the morning, peering through the chain-link, I had noticed that the hardware on the plank doors appeared ancient. It might have been installed back when California's governor believed in the healing potential of crystals, confidently predicted the obsolescence of the automobile by 1990, and dated a rock star named Linda Ronstadt.

On closer inspection, I saw that the lock cylinder was not only old but cheap. The collar did not feature a guard ring. This offered a level of security half a step up from a padlock.

During the walk here from the Grille, I had paused in Memorial Park to take a pair of sturdy locking tongs from my backpack. Now I withdrew them from under my belt and used them to rip the lock cylinder out of the door.

That was a noisy business, but it lasted no more than half a minute. Boldly, as if I belonged there, I went inside, found a light switch, and closed the doors behind me.

The shed contained a rack of tools, but primarily it served as a vestibule from which to gain access to the network of storm drains under Pico Mundo. Wide spiral stairs led down.

On the twisting staircase, picking out the perforated metal treads with my flashlight, I was reminded of the back stairs at the Jessup house. For a moment, it seemed that I had been swept into some dark game in which I had already once circled the board and had been brought by the roll of the dice to another dangerous descent.

I didn't turn on the stair lights because I didn't know if perhaps the same switch activated service lamps in the storm drains, which would announce my presence sooner than necessary.

I counted the steps, calculating eight inches for each riser. I descended over fifty feet, much deeper than I expected.

At the bottom, a door. The half-inch-diameter latch bolt could be operated from either side.

I thumbed off the flashlight.

Although I expected the bolt to scrape, the hinges to creak, instead the door opened without protest. It was remarkably heavy but smooth in action.

Blind and breathless, listening for a hostile presence, I heard nothing. When I had heard enough of it, I felt sufficiently safe to use the flashlight again.

Beyond the threshold lay a corridor that led to

my right: twelve feet long, five feet wide, a low ceiling. Following it, I discovered that it was an L, with an eight-foot short arm. Here stood another heavy door with a bolt action that worked from both sides.

This arrangement of access to the storm drains was more elaborate than I had imagined—and seemed unnecessarily complicated.

Again I doused the flashlight. Again the door eased open with not a sound.

In the absolute darkness, I listened and heard a faint silken sinuous sound. My mind's eye conjured an immense serpent slithering through the gloom.

Then I recognized the whisper of easy-flowing water as it slid without turbulence along the smooth walls of the conduit.

I switched on the flashlight, crossed the threshold. Immediately beyond lay a two-foot-wide concrete walkway, which seemed to lead to infinity both to my left and to my right.

A foot and a half below the walkway, gray water, perhaps taking much of its color by reflection from the concrete walls of the drain, swept past not in a churning rush but in a stately flow. The beam of the flashlight stitched silver filigrees across the gently undulating surface.

Based on the arc of the walls, I estimated that the water in the center of the channel measured, at its deepest, eighteen inches. Next to the walkway, it would plumb at less than a foot.

The storm drain appeared to be approximately twelve feet in diameter, a massive artery in the body of the desert. It bored away toward some distant dark heart.

I'd been concerned that switching on the service lamps in this maze would alert Simon that I was coming. But a flashlight would pinpoint me for anyone waiting in the darkness ahead.

Taking the only logical alternative to feeling my way in the dark, I retreated through the stairwell door and found a pair of switches. The nearest one brightened the drain.

Returning to the walkway, I saw that sandwiches of glass and wire protected lamps embedded in the ceiling of the tunnel at thirty-foot intervals. They did not shed the equivalent of daylight in this deep realm; repetitive bat-wings of shadow scalloped the walls, but visibility proved good enough.

Although this was a storm drain, not a sewer, I had expected a foul smell if not a full stink. The cool air had a dank scent, but it wasn't offensive, and had that almost appealing limy smell common to concrete places.

Most of the year, these passages carried no water. They dried out and therefore did not support lingering molds of any kind.

I considered the moving water for a moment. We'd not had rain in five days. This couldn't be the last runoff from the heights in the eastern part of the county. The desert isn't that slow to drain.

The clouds crawling down the northeast sky when I'd left Terri's place might have been the outrunners of a storming horde still hours distant.

You might wonder why a desert county would need flood-control tunnels as elaborate as these. The answer has two parts, one involving climate and terrain, the other geopolitics.

Although we have little rain in Maravilla County, when storms come, they are frequently fierce deluges. Large parts of the desert are less sand than shale, less shale than rock, with little soil or vegetation to absorb a downpour or to slow the runoff from higher elevations.

Flash floods can turn low-lying desert areas into vast lakes. Without aggressive diversion of storm runoff, a significant portion of Pico Mundo would be at risk.

We can go a year without a monster storm that makes us think nervously of Noah—and then have five the next year.

Nevertheless, flood control in desert towns usually consists of a network of concrete V ditches, weather-carved arroyos, and culverts feeding either a natural dry riverbed or one engineered to carry water away from human habitations. If not for the fact that Fort Kraken, a major air-force base, backed up to Pico Mundo, we would be served by an equally low-tech and imperfect system.

For six decades, Fort Kraken had been one of the nation's most vital military resources. The flood-control system that benefited Pico Mundo had been constructed largely to ensure that the runways and the vast facilities of the base were protected from Mother Nature in her most thunderous moods.

Some believe that under Kraken lies a deep-rock command-and-control complex that was designed to ride out nuclear strikes by the former Soviet Union and to serve as a governmental center for the reconstruction of the southwestern United States subsequent to an atomic war.

Following the end of the Cold War, Fort Kraken was downsized but not decommissioned as were many other military bases. Some say that because a chance exists that we may one day face an aggressive China armed with thousands of nuclear missiles, this hidden facility is maintained in readiness.

Rumors have it that these tunnels serve clandestine functions in addition to flood control. Maybe they disguise the venting of that deep-rock complex. Maybe some of them double as secret entrances.

All this may be true or it may be the equivalent of the urban legend that claims pet alligators, flushed down toilets when they were babies and grown to full adulthood, live in the New York City sewer system, feeding on rats and unwary sanitation workers.

One of the people who believe all or part of the Kraken story is Horton Barks, publisher of the *Maravilla County Times*. Mr. Barks also claims that twenty years ago, while hiking in the Oregon woods, he had a pleasant dinner of trail mix and canned sausages with Big Foot.

Being the person I am, with the experiences I've had, I tend to believe him about the Sasquatch.

Now, in search of Danny Jessup, trusting to my unique intuition, I turned right and followed the service walkway upstream, through ordered patterns of shadow and light, toward one kind of storm or another.

16

A BOBBING TENNIS BALL, A PLASTIC BAG pulsing as if it were a jellyfish, a playing card—the ten of diamonds—a gardening glove, a cluster of red petals that might have been cyclamen: Every object on the gray tide was luminous with mysterious meaning. Or so it all seemed to me, for I had fallen into a *mood* for meaning.

Because this water poured into the flood-control system not from Pico Mundo but from a storm far to the east, it carried less flotsam than it would later if the volume increased and the downpour washed in from city streets.

Tributary tunnels fed the one in which I walked. Some were dry, but others added to the flow. Many were about two feet in diameter, although several loomed as large as this passage by which I had entered.

At each intersection, the walkway ended but resumed on the farther side. At the first ford, I considered taking off my shoes and rolling up my jeans. Barefoot, I might step on something sharp in the water—a concern that kept me shod.

My new white sneakers were at once a mess. Terrible Chester might as well have peed on them.

Mile by mile, as I moved eastward, barely aware of the gradual incline, I found the subterranean structure increasingly impressive. The pleasurable curiosity that arises from exploration gradually matured into admiration for the architects, engineers, and skilled tradesmen who had conceived and executed this project.

Admiration began to ripen into something almost like wonder.

The complex of tunnels proved to be immense. Of those large enough to provide human passage, some were lighted, but others were dark. Those that were illuminated either dwindled away as if to infinity or curved gracefully out of sight.

I saw no terminations, only the openings to new branches.

A fantastic perception arose that I had ventured into a construction that stood between worlds, or linked them, as if uncountable nautilus shells intersected in myriad dimensions, the fluid geometries of their spiral passages offering pathways to new realities.

Beneath the city of New York supposedly lie seven levels of infrastructure. Some are cramped and tortuous to service, others grand in scale.

But this was Pico Mundo, home of the Gila Monsters. Our biggest cultural event is the annual cactus festival.

At key stress points, arches and buttresses lent reinforcement, and in some places the curved walls were ribbed. These elements had been executed with rounded edges that didn't detract from the organic quality of the whole.

The immense volume of these tunnels seemed excessive for their reputed purpose. I found it difficult to believe that, with so many routes to follow, the runoff from even a hundred-year storm would rise as far as the midpoint of one of the larger arteries.

I had no difficulty, however, believing that these tunnels were only secondarily drains and were primarily one-lane highways. Trucks could travel through them, even eighteen-wheelers, and transfer from one passage to another with a two-maneuver turn.

Ordinary trucks or mobile missile launchers.

I suspected that this labyrinth lay under not only Fort Kraken and Pico Mundo. It also extended miles north and south through the Maravilla Valley.

If you needed to move around hot-target nuclear assets during the first hours of the Last War, to get them out of the devastation of the initial strike zone to points from which they could be taken to the surface and launched, these subterranean highways might meet your requirements. They had been constructed at sufficient depth to allow considerable hardening against blast penetration.

Indeed, having accumulated this far below the surface, storm runoff eventually must be dumped not into a reservoir but into an underground lake or other geological formation that supported the area water table.

How peculiar to think of myself, in the days before my loss, at the griddle of the Pico Mundo Grille, frying cheeseburgers, wrecking eggs, turning bacon, dreaming of marriage, unaware that far beneath me, the highways of Armageddon lay in silent anticipation of sudden convoys of death.

Although I see the dead, whom others cannot see, the world wears many veils and is layered with secrets that cannot be perceived with merely a sixth sense.

Mile after mile, I progressed less quickly than I would have preferred. My psychic magnetism served me less well than usual, often leaving me standing in uncertainty when I arrived at the option of another conduit.

Doggedly nonetheless, I proceeded eastward, or suspected that I did. Holding fast to an accurate sense of direction underground is not easy.

For the first time, I encountered a depth-marker post—white with black numbers at one-foot intervals—situated in the center of the watercourse. This six-inch-square fixture rose eleven and a half feet, nearly to the apex of the curved ceiling.

The gray water reached three or four inches shy of the two-foot line, close to the estimation that I'd made earlier, but of greater interest was the corpse. It had snared on the post.

The cadaver bobbed facedown in the flow. The murky water, the billowing pants and shirt, prevented me from determining even the sex of the deceased from where I stood on the elevated walkway.

My heart knocked, knocked, and the sound of it echoed through me as though I were an empty house.

If this was Danny, I was done. Done not just with the search for him, but finished.

Two feet of fast-moving water could in an instant sweep a grown man off balance. This conduit had only a minimal slope, however, and the unchanging depth of the flow, plus the lazy look of it, suggested that the velocity was—and would continue to be for a while—less than overwhelming.

After dropping my backpack on the walkway, I stepped down into the channel and waded toward the marker post. As lazy as the water appeared to be, it still had power.

Rather than dawdle in midstream and tempt

the gods of the drain, I didn't at once try to roll the body over and look at its face, but grabbed a fistful of its clothing and towed it to the walkway.

Although I am comfortable with the spirits of the dead, cadavers spook me. They seem like empty vessels in which a new and malevolent entity might take up residence.

I've never actually known this to happen, though there's a clerk at the Pico Mundo 7-Eleven that I wonder about.

On the walkway, I flopped the body on its back and recognized the snaky man who had Tasered me.

Not Danny. A thin whimper of relief escaped me.

At the same time my nerves coiled tight and I shuddered. The dead man's face was unlike the faces of other corpses that I had seen.

His eyes had rolled so far back in his head that I could not see the thinnest crescent of green. Although he could have been dead, at most, only a couple hours, his eyes also seemed to swell forward as though pressure within the skull might force them from their sockets.

Had his face been a bloodless white, I wouldn't have been surprised. Had the skin already turned a pale green, as it always will within a day of death, I would have wondered what had hastened the process of decomposition, but I would not have been startled.

The skin was neither bloodless nor pale green, nor even livid, but several shades of gray, mottled from ash-pale to charcoal. He looked drawn, too, as if life were a juice that had been sucked out of him.

His mouth hung open. His tongue was gone. I didn't think anyone had cut it out. He appeared to have swallowed it. Aggressively.

His head bore no obvious injuries. Although I was curious about the cause of death, I had no intention of undressing him in a search for wounds.

I *did* roll him over, facedown, to check for a wallet. He wasn't carrying one.

If this man had not died accidentally, if he had been murdered, surely Danny Jessup had not killed him. Which seemed to leave only the possibility that he had been offed by one of his associates.

After retrieving my backpack and shrugging my arms through the straps, I continued in the direction that I had been headed. Several times, I glanced back, half expecting to discover that he had risen, but he never did.

17

EVENTUALLY I TURNED EAST-SOUTHEAST INTO another tunnel. This one was dark.

Sufficient light intruded past the intersection to reveal the GFI switch on the wall of the new passage. The stainless-steel plate was set at six feet, suggesting the designers of the flood-control system had not expected water ever to rise within a foot of that mark, confirming that the volume of the drains was far greater than a worst-case storm required.

I flicked the switch. The tunnel ahead brightened, as perhaps did other branches related to it.

Because I now proceeded east-southeast and because the storm was evidently coming in from the north, this new passageway brought no water toward me.

The concrete had nearly dried from its most recent soaking. The floor featured a skin of pale sediment littered with small items that had fallen out of the last spate of runoff from a previous storm.

I looked for footprints in the silt, but saw none. If Danny and his captors had come this way, they had stayed on the elevated walkway that I used.

My sixth sense compelled me forward. As I walked somewhat faster than before, I wondered . . . .

In the streets of Pico Mundo are manhole covers. Those heavy cast-iron discs must be disengaged from integrating latch slots and lifted with a special tool.

Logic argued that the conduits belonging to the department of power and water and those under the authority of the sewer department must be systems separate from—and much more humble than—the flood-control tunnels. Otherwise, I would by now have encountered numerous maintenance shafts with stairs or ladders.

Although I had walked miles in the first tunnel, I had not seen a single service entrance after the one through which I had arrived. Less than two hundred yards into the new passageway, I came to an unmarked steel door in the wall.

The psychic magnetism that drew me toward Danny Jessup did not pull me toward this exit. Simple curiosity motivated me.

Beyond the door—heavy to the point of massiveness, as had been the two through which

I had entered—I located a light switch and a T-shaped corridor. Other doors stood at the ends of the short arms of the T.

One of these revealed a vestibule where an open spiral of metal stairs led up to what was clearly another slump-stone shed like the one into which I had broken, property of the Maravilla County Flood-Control Project.

At the other end of the T, a door opened into a high-ceilinged transition space that housed a steep flight of conventional stairs. They rose twenty feet to a door marked PMDPW.

I interpreted this to mean *Pico Mundo Department of Power and Water*. Also stenciled on the steel was 16S-SW-V2453, which meant nothing to me.

I explored no farther. I had discovered that the subterranean systems of the department of power and water interfaced with the flood-control-project tunnels at least at a few points.

Why this might eventually be useful information, I didn't know, but I felt that it would.

After returning to the drain and discovering that the white-eyed snaky man was not waiting for me, I proceeded east-southeast.

When another tunnel met this one, the elevated walkway ended. In the powdery sediment below were footprints crossing the intersection to the place where the walkway resumed.

I dropped two feet to the drain floor and studied the prints in the silt.

Danny's tracks were different from the others. His numerous fractures over the years—and the unfortunate distortions in the bones that often accompanied healing in a victim of osteogenesis imperfecta—had left his right leg an inch shorter than his left, and twisted. He hobbled with a roll of the hips and tended to drag his right foot.

If I was also hunchbacked, he had once said, *I'd have a lifelong job in the bell tower at Notre Dame, with good fringe benefits, but as usual, Mother Nature hasn't played fair with me.*

In keeping with his diminutive stature, his feet were no bigger than those of a ten- or twelve-year-old. In addition, his right was a size larger than his left.

No one else could have made these tracks.

When I considered how far they had brought him on foot, I felt sick, angry, and afraid for him.

He could take short walks—a few blocks, a tour of the mall—without pain, sometimes even without discomfort. But a trek as long as this would be agony for him.

I had thought Danny had been taken by two men—his biological father, Simon Makepeace, and the nameless snaky man, now deceased. In the powdery silt, however, were *three* additional sets of footprints.

Two were the prints of grown men, one with larger feet than the other. The third appeared to have been made by a boy or a woman.

I tracked them across the confluence of tunnels to the next section of walkway. Thereafter, I again had nothing to follow except my uniquely intense intuition.

This dry section of the labyrinth lacked even the silken whisper of shallow water flowing unimpeded. This was deeper than a silence; this was a *hush*.

I have a light tread; and having proceeded at a measured pace, I was not breathing hard. Even as I walked, I could listen to the tunnel without masking any noises my quarry might make. But no telltale footfalls or voices came to me.

A couple of times, I halted, closed my eyes to concentrate on listening. I heard only a deep hollow *potential* for sound, and not a throb or gurgle that wasn't internal to me.

The evidence of such profound silence suggested that somewhere ahead, the four had departed the flood tunnels.

Why would Simon have kidnapped a son he didn't want and whom he refused to believe he had fathered?

Answer: If he thought that Danny was the offspring of the man with whom Carol had cuckolded him, Simon might take satisfaction in killing him. He was a sociopath. Neither logic nor ordinary emotions served as a foundation for his actions. Power—and the pleasure he got from exercising it—and survival were his only motivations.

That answer had satisfied me thus far—but no longer.

Simon could have murdered Danny in his bedroom. Or if my arrival at the Jessup house had interrupted him, he could have done the job in the van, while the snaky guy drove, and would have had time for torture if that was what he wanted.

Bringing Danny into this maze and hiking him through miles of tunnels qualified as a form of torture, but it was neither dramatic enough nor physically invasive enough to thrill a homicidal sociopath who liked *wet* work.

Simon—and his remaining two companions—had some use for poor Danny that eluded me.

Neither had they come this way to circumvent the roadblocks, nor the sheriff's-department aerial patrols. They could have found better places in which to lie low until the blockades were removed.

With grim expectations, I walked faster now, not because psychic magnetism pulled me more effectively, which it did not, but because at each intersection, I had the confirmation of their footprints in the silt.

The endless gray walls, the monotony of the patterns of shadow and light thrown by the overhead lamps, the silence: This might have served as Hell for any hopeless sinner whose two greatest fears were solitude and boredom.

Following the discovery of the first footprints,

I hurried along for more than another thirty minutes, not running but walking briskly—and came to the place at which they had exited the maze.

18

WHEN I TOUCHED THE STAINLESS-STEEL service door in the wall of the tunnel, a psychic hook bit deep, and I felt myself being reeled forward, as if my quarry were the fishermen and I the fish.

Beyond the door, an L-shaped hallway. At the end of the L, a door. Pushing through the door, I found a vestibule, spiral stairs, and at the top another slump-stone shed with tool rack.

Although the February day was pleasantly warm, not blistering, the air in here was stuffy. The smell of dry rot settled from the rafters under the sun-baked metal roof.

Apparently Simon had picked the lock as he had done at the first shed off the alleyway near the Blue Moon Cafe. Leaving, they had closed the door, and it had latched securely behind them.

With my laminated driver's license, I could spring a simple latch, but although cheap and flimsy, this model would be impervious to a plastic loid. I retrieved the pair of locking tongs from my backpack.

I was not concerned about the noise alerting Simon and his crew. They would have passed this way hours ago; and I had every reason to believe that they had kept moving.

As I was about to apply the tongs to the lock cylinder, Terri's satellite phone rang, startling me.

I fumbled it from my pocket and answered on the third ring. "Yeah?"

"Hi."

From that single word, I recognized the smoky-voiced woman who had called while I'd been sitting under the branches of the poisonous brugmansia behind the Ying house, the previous night.

"You again."

"Me."

She could have obtained this number only by calling my recharged cell phone and talking to Terri.

"Who are you?" I asked.

"You still think I have the wrong number?"

"No. Who are you?"

She said, "You have to ask?"

"Didn't I just?"

"You shouldn't have to ask."

"I don't know your voice."

"So many men know it well."

If she wasn't speaking in riddles, she was at least being obscure, taunting.

"Have I ever met you?" I asked.

"No. But can't you dream me up?"

"Dream you up?"

"I'm disappointed in you."

"Again?"

"Still."

I thought of the footprints in the silt. One pair had belonged to either a boy or a woman.

Not sure of the game, I waited.

She waited, too.

In most of the rafter junctions, spiders had spun webs. Those architects hung, glossy and black, among the pale carcasses of flies and moths on which they had feasted.

Finally I said, "What do you want?"

"Miracles."

"By which you mean—what?"

"Fabulous impossible things."

"Why call me?"

"Who else?"

"I'm a fry cook."

"Astonish me."

"I sling hash."

She said, "Icy fingers."

"What?"

"That's what I want."

"You want icy fingers?"

"Up and down my spine."

"Get an Eskimo masseuse."

"Masseuse?"

"For the icy fingers."

The humorless always need to ask, and she did: "Is that a joke?"

"Not a great one," I admitted.

"You think everything's funny? Is that the way you are?"

"Not everything."

"Not very much at all, asshole. You laughing now?"

"No, not now."

"You know what I think would be funny?"

I didn't reply.

"What I think would be funny is I take a hammer to the little creep's arm."

Overhead, an eight-legged harpist moved, and silent arpeggios trembled through taut strings of spider silk.

She said, "Will his bones shatter like glass?"

I didn't at once respond. I thought before I spoke, then said, "I'm sorry."

"What're you sorry for?"

"I'm sorry for offending you with the joke about the Eskimo."

"Baby, I don't offend."

"I'm glad to hear that."

"I just get pissed off."

"I'm sorry. I mean it."

"Don't be boring," she said.

I said, "Please don't hurt him."

"Why shouldn't I?"

"Why should you?"

"To get what I want," she said.

"What do you want?"

"Miracles."

"Maybe it's me, I'm sure it is, but you aren't making sense."

"Miracles," she repeated.

"Tell me what I can do?"

"Amazements."

"What can I do to get him back unhurt?"

"You disappoint me."

"I'm trying to understand."

"He's proud of his face, isn't he?" she asked.

"Proud? I don't know."

"It's the only part of him not screwed up."

My mouth had gone dry, but not because the shed was hot and layered with dust.

"He's got a pretty face," she said. "For now."

She terminated the call.

Briefly I considered pressing *69 to see if I could ring her back even though she had a block on her caller ID. I did not do it because I suspected this would be a mistake.

Although her cryptic statements shed no light on her enigmatic agenda, one thing seemed clear. She was accustomed to control, and at the mildest challenge to it, she responded with hostility.

Having assigned to herself the aggressive role

in this, she expected me to be passive. If I star-sixty-nined her, she would no doubt be pissed off.

She was capable of cruelty. What anger I inspired in her, she might vent on Danny.

The smell of dry rot. Of dust. Of something dead and desiccated in a shadowy corner.

I returned the phone to my pocket.

On a silken thread, a spider descended from its web, lazily turning in the still air, legs trembling.

19

I RIPPED OUT THE LOCK CYLINDER, SHOVED open the door, and left the spiders to their preying.

So otherworldly and disturbing had been the flood-control system, so eerie the phone conversation that followed, had I stepped across the threshold into Narnia, I would not have been more than mildly surprised.

In fact, I found myself beyond the limits of Pico Mundo, but not in a land ruled by magic. On all sides lay desert scrub, rocky and remorseless.

This shed stood on a concrete pad twice its size. A chain-link fence enclosed the facility.

I walked the perimeter of this enclosure, studying the rugged landscape, seeking any sign of an observer. The encircling terrain offered no good hiding places.

When it appeared that retreat to the shed, to avoid gunfire, would not be necessary, I climbed the chain-link gate.

The stony ground immediately before me took no impressions. Relying on intuition, I headed south.

The sun had reached its apex. Perhaps five hours of daylight remained before the early winter nightfall.

To the south and west, the pale sky looked three shades short of the ideal blue, as though it had been faded by millennia of sunshine reflected upon it from the Mojave.

In contrast, behind me, the northern third of the heavens had been consumed by ravenous masses of threatening clouds. They were dirty, as they had been earlier, but now also bruised.

Within a hundred yards, I topped a low hill and descended into a swale where the soft soil took prints. Before me again were the tracks of the fugitives and their captive.

Danny had been dragging his right foot worse here than in the flood tunnels. The evidence of his gait suggested acute pain and desperation.

Most victims of osteogenesis imperfecta—OI—experience a marked decrease in fractures following puberty. Danny had been one of those.

Upon reaching adulthood, the most fortunate discover that they are only minimally—if at all—more prone to broken bones than are people without their affliction. They are left with the legacy of bodies distorted by deformed healing and abnormal bone growth, and some of them eventually go deaf from otosclerosis, but otherwise the worst ravages of this genetic disorder are behind them.

While not ten percent as fragile as he had been as a child, Danny was one of an unfortunate minority of OI adults who must remain cautious. He had not in a long time *casually* broken a bone, as when he had at the age of six cracked his wrist while snap-dealing Old Maid. But a year ago, in a fall, he had fractured his right radius.

For a moment I studied the woman's footprints, wondering who she was, what she was, why.

I followed the swale about two hundred yards before the tracks departed it. They vanished on a stony slope.

As I started to climb the hillside, the satellite phone rang.

She said, "Odd Thomas?"

"Who else?"

"I've seen your picture," she said.

"My ears always photograph bigger than they are."

"You have the look," she said.

"What look?"

"Mundunugu."

"Is that a word?"

"You know what it means."

"I'm sorry, but I don't."

"Liar," she said, but not angrily.

This was the equivalent of table conversation at the Mad Hatter's tea party.

She said, "You want the little creep?"

"I want Danny. Alive."

"You think you can find him?"

I said, "I'm trying."

"You were so fast, now you're damn slow."

"What do you think you know about me?"

In a coy voice, she said, "What is there to know, baby?"

"Not much."

"For Danny's sake, I hope that's not true."

I began to have the queasy if inexplicable feeling that somehow Dr. Jessup had been murdered . . . because of me.

"You don't want to be in trouble this bad," I said.

"Nobody can hurt me," she declared.

"Is that right?"

"I'm invincible."

"Good for you."

"You know why?"

"Why?"

"I have thirty in an amulet."

"Thirty what?" I asked.

"Ti bon ange."

I had never heard the term before. "What does that mean?"

"You know."

"Not really."

"Liar."

When she didn't hang up but didn't immediately say anything more, either, I sat on the ground, facing west again.

Except for an occasional clump of mesquite and a bristle of bunch-grass, the land was ash-gray and acid-yellow.

"You still there?" she asked.

"Where would I go?"

"So *where* are you?"

I traded another question: "Can I speak to Simon?"

"Simple or says?"

"What's that mean?"

"Simple Simon or Simon Says?"

"Simon Makepeace," I said patiently.

"You think he's here?"

"Yes."

"Loser."

"He killed Wilbur Jessup."

"You're half-assed at this," she said.

"At what?"

"Don't disappoint me."

"I thought you said I already had."

"Don't disappoint me *anymore*."

"Or what?" I asked, and immediately wished that I had not.

"How about this. . . ."

I waited.

Finally she said, "How about, you find us by sundown or we break both his legs."

"If you want me to find you, just tell me where you are."

"What would be the point of that? If you don't find us by nine o'clock, we also break both his arms."

"Don't do this. He never harmed you. He never harmed anyone."

"What's the first rule?" she asked.

Remembering our shortest and most cryptic conversation, from the previous night, I said, "I have to come alone."

"You bring cops or anyone, we break his pretty face, and then the rest of his life, he'll be butt ugly from top to bottom."

When she hung up, I pressed END.

Whoever she might be, she was crazy. Okay. I'd dealt with crazy before.

She was crazy *and* evil. Nothing new about that, either.

20

I SHRUGGED OUT OF MY BACKPACK AND rummaged in it for an Evian bottle. The water wasn't cold but tasted delicious.

The plastic bottle did not actually contain Evian. I had filled it at the tap in my kitchen.

If you would pay a steep price for bottled water, why wouldn't you pay even more for a bag of fresh Rocky Mountain air if someday you saw it in the market?

Although I am not a skinflint, for years I have lived frugally. As a short-order cook with plans to marry, paid a fair but not lavish salary, I had needed to save for our future.

Now she is gone, and I am alone, and the last thing I need money for is a wedding cake. Yet from long habit, when it comes to spending on myself, I still pinch each penny hard enough to press it into the size of a quarter.

Given my peculiar and adventurous life, I don't

expect to live long enough to develop an enlarged prostate, but if I *do* miraculously reach ninety before I croak, I'll probably be one of those eccentrics who, assumed to be poor, leaves a million dollars' cash rolled up in old coffee cans with instructions to spend it on the care of homeless poodles.

After finishing the faux Evian, I returned the empty bottle to my backpack, and then watered a patch of desert with Odd's finest.

I suspected that I had drawn close to my objective, and now I had a deadline. Sundown.

Before completing the final leg of the journey, however, I needed to know about a few things that were happening in the real world.

None of Chief Porter's numbers were programmed for speed dial on Terri's phone, but I had long ago memorized all of them.

He answered his mobile phone on the second ring. "Porter."

"Sir, sorry to interrupt."

"Interrupt what? You think I'm in a whirl of busy police work?"

"Aren't you?"

"Right now, son, I feel like a cow."

"A cow, sir?"

"A cow standing in a field, chewing its cud."

"You don't sound as relaxed as a cow," I said.

"It's not cow-relaxed I'm feeling. It's cow-dumb."

"No leads on Simon?"

"Oh, we've got Simon. He's jailed in Santa Barbara."

"That's pretty fast work."

"Faster than you think. He was arrested two days ago for starting a bar fight. He struck the arresting officer. They're holding him for assault."

"Two days ago. So the case . . ."

"The case," he said, "isn't what we thought it was. Simon didn't kill Dr. Jessup. Though he says he's happy someone did."

"Was it maybe murder-for-hire?"

Chief Porter laughed sourly. "With Simon's prison record, the job he was able to get was pumping out septic tanks. He lives in a rented room."

"Some people would do a hit for a thousand bucks," I said.

"They sure would, but the most they'd be likely to get from Simon is a free septic clean-out."

The dead desert did a Lazarus, breathed and seemed about to rise. Bunch-grass shivered. Jimsonweed whispered briefly, but then fell silent as the air went still.

Gazing north, toward the distant thunderheads, I said, "What about the white van?"

"Stolen. We didn't get any prints off it worth spit."

"No other leads?"

"Not unless county CSI finds some strange DNA or other trace evidence at the Jessup place. What's the situation with you, son?"

I surveyed the surrounding wasteland. "I'm out and about."

"Feeling at all magnetic?"

Lying to him would be harder than lying to myself. "I'm being pulled, sir."

"Pulled where?"

"I don't know yet. I'm still on the move."

"Where are you now?"

"I'd rather not say, sir."

"You're not gonna Lone Ranger this," he worried.

"If that seems best."

"No Tonto, no Silver—that's not smart. Use your head, son."

"Sometimes you've got to trust your heart."

"No point in me arguing with you, is there?"

"No, sir. But something you could do is run a search of Danny's room, look for evidence that a woman might've come into his life lately."

"You know I'm not cruel, Odd, but as a cop, I have to stay *real*. If that poor kid went on a date, it would be all over Pico Mundo the next morning."

"This might be a discreet relationship, sir. And I'm not saying Danny got anything from it that he hoped to. Fact is, maybe he got a world of hurt."

After a silence, the chief said, "He would be vulnerable, you mean. To a predator."

"Loneliness can lower your defenses."

The chief said, "But they didn't steal anything. They didn't ransack the house. They didn't even bother taking the money out of Dr. Jessup's wallet."

"So they wanted something other than money from Danny."

"Which would be—what?"

"That's still a blind spot for me, sir. I can sort of feel a shape in it, but I can't yet see the thing."

Far to the north, between the charred sky and the ashen earth, the rain resembled shimmering curtains of smoke.

"I have to get moving," I said.

"If we turn up anything about a woman, I'll call you."

"No, sir, I'd rather you didn't. I need to keep the line open and save the battery. I just called because I wanted you to know there's a woman in it, so if anything happens to me, you've got a starting place. A woman and three men."

"Three? The one who Tasered you—and who else?"

"Thought one must be Simon," I said, "but now he can't be. All I know about the others is, one of them has big feet."

"Big feet?"

"Say a prayer for me, sir."

"I do each night."

I terminated the call.

After hoisting my backpack, I continued the climb that had been interrupted by the woman's call. The slope rose a long way but at a gentle incline. Rotten shale crunched and slid from under my feet, repeatedly testing my agility and balance.

A few small lizards skittered out of my way. I remained watchful for rattlesnakes.

Rugged leather hiking boots would have been better than the softer sneakers that I was wearing. Eventually, I would probably have to do some sneaking, and these once-white shoes would be ideal for that.

Maybe I shouldn't have worried about footwear, snakes, and balance if I was destined to be killed by someone waiting behind a white paneled door. On the other hand, I didn't want to rely on the theory that the repetitive dream was reliably predictive, because perhaps it had just been the consequence of too much fried food and spicy salsa.

Distant and celestial, a great door rolled open, rumbling in its tracks, and a breeze stirred the day again. When the faraway thunder faded, the air did not fall still as it had earlier, but continued to chase through the sparse vegetation, like a ghost pack of coyotes.

When I reached the top of the hill, I knew that

my destination lay before me. Danny Jessup would be found here, captive.

In the distance lay the interstate. A four-lane approach road led from that highway to the plain below. At the end of the road stood the ruined casino and the blackened tower, where Death had gone to gamble and had, as always, won.

21

THEY WERE THE PANAMINT TRIBE, OF THE Shoshoni-Comanche family. These days we are told that throughout their history—like all the natives of this land prior to Columbus and the imposition of Italian cuisine on the continent—they had been peaceful, deeply spiritual, selfless, and unfailingly reverent toward nature.

The gambling industry—feeding on weakness and loss, indifferent to suffering, materialistic, insatiably greedy, smearing across nature some of the ugliest, gaudiest architecture in the history of human construction—was seen by Indian leaders as a perfect fit for them. The state of California agreed, granting to Native Americans a monopoly on casino gambling within its borders.

Concerned that the Great Spirit alone might not provide enough guidance to squeeze every possible drop of revenue out of their new enterprises, most tribes made deals with experienced gaming companies to manage their casinos. Cash rooms were established, games were set up and staffed, the doors were opened, and under the watchful eyes of the usual thugs, the river of money flowed.

The golden age of Indian wealth loomed, every Native American soon to be rich. But the flow did not reach as deeply or as quickly into the Indian population as expected.

Funny how that happens.

Addiction to gambling, impoverishment therefrom, and associated crime rose in the community.

Not so funny how that happens.

On the plain below the hilltop where I stood, about a mile away, on tribal land, waited the Panamint Resort and Spa. Once it had been as glittering, as neon-splashed, as tacky as any facility of its kind, but its glory days were gone.

The sixteen-story hotel had all the grace of a high-rise prison. Five years ago, it had withstood an earthquake with minor damage, but it had failed to weather the subsequent fire. Most of its windows had been shattered by the temblor or had exploded from the heat as the rooms blazed. Great lapping tongues of smoke had licked black patterns across the walls.

The two-story casino, wrapping three sides of the tower, had collapsed at one corner. Cast in tinted concrete, a facade of mystic Indian symbols—many of which were not actual Indian symbols but New Age interpretations of Indian spiritualism as previously conceived by Hollywood film designers—had mostly torn away from the building and collapsed into the surrounding parking lot. A few vehicles remained, crushed and corroding under the debris.

Concerned that a sentinel with binoculars might be surveying the approaches, I retreated from the hilltop, hoping that I had not been spotted.

Within days of the resort disaster, many had predicted that, considering the money to be made, the place would be rebuilt within a year. Four years later, demolition of the burned-out hulk had not begun.

Contractors were accused of having cut corners in construction that weakened the structure. County building inspectors were brought up on charges of having accepted bribes; they in turn blew the whistle on corruption in the county board of supervisors.

So much blame could be widely assessed that a farrago of both legitimate and frivolous litigation, of battling public-relations firms, resulted in several bankruptcies, two suicides, uncounted divorces, and one sex-change operation.

Most of those Panamints who had made fortunes had been stripped of them by settlements or were hemorrhaging still to attorneys. Those who had never gotten wealthy but had become compulsive gamblers were inconvenienced by the need to travel farther to lose what little they had.

Currently, half the litigations await final resolution, and no one knows if the resort will rise like a phoenix. Even the right—some would say the obligation—to bulldoze the ruins has been frozen by a judge pending the fate of an appeal of a key court decision.

Staying below the crest, I traversed south until the rocky slope rolled into a declivity.

Numerous hills fold to form a crescent collar around the west, south, and east of the plain on which the ravaged resort stands, with flatlands and bustling interstate to the north. Among these folds, I followed a series of narrow divides that eventually widened into a dry wash, progressing east by a serpentine route forced upon me by the topography.

If Danny's kidnappers had camped on one of the higher floors of the hotel, the better to keep a lookout, I needed to approach from an unexpected direction. I wanted to get as close to the property as possible before coming out in the open.

How the nameless woman knew that I would be able to follow them, how she knew that I would be compelled to follow, why she *wanted* me to follow, I couldn't explain with certainty. Reason, however, led me to the inescapable suspicion that Danny had shared with her the secret of my gift.

Her cryptic conversation on the phone, her taunting, seemed designed to tease admissions from me. She sought confirmation of facts that she already knew.

A year ago, he had lost his mother to cancer. As his closest friend, I had been a companion in his grief—until my own loss in August.

He was not a man with many friends. His physical limitations, his appearance, and his acerbic wit limited his social opportunities.

When I had turned inward, giving myself entirely to my grief, and then to writing about the events of August, I had not comforted him any longer, not as generously as I should have done.

For consolation, he had his adoptive father. But Dr. Jessup had been grieving, too, and being a man of some ambition, had probably sought solace in his work.

Loneliness comes in two basic varieties. When it results from a desire for solitude, loneliness is a door we close against the world. When the world instead rejects us, loneliness is an open door, unused.

Someone had come through that door when Danny was at his most vulnerable. She had a smoky, silken voice.

22

IN A BELLY CRAWL, OUT OF THE DRY WASH, onto flat land, leaving the hills behind, I squirmed fast through bush sage three feet high, which gave me cover. My objective was a wall that separated the desert from the grounds of the resort.

Jackrabbits and a variety of rodents shelter from the sun and nibble leaves in just such vegetation. Where rabbits and rats went, snakes would follow, feeding.

Fortunately snakes are shy; not as shy as church mice, but shy enough. To warn them off, I made plenty of noise before slithering out of the wash and into the sage, and as I moved, I grunted and spat dirt and sneezed and, in general, produced enough noise to annoy all wildlife into relocating.

Assuming that my adversaries had camped high in the hotel, and considering that I was still a few hundred yards from that structure, what noise I made would not alert them.

If they happened to be looking in this direction, they would be scanning for movement. But the rustle of the bush sage would not draw special notice; the breeze out of the north had stiffened, shuddering all the scrub and weeds. Tumbleweed tumbled, and here and there a dust devil danced.

Having avoided the bite of snake, the sting of scorpion, the nip of spider, I reached the edge of the resort grounds. I got to my feet and leaned with my back against the wall.

I was covered in pale dust and in a powdery white substance acquired from the undersides of the sage leaves.

The unfortunate consequence of psychic magnetism is not only that it too often draws me into dangerous circumstances but also into dirty places. I'm perpetually behind in my laundry.

After brushing myself off, I followed the resort wall, which gradually curved northeast. On this side, exposed concrete block had been painted white; on the farther side, where paying customers had been able to see it, the eight-foot-high barrier had been plastered and painted pink.

Following the quake and the fire, tribal officials posted metal signs at hundred-foot intervals, sternly warning would-be trespassers of the dangers of the damaged structures beyond and of toxic residues they might contain. The Mojave sun had faded those warnings, but they remained readable.

Along the wall, on the grounds of the resort, were irregularly planted clusters of palm trees. Because they were not native to the Mojave and hadn't been watered after the quake wrecked the landscape-irrigation system, they were dead.

Some of the fronds had fallen off; others hung as if limp; and the rest bristled, shaggy and brown. Nevertheless, I found a cluster that screened a portion of the wall from the hotel.

I jumped, got a handhold, clambered up, over, and dropped into a drift of debris from the palms, not as fluidly as those words imply, but with enough thrashing and elbow-knocking to prove beyond doubt that I couldn't have descended from apes. I crouched behind the thick palm boles.

Beyond the ragged trees lay an enormous swimming pool crafted to imitate a natural rock formation. Man-made waterfalls doubled as water slides.

Nothing fell from the falls. The drained pool was half full of windblown debris.

If Danny's captors were keeping a watch, they would most likely focus their attention to the west, the direction from which they themselves had come. They might also be monitoring the road that linked the resort and the interstate in the north.

The three of them could not guard four sides of the hotel. Furthermore, I doubted that each would go off alone to a separate post. At most, their vigilance encompassed two of the approaches.

Chances were that I could get from the palms to the building without being seen.

They would have more weapons than the shotgun, but I didn't worry about taking a bullet. If they had wanted to kill me, I would not have been Tasered at the Jessup house; I would have been shot in the face.

Later, perhaps, they would be pleased to kill me. Now they wanted something else. Miracles. Amazements. Icy fingers. Fabulous impossible things.

So . . . get inside, scout the terrain, find out where they were holding Danny. Once I understood the situation, if I could not spring him without help, I'd have to call Wyatt Porter regardless of the fact that in this case my intuition equated police involvement with certain death.

I broke from the cover of the trees and raced across artificial-stone decking where once well-oiled sunbathers had drowsed on padded lounge chairs, prepping themselves for melanoma.

Instead of tropical rum drinks, an open-air tiki-style poolside bar offered formidable piles of bird droppings. These were produced by feathered presences that I could not see, but that I heard. The flock roosted on the crisscrossing lengths of imitation bamboo that supported the densely thatched roof of plastic palm fronds, and as I hurried past, they flapped and shrilled to warn me off.

By the time I rounded the pool and reached the back entrance to the hotel, I'd had a chance to draw a lesson from the unseen birds. Broken, burned, abandoned, wind-worn, sand-scoured, even if more structurally sound than not, the Panamint Resort and Spa no longer merited even a single star in the Michelin Guide; but it might have become the home to various desert fauna that found the place more hospitable than their usual holes in the ground.

In addition to the threat posed by the mystery woman and her two murderous male friends, I would need to be alert for predators that had no mobile phones.

The sliding glass doors at the back of the hotel, shattered in the quake, had been replaced with sheets of plywood to deny easy access to the morbidly curious. Stapled to these panels were plastic sleeves holding notices of the vigorous civil actions that would be taken against anyone caught on the premises.

The screws that held one of the sheets of plywood in place had been removed, and the panel had been laid aside. Judging by the sand and scraps of weeds that had drifted over the panel, it had not been taken down as recently as the past twenty-four hours, but weeks or months ago.

For two years or so after the destruction of the

resort, the tribe had paid for a roving security patrol 24/7. As the suits and countersuits proliferated and the likelihood grew that the property might be surrendered to creditors—much to the creditors' horror—the patrols had become an expense it no longer made sense to incur.

With the hotel open before me, with a breeze churning itself into a wind at my back, with a storm coming and Danny at risk, I nevertheless hesitated to cross the threshold. I am not as fragile as Danny Jessup, neither physically nor emotionally, yet everyone has a breaking point.

I delayed not because of the people or the other living menaces that lurked in the ruined resort. I was given pause, instead, by the thought of the lingering dead who might still haunt its soot-stained spaces.

23

INSIDE THE REAR DOORS OF THE HOTEL LAY what might have been a secondary lobby illuminated only by ashen light that sifted through the gap in the plywood barrier.

My shadow before me, a gray ghost, was visible from its legs to its neck. Its head became one with the murk, as though it were cast by a decapitated man.

I switched on a flashlight and swept the walls. The fire itself had not raged here, but smoke stains mottled everything.

At first the presence of furniture—sofas, armchairs—surprised me, as it seemed they should have been salvaged. Then I realized that their grungy condition resulted not simply from smoke and from five years of abandonment, but also from having been saturated by fire hoses, which had left their stuffing sodden and their frames badly warped.

Even five years after the tragedy, the air smelled of char, of scorched metal, of melted plastics, of fried insulation. Underlying that miasma were other smells less astringent but also less pleasing, which perhaps were best left unanalyzed.

Footprints patterned the carpet of soot, ashes, dust, and sand. Danny's unique tracks were not among them.

On closer inspection, I saw that none of the tread patterns of the shoes appeared crisp. They had been smoothed by drafts, softened by later siftings of ashes and dust.

These prints had been made weeks if not months ago. My quarry had not entered by this route.

A set or perhaps two sets of paw prints looked fresh. Maybe the Panamints of a hundred years ago—close to nature and unfamiliar with the roulette wheel—could have read these impressions at a glance.

With nothing of the tracker in my heritage and nothing in my fry-cook training applicable to the problem, I had to rely not on knowledge but on imagination to summon a creature to fit those tracks. My mind leapt directly to an image of a saber-toothed tiger, though that species had been extinct over ten thousand years.

In the unlikely event that a single immortal sabertooth had survived millennia beyond all others of his species, I supposed I could escape intact from a confrontation. After all, I had thus far survived Terrible Chester.

To the left of this lobby had been a coffee shop with a view of the hotel pool. A partial collapse of the ceiling, just beyond the entrance to the restaurant, presented extreme geometries of Sheetrock and two-by-fours.

To the right, a wide hallway led into darkness that a flashlight could not entirely relieve, into silence. Bronze letters fixed to the wall above the entrance to that passage promised REST ROOMS, CONFERENCE ROOMS, LADY LUCK BALLROOM.

Luckless people had died in the ballroom. A massive chandelier, suspended not from a red-steel beam as the construction drawings had required, but from a wooden beam, had fallen on the crowd, crushing and skewering those under it, when the initial shock of the quake had cracked some four-by-sixes as though they were balsa wood.

I crossed the littered lobby, weaving through the sagging sofas and the overturned armchairs, and departed by a third route, another wide hall that evidently led toward the front of the hotel. The tracks of the sabertooth also proceeded in that direction.

Belatedly, I thought of the satellite phone. I took it from my pocket, switched off the ringer, and set it to vibrate instead. If the seeker of miracles called me again, and if I happened to be close to her position in the hotel, I didn't want the phone to reveal my presence.

I'd never visited this place during the years that it had been a thriving enterprise. When it is within my power to do so, when the dead are making no demands on me, I seek serenity, not excitement. The turn of the cards and the roll of the dice offer me no chance to win freedom from the destiny that my gift imposes upon me.

My unfamiliarity with the resort, combined with the damage wrought by the earthquake and the fire, presented me with a man-made wilderness: hallways and rooms no longer always clearly defined due to the collapse of partitions, a maze of passages and spaces, here barren and bleak, here chaotic and threatening, revealed only in wedges defined by the flashlight beam.

By a route that I could not have retraced, I entered the burned-out casino.

Casinos have no windows, no clocks. The masters of the games want their customers to forget the passage of time, to lay down just one more bet, and then one more. Cavernous, larger than a football field, the room was too long for my light to find the farther end.

One corner of the casino had suffered partial collapse. Otherwise, the immense chamber remained structurally intact.

Hundreds of broken slot machines were

tumbled on the floor. Others stood in long rows, as they had before the quake, half-melted but at attention, like ranks of war machines, robot soldiers halted in their march when a blast of radiation had fried their circuits.

Most of the games and pit-boss stations had been reduced to charred debris. A couple of scorched craps tables remained, filled with blackened chunks of plaster ornamentation that had fallen from the ceiling.

Amidst the charred and splintered rubble, two damaged blackjack games stood upright. A pair of stools waited at one of those games, as though the devil and his date had been playing when the fire broke out, had wished not to be distracted from their cards, commanding respect from the flames.

Instead of the devil, a pleasant-looking man with receding hair perched on a stool. He had been sitting in the dark until my light found him. His arms rested on the padded rim of the crescent-shaped table, as if he were waiting for a dealer to shuffle the deck.

This did not appear to be the kind of man who would collaborate in murder and assist with a kidnapping. Fiftyish, pale, with a full mouth and a dimpled chin, he might have been a librarian or a small-town pharmacist.

As I approached and he looked up, I could not be certain of his status. I knew that he was a spirit only when I saw him register surprise as he realized that I could see him.

On the day of the disaster, perhaps he had been brained by falling debris. Or burned alive.

He did not reveal to me the true condition of his corpse at the time he died, a courtesy for which I was grateful.

Peripheral movement in the shadows snared my attention. From out of the darkness came the lingering dead.

24

STEPPING INTO THE LIGHT BEFORE ME, A pretty young blonde in a blue-and-yellow cocktail dress revealed immodest decolletage. She smiled, but at once her smile faltered.

From my right came an old woman with a long face, eyes vacant of hope. She reached out to me, then frowned at her hand, withdrew it, lowered her head, as if she thought, for whatever reason, that I would find her repellent.

From my left appeared a short, red-headed, cheerful-looking man whose anguished eyes belied his amused smile.

I turned, revealing others with my flashlight. A cocktail waitress in her Indian-princess uniform. A casino guard with a gun on his hip.

A young black man dressed in cutting-edge fashion ceaselessly fingered his silk shirt, his jacket, the jade pendant that hung from his neck, as though in death he was embarrassed to have been so fashion-conscious in life.

Counting the player at the blackjack table, seven appeared to me. I couldn't know if all had perished in the casino or if some had died elsewhere in the hotel. Perhaps they were the only ghosts haunting the Panamint, perhaps not.

One hundred and eighty-two people had perished here. Most would have moved on the moment they expired. At least, for my sake, I hoped that was true.

Most commonly, spirits who have dwelled this long in a self-imposed state of purgatory will manifest in a mood of melancholy or anxiety. These seven conformed to that rule.

Yearning draws them to me. I am not always certain for what it is they yearn, though I think most of them desire resolution, the courage to let go of this world and to discover what comes next.

Fear inhibits them from doing what they must. Fear and regret, and love for those they leave behind.

Because I can see them, I bridge life and death, and they hope I can open for them the door they are afraid to open for themselves. Because I am who I am—a California boy who looks like surfers looked in *Beach Blanket Bingo,* half a century ago, less coiffed and even less threatening than Frankie Avalon—I inspire their trust.

I'm afraid that I have less to offer them than

they believe I do. What counsel I give them is as shallow as Ozzie *pretends* his wisdom is.

That I will touch them, embrace them, seems always to be a comfort for which they're grateful. They embrace me in return. And touch my face. And kiss my hands.

Their melancholy drains me. Their need exhausts me. I am wrung by pity. Sometimes it seems that to exit this world, they must go through my heart, leaving it scarred and sore.

Moving now from one to the other, I told each of them what I intuited he or she needed to hear.

I said, "This world is lost forever. There's nothing here for you but desire, frustration, sadness."

I said, "You know now that part of you is immortal and that your life had meaning. To discover that meaning, embrace what comes next."

And to another, I said, "You think you don't deserve mercy, but mercy is yours if you'll put aside your fear."

As one by one I spoke to the seven, an eighth spirit appeared. A tall, broad brick of a man, he had deep-set eyes, blunt features, and buzz-cut hair. He stared at me over the heads of the others, his gaze the color of bile and no less bitter.

To the young black man who fussed ceaselessly and with apparent embarrassment at his fine clothes, I said, "Truly evil people aren't given the license to linger. The fact that you've been here so long since death means you don't have any reason to fear what comes next."

As I turned from one of the encircling dead to the next, the newcomer prowled beyond the perimeter of the group, keeping my face in sight. His mood appeared to darken as he listened to me.

"You think what I'm telling you is bullshit. Maybe it is. I haven't been across. How can I know what waits on the other side?"

Their eyes were lustrous pools of longing, and I hoped they recognized in me not pity, but sympathy.

"The grace and beauty of this world enchant me. But it's all broken. I want to see the version we didn't screw up. Don't you?"

Finally, I said, "The girl I love . . . she thought we might have three lives, not two. She called this first life *boot camp*."

I paused. I had no choice. For a moment, I belonged more to their purgatory than I did to this world, in the sense that words failed me.

Eventually I continued: "She said we're in boot camp to learn, to fail or succeed of our own free will. Then we move on to a second life, which she called *service*."

The red-haired man, whose cheerful smile was belied by anguished eyes, came to me and put a hand on my shoulder.

"Her name is Bronwen, but she prefers to be called Stormy. In service, Stormy said, we have fantastic adventures in some cosmic campaign, some wondrous undertaking. Our reward comes in our third life, and that one lasts forever."

Reduced to silence again, I could not meet their stares with the confidence I owed them, and so I closed my eyes and in memory saw Stormy, who gave me strength, as she had always done.

Eyes closed, I said, "She is a kick-ass kind of girl, who not only knows what she wants, but what she *should* want, which makes all the difference. When you meet her in service, you'll know her, sure enough. You'll know her, and you'll love her."

After a further silence, when I opened my eyes and turned in a circle, probing with my flashlight, four of the initial seven were gone: the young black man, the cocktail waitress, the pretty blonde, and the red-haired man.

I can't be sure if they moved Beyond or merely elsewhere.

The big man with the buzz-cut looked angrier than ever. His shoulders were hunched, as if under a burden of rage, and his hands curled into fists.

He stalked away into the burned-out room, and though he had no physical substance that could affect this world, gray ashes rose in shimmering shapes around him, and settled to the floor again in his wake. Lightweight debris—

scorched playing cards, splintery scraps of wood—trembled as he passed. A five-dollar casino chip stood on edge, spun, wobbled, fell flat once more, and heat-yellowed dice rattled on the floor.

He had poltergeist potential, and I was glad to see him go.

25

A DAMAGED FIRE DOOR HUNG OPEN AND askew on two of three hinges. The stainless-steel threshold reflected the flashlight in those few places where it was not crusted with dark material.

If memory served me well, people had been trampled to death in this doorway when the crowd of gamblers stampeded for the exits. No horror came over me at that recollection, only a deeper sadness.

Beyond the door, patinaed by smoke and water, spalling from the effects of efflorescing lime, looking as if they had been transported from an ancient temple of a long-forgotten faith, thirty flights of wide concrete emergency stairs led to the north end of the sixteenth floor. Perhaps two additional flights ascended all the way to the roof of the hotel.

I climbed only halfway to the first landing

before I halted, cocked my head, and listened. I don't believe a sound had alarmed me. No tick, no click, no whisper stepped down to me from higher floors.

Perhaps a scent alerted me. Compared to other spaces in the devastated structure, the stairwell smelled less of chemicals and hardly at all of char. This cooler, limy air was clean enough to allow the recognition of an odor as exotic as—but different from—those of the fire's aftermath.

The faint essence I could not identify was musky, mushroomy. But it also had a quality of fresh raw meat, by which I don't mean a bloody stink, but that subtle smell you get from a butcher's case, where ready flesh is presented.

For a reason I could not define, into my mind's eye came the dead face of the man I had fished from the storm drain. Mottled gray skin. Eyes rolled back in a blind white gaze.

The fine hairs on the nape of my neck quivered as if the air had been charged by the advancing storm.

I switched off the flashlight and stood in absolute, monster's-gonna-get-you blackness.

Because the stairs were enclosed by concrete walls, the sharp turn at each landing provided an effective baffle to light. A sentry one floor above, or at most two, might have noticed the radiant bloom below, but no light could have transferred, angle after angle, to any higher floors.

After a minute, when I hadn't heard the rustle of clothing or the scrape of a shoe on concrete, when no scaly tongue had licked my face, I backed cautiously out of the stairwell, across the threshold. I retreated into the casino before switching on the flashlight.

A few minutes later, I located the south stairs. Here the door still hung from all its hinges, but it stood open like the first.

Shuttering the lens of the flash with my fingers, to reduce its reach, I ventured across the threshold.

This silence, like that in the north stairwell, had an expectant quality, as though I might not be the only listening presence. Here, too, after a moment, I detected that subtle and disturbing smell that had discouraged me from ascending at the other end of the building.

As before, into my mind came the dead face of the man who had Tasered me: eyes protuberant and white, mouth open wide and tongue swallowed.

On the basis of a bad feeling and a smell, real or imagined, I decided that the emergency stairs were under observation. I could not use them.

Yet my sixth sense told me that Danny lay imprisoned somewhere high above. He (the magnet) waited, and I (the magnetized), in some strange power's employ, was drawn upward with an insistence that I could not ignore.

26

OFF THE MAIN LOBBY, I LOCATED AN ALCOVE with ten elevators, five on each side. Eight sets of doors were closed, though I'm sure I could have pried them open.

The last two sets of doors on the right were fully retracted. In the first of these openings, an empty cab waited, its floor a foot below the floor of the alcove. The second offered only a void.

Leaning into the shaft, I played the flashlight up and down, over guide rails and cables. The missing cab lay two floors below, in the sub-basement.

To the right, the wall featured a service ladder. It receded to the very top of the building.

After raiding my backpack for a spelunker's flashlight strap, I fitted the handle of the light in the tight collar, and secured the Velcro fastener around my right forearm. Like a telescopic sight on a shotgun barrel, the light surmounted my arm, the beam spearing across the back of my hand and out past my fingertips into the dark.

With both hands free, I was able to get a grip on a rung and swing off the alcove threshold. I mounted the ladder.

After ascending several rungs, I paused to savor the odors in the shaft. I didn't detect the scent that had warned me off both the north and the south stairs.

The shaft was resonant, however; it would amplify every sound. If the wrong set of doors stood open above, and if someone was near that alcove, he would hear me coming.

I needed to climb as silently as possible, which meant not so fast that I began to breathe hard with the exertion.

The flashlight seemed problematic. Holding the ladder with my right hand, I used my left to switch off the beam.

How unsettling: to climb into perfect darkness. In the most primitive foundations of the mind, at the level of race memory or even deeper, lay the expectation that any ascent should be toward light. Rising higher, higher into unrelenting blackness proved to be disorienting.

I estimated eighteen feet of height for the first story, twelve feet per story thereafter. I guessed there were twenty-four rungs in twelve feet.

By that measure, I had climbed two stories when a protracted rumble passed through the shaft. I thought *Earthquake,* and I froze on the ladder, held fast, expecting plummeting masonry and further destruction.

When the shaft did not shake, when the cables did not sing with vibrations, I realized that the rumble was a long peal of thunder. Although still distant, it sounded closer than it had been earlier.

Hand over hand, foot after foot, climbing again, I wondered how I would get Danny down from his high prison, assuming that I would be able to free him. If armed sentries had been posted on the stairs, we could not escape the hotel by either of those routes. Considering his deformities and his physical uncertainty, he could not descend on this ladder.

One thing at a time. First, find him. Second, free him.

Thinking too far ahead might paralyze me, especially if every strategy that I considered led inevitably to the need to kill one or all of our adversaries. The determination to kill did not come easily to me, not even when survival depended on it, not even when my target was unarguably evil.

You don't get James Bond with me. I'm even less bloodthirsty than Miss Moneypenny.

At what must have been the fifth floor, I encountered an open set of elevator doors, the first since I had entered the shaft on the lobby level. The gap revealed itself as a dark-gray rectangle in an otherwise pitch landscape.

The alcove beyond the retracted doors would open onto a fifth-floor hall. Along that corridor, the doors to some guest rooms would be standing open; others would have been broken down by firemen or would have burned away. The windows in those rooms, which had not been boarded over to keep out trespassers, as on the ground floor, admitted light to the public hall; and meager rays filtered from there into the alcove.

Intuition told me that I had not climbed high enough. The low voice of faraway thunder spoke again when I was between the seventh and eighth floors. Just past the ninth floor, I wondered how many bodachs had swarmed the hotel prior to the catastrophe.

A bodach is a mythical beast of the British Isles, a sly thing that comes down chimneys during the night to carry away naughty children.

In addition to the lingering dead, I occasionally see menacing spirits that I call bodachs. That's not what they are, but I need to call them something, and that name seems to fit.

A young English boy, the only person I have known who shared my gift, called them bodachs in my presence. Minutes after he had used that word, he was crushed to death by a runaway truck.

I never speak of the bodachs when they are

near. I pretend not to see them, do not react to them either with curiosity or fear. I suspect that if they knew I see them, there would be a runaway truck for me.

These creatures are utterly black and without features, so thin they can slip through a crack in a door, or enter by a keyhole. They have no more substance than shadows.

They are soundless in movement, often slinking like cats, though cats as big as men. Sometimes they run semi-erect and seem to be half man, half dog.

I have written about them before, in my first manuscript. I will not spend many words on them here.

They are not human spirits, and they do not belong here. Their natural realm, I suspect, is a place of eternal darkness and much screaming.

Their presence always signifies an oncoming event with a high body count—like the shootings at the mall last August. A single murder, like that of Dr. Jessup, does not draw them forth from wherever they dwell. They thrill only to natural disasters and to human violence on an operatic scale.

In the hours before the quake and the fire, they surely swarmed the casino and the hotel by the hundreds, in frenzied anticipation of the impending misery, pain, and death, which is their favorite three-course meal.

Two deaths in this case—Dr. Jessup and the snaky man—elicited no bodach interest. Their continued absence suggested that whatever show-down lay ahead might not result in a bloodbath.

Nevertheless, as I climbed, my churning imagination populated the lightless shaft with bodachs that, like cockroaches, crawled the walls, fleet and quivering.

27

AT THE NEXT SET OF RETRACTED ELEVATOR doors, on the twelfth floor, I knew in a certain-to-the-bones way that I had climbed past the stairwell guards. In fact, I sensed that I had arrived at the level on which the kidnappers were holding Danny.

The muscles of my arms and legs burned, not because the climb had been physically demanding, but because I had ascended in a state of extreme and constant tension. Even my jaws ached because I'd been grinding my teeth.

I preferred not to transition from the shaft to the elevator alcove in darkness. But I dared risk using the light only briefly, to locate the first of the recessed handholds and footholds that allowed transfer from the service ladder to the doorway.

I switched on the flashlight, quickly studied the situation, and switched it off.

Although I had repeatedly blotted them on my jeans, my hands were slippery with sweat.

No matter how ready I may be to join Stormy in service, I do not have nerves of steel. If I'd been wearing boots instead of sneakers, I would have quaked in them.

I reached into the thwarting gloom, located the first of the recessed handgrips, which was like an in-wall holder for a roll of toilet paper, but three times as wide. I clutched it with my right hand, hesitated as I was overcome with nostalgia for the griddle and the grill and the deep-fryer, then grabbed it with my left hand, as well, and stepped off the ladder.

For a moment I hung from my arms, by my sweaty hands, toeing the wall in search of the footholds. When it seemed that I would never find them, I found them.

Having left the ladder, the act of leaving the ladder now struck me as folly.

The top of the elevator cab was in the subbasement, thirteen floors below. Thirteen stories is a long fall in any lighting condition, but the prospect of plunging that far in inky darkness struck me as especially terrifying.

Lacking a safety harness, I also did not have a sturdy tether to snap to the handhold. Or a parachute. I had committed myself to total freestyle.

Among other items in my rucksack were

Kleenex, a couple of coconut-raisin protein bars, and foil packets of lemon-scented moist towelettes. My packing priorities had seemed entirely sensible at the time.

If I plummeted thirteen floors onto the roof of the elevator cab, at least I would be able to blow my nose, have a last snack, and scrub my hands, thereby avoiding the indignity of dying with snotty nostrils and sticky fingers.

By the time that I had fumbled sideways from the ladder to the open doorway and had swung across the threshold into the elevator alcove, the *compelling* nature of psychic magnetism, the *irresistible* insistence of it had been forcefully impressed upon me, although not for the first time.

I leaned against a wall, relieved not to have a yawning void at my back, waiting for my clammy palms to stop perspiring, for my heart to cease hammering. Repeatedly I flexed and extended my left arm to work a mild cramp out of the biceps.

Beyond the shadow-cloaked alcove, there appeared to be sources of watery-gray light both from north and from south along the public hallway.

No voices. If I could judge by her performance on the phone, the mystery woman was a talker. She liked the sound of herself.

When I eased to the open end of the alcove

and peered cautiously around the corner, I saw a long, deserted hall. Here and there, open doorways on both sides admitted daylight from guest rooms, as I had expected.

The I-shaped hotel featured a shorter hall with more rooms at each end of the main corridor. The guarded stairs that I had chosen to avoid were in those secondary wings.

Left or right would have been a choice to ponder for any other searcher, but not for me. Less equivocal here than it had been in the storm drains, my sixth sense drew me to the right, south.

From the foundation to the highest level, the floors of the hotel were steel-reinforced concrete. The fire had not been intense enough to buckle let alone collapse them.

Consequently, the flames had worked upward through the structure by way of plumbing and electrical chases. Only about sixty percent of those internal pathways had been fully fireproofed and sprinklered as specified by the construction documents.

This resulted in a hopscotch pattern of destruction. Some floors were virtually gutted, while others fared far better.

The twelfth story had suffered extensive smoke and water damage, but I encountered nothing eaten by flames, nothing scorched. Carpet matted with soot and filth. Wallpaper stained, peeling. A few glass shades had been shaken loose of ceiling lights; sharp shards required wariness.

A Mojave vulture evidently had swooped in through one shattered window or another and had not been able to find its way out. In its frantic search, it had broken a wing against a wall or a door frame. Now its macabre carcass, having half rotted before it desiccated in the dry heat, lay with tattered pinions spread in the center of the corridor.

Although the twelfth floor might be in good shape by comparison to other levels of the hotel, you wouldn't want to check in for your next vacation.

I moved cautiously from open room to open room, scouting each from its threshold. None was occupied.

The furniture violently redistributed by the quake, tipped on its side, jammed the same end of each room, where the power of the temblor had thrown it. Everything was soiled and sagging and not worth the effort to salvage.

Beyond those windows that were broken out or that were free of soot, the lowering sky revealed a metastasis of storm clouds, healthy blue holding only in the south, and even there succumbing.

The closed doors didn't concern me. I would be warned by a rasp of rusted knob and a screech of corroded hinges if one began to open. Besides, these were neither white nor paneled, as were the mortal doors of my dream.

Halfway between the elevator alcove and the intersection with the next corridor, I came to a closed door that I was not able to pass. Tarnished metal numbers identified it as Room 1242. As though guided by a puppet master whose strings were invisible, my right hand reached for the knob.

I restrained myself long enough to rest my head against the jamb and listen. Nothing.

Listening at a door is always a waste of time. You listen and listen, and when you feel confident that the way ahead is safe, you open the door, whereupon some guy with BORN TO DIE tattooed on his forehead shoves a monster revolver in your face. It's almost as reliable as the three laws of thermodynamics.

When I eased open the door, I encountered no tattooed thug, which meant that gravity would soon fail and that bears would henceforth leave the woods to toilet in public lavatories.

Here as elsewhere, the earthquake five years ago had rearranged the furniture, shoving everything to one end of the space, stacking the bed on top of chairs, on top of a dresser. Search dogs would have been needed to certify that no victims, either alive or dead, had remained under the debris.

In this instance, a single chair had been

retrieved from the scrap heap and placed in the quake-cleared half of the room. In the chair, secured to it by duct tape, sat Danny Jessup.

28

EYES CLOSED, PALE, UNMOVING, DANNY looked dead. Only the throb of a pulse in his temple and the tension in his jaw muscles revealed that he was alive, and in the grip of dread.

He resembles that actor, Robert Downey Jr., though without the edge of heroin-addict glamour that would give him true star quality in contemporary Hollywood.

Past the face, the resemblance to *any* actor drops to zero. Danny has a lot better brain than any movie star of the past few decades.

His left shoulder is somewhat misshapen from excess bone growth during the healing of a fracture. That arm twists unnaturally from shoulder to wrist, with the consequence that it doesn't hang straight at his side, and the hand twists away from his body.

His left hip is deformed. The right leg is shorter than the other. The right tibia thickened and bowed as it healed from a break. His right ankle contains so much excess bone that he has only forty percent function in that joint.

Strapped to the hotel-room chair, dressed in jeans and a black T-shirt with a yellow lightning bolt on the chest, he could have been a fairy-tale character. The handsome prince suffering under a witch's spell. The love child of a forbidden romance between a princess and a kind troll.

I closed the door behind me before I said softly, "Wanna get out of here?"

His blue eyes opened, owlish with surprise. Fear made room for mortification, but he didn't appear to be at all relieved.

"Odd," he whispered, "you shouldn't have come."

Dropping the backpack, zipping it open, I whispered, "What am I gonna do? There was nothing good on TV."

"I knew you'd come, but you shouldn't, it's hopeless."

From the backpack, I withdrew a fishing knife, flipped the blade out of the handle. "Always the optimist."

"Get out of here while you can. She's crazier than a syphilitic suicide bomber with mad-cow disease."

"I don't know anybody else who says stuff like that. Can't leave you here when you talk that good."

His ankles were bound to the chair legs with numerous turns of duct tape. Bonds of tape wound around his chest, securing him to the back of the chair. In addition, his arms were taped to the arms of the chair at the wrists and at the crooks of the elbows.

I started sawing rapidly at the loops of tape that bound his left wrist.

"Odd, stop it, listen, even if you have time to cut me loose, I can't stand up—"

"If your leg's broken or something," I interrupted, "I can carry you at least to a hiding place."

"Nothing's broken, that's not it," he said urgently, "but if I stand up, it'll detonate."

Although I finished freeing his left wrist, I said, "*Detonate*. That's a word I like even less than *decapitate*."

"Check out the back of the chair."

I went around behind him to have a look. Being a guy who has seen a few movies as well as some weird action in real life, I at once recognized the kilo of plastic explosives held to the back of the chair by the same tape that bound Danny.

A battery, lots of colorful wires, an instrument that resembled a small version of a carpenter's level (with the indicator bubble measuring a perfect horizontal plane), and other arcane paraphernalia suggested that whoever had put the bomb together had a flair for such work.

Danny said, "The instant I raise my ass off the chair—boom. If I try to *walk* with the chair and the level measures too far off the horizontal—boom."

"We have a problem here," I agreed.

29

IN WHISPERS, IN MURMURS, WITH BATED breath, *sotto voce,* in *voce velata,* softly we conducted the conversation, not solely because the syphilitic-suicide-bomber-mad-cow woman and her pals might hear us, but I think also because we superstitiously felt that the wrong word, spoken too loud, would trigger the bomb.

Stripping the spelunker's strap off my arm and setting it aside with the flashlight, I said, "Where are they?"

"I don't know. Odd, you have to get out of here."

"Do they leave you by yourself for long periods?"

"They check in maybe once an hour. She was just here about fifteen minutes ago. Call Wyatt Porter."

"This isn't in his jurisdiction."

"So he'll call Sheriff Amory."

"If police get into this, you'll die."

"So who do you want to call—the sanitation department?"

"I just know you'll die. The way I know things. Can this package be detonated whenever they want?"

"Yeah. She showed me a remote control. She said it would be as easy as changing TV channels."

"Who is she?"

"Her name's Datura. Two guys are with her. I don't know their names. There was a third sonofabitch."

"I found his body. What happened to him?"

"I didn't see it. He was . . . strange. So are the other two."

As I began to cut the tape on his left forearm, I said, "What's her first name?"

"Datura. I don't know her last. Odd, what're you doing? I can't get up from this chair."

"You might as well be *ready* to get up in case the situation changes. Who is she?"

"Odd, she'll kill you. She will. You've got to get out of here."

"Not without you," I said, sawing the tape that bound his right wrist to the chair.

Danny shook his head. "I don't want you to die for me."

"Then who am I gonna die for? Some total stranger? What sense does that make? Who is she?"

He let out a low sound of abject misery. "You're gonna think I'm such a loser."

"You're not a loser. You're a geek, I'm a geek, but we're not losers."

"You're not a geek," he said.

Cutting the second set of bonds on his right arm, I said, "I'm a fry cook *when* I'm working, and when I added a sweater vest to my wardrobe it was more change than I could handle. I see dead people, and I talk to Elvis, so don't tell me I'm not a geek. Who is she?"

"Promise you won't tell Dad."

He wasn't talking about Simon Makepeace, his biological father. He meant his stepfather. He didn't know Dr. Jessup was dead.

This wasn't the best time to tell him. He would be devastated. I needed him to be focused, and game.

Something he saw in my eyes, in my expression, made him frown, and he said, "What?"

"I won't tell him," I promised, and turned my attention to the bonds securing his right ankle to the leg of the chair.

"You swear?"

"If I ever tell him, I'll give back my Venusian-methane-slime-beast card."

"You still have it?"

"I *told* you I'm a geek. Who is Datura?"

Danny took a deep breath, held it until I thought that he was going after a Guinness World Record, then let it out with two words: "Phone sex."

I blinked at him, briefly confused. "Phone sex?"

Blushing, mortified, he said, "I'm sure this is a colossal surprise to you, but I've never done the real thing with a girl."

"Not even with Demi Moore?"

"Bastard," he hissed.

"Could *you* have passed up a shot like that?"

"No," he admitted. "But being a virgin at twenty-one makes me the king of losers."

"No way I'm gonna start calling you *Your Highness*. Anyway, a hundred years ago, guys like you and me would be called gentlemen. Funny what a big difference a century makes."

"You?" he said. "Don't try to tell me *you* are a member of the club. I'm inexperienced but I'm not naive."

"Believe what you want," I said, sawing the bonds at his left ankle, "but I'm a member in good standing."

Danny knew that Stormy and I had been an item since we were sixteen, in high school. He didn't know that we'd never made love.

As a child, she had been molested by an adoptive father. For a long time, she'd felt unclean.

She wanted to wait for marriage before we did the deed because she felt that by delaying our gratification, we would be purifying her past. She was determined that those bad memories of abuse would not haunt her in our bed.

Stormy had said sex between us should feel clean and right and wonderful. She wanted it to be sacred; and it would have been.

Then she died, and we never experienced that one bliss together, which was all right, because we experienced so many others. We packed a lifetime into four years.

Danny Jessup didn't need to hear any details. They are my most private memories, and precious to me.

Without looking up from his left ankle, I said, "Phone sex?"

After a hesitation, he said, "I wanted to know what it was like to talk about it, you know, with a girl. A girl who didn't know what I look like."

I took longer cutting the tape than was required, keeping my head down, giving him time.

He said, "I have some money of my own." He designs web sites. "I pay the bills for my phone. Dad didn't see the nine-hundred-number charges."

Having freed his ankle, I busied myself cleaning the tape-gummed blade of the knife on my jeans. I couldn't cut the bonds around his chest because the same loops held the bomb level and in place.

"For a couple minutes," he continued, "it was exciting. But then pretty soon it seemed gross. Ugly." His voice quavered. "You probably think I'm a pervert."

"I think you're human. I like that in a friend."

He took a deep breath and went on: "It seemed gross . . . and then stupid. So I asked the girl, could we just talk, not about sex, about other things, anything. She said sure, that was all right."

Phone-sex services charge by the minute. Danny could have held forth for hours about the qualities of various laundry soaps, and she would have pretended to be enthralled.

"We chatted half an hour, just about things we like and don't like—you know, books, movies, food. It was wonderful, Odd. I can't explain how wonderful it was, the *glow* I got from it. It was just . . . it was so nice."

I wouldn't have thought that the word *nice* could break my heart, but it almost did.

"That particular service will let you make an appointment with a girl you like. I mean for another conversation."

"This was Datura."

"Yes. The second time I talked to her, I found out she has this real fascination with the supernatural, ghosts and stuff."

I folded shut the knife and returned it to my backpack.

"She's read like a thousand books on the subject, visited lots of haunted houses. She's into all kinds of paranormal phenomena."

I went around behind his chair and knelt on the floor.

"What're you doing?" he asked nervously.

"Nothing. Relax. I'm just studying the situation. Tell me about Datura."

"This is the hardest part, Odd."

"I know. It's okay."

His voice grew even softer: "Well . . . the third time I called her, pretty much the *only* thing we talked about was supernatural stuff—from the Bermuda Triangle to spontaneous human combustion to the ghosts that supposedly haunt the White House. I don't know . . . I don't know why I wanted so bad to impress her."

I am no expert on bomb-making. I had encountered only one other in my life—the previous August, in the same incident that involved the mall shootings.

"I mean," Danny said, "she was just this girl who talked filthy to men for money. But it was important to me that she liked me, maybe even thought I was a little cool. So I told her I had a friend who could see ghosts."

I closed my eyes.

"I didn't use your name at first, and at first she didn't really believe me. But the stories I told her about you were so detailed and so unusual, she began to realize they were true."

The bomb at the mall had been a truck packed with hundreds of kilos of explosives. The detonator had been a crude device.

"Our talks got to be so much fun. Then the

sweetest thing. It *seemed* so sweet. She started calling me on her own time. It didn't cost me anything anymore."

I opened my eyes and gazed at the package on the back of Danny's chair. This was a lot more sophisticated than the truck bomb at the mall. It was meant to challenge me.

"We didn't always get around to talking about you," Danny said. "I realize now, she was clever. She didn't want to be obvious."

Careful not to disturb the carpenter's level, I traced a coiled red wire with one finger, and then a straighter yellow wire. Then green.

"But after a while," Danny continued, "I didn't have any more to tell her about you . . . except the thing at the mall last year. That was such a big story nationwide, all over the newspapers and TV, so then she knew your name."

Black wire, blue wire, white wire, red again. . . . Neither the sight of them nor the feel of them against my fingertip engaged my sixth sense.

"I'm so sorry, Odd. So damn sorry. I sold you out."

I said, "Not for money. For love. That's different."

"I don't love her."

"All right. Not love. For the *hope* of love."

Frustrated by the indecipherable wiring of the bomb, I went around to the front of the chair.

Danny rubbed his right wrist, around which

the duct tape had been drawn so tight that it had left angry red impressions in his skin.

"For the *hope* of love," I repeated. "What friend wouldn't cut you a little slack in a case like that?"

Tears welled in his eyes.

"Listen," I said, "you and I weren't meant to have our tickets punched in a cheesy casino resort. If fate says we've got to croak in a hotel, then we'll rent a suite someplace that rates five stars. You okay?"

He nodded.

Tucking my backpack in among the earthquake-pitched furniture where it was unlikely to be found, I said, "I know why they brought you here, of all places. If she thinks somehow I can conjure spirits, she figures a bunch of them have to be hanging around this joint. But why through the flood-control tunnels?"

"She's beyond psychotic, Odd. It never came across on the phone, or maybe I didn't want to hear it when I was . . . romancing her. Damn. That's pathetic. Anyway, she's a weird kind of crazy, delusional but not stupid, a real hard-nosed nutty bitch. She wanted to bring me to the Panamint by an unusual route, something that would be a serious test of your psychic magnetism, prove to her it was real. And there's something else going on with her. . . ."

His hesitation told me that this something else would not be a cheerful revelation, such as that

Datura had taken up gospel singing or that she had baked my favorite cake.

"She wants you to show her ghosts. She thinks you can summon them, make them speak. I never told her anything like that, it's just what she insists on believing. But she wants something else, too. I don't know why. . . ." He thought about it, shook his head. "But I get the feeling she wants to kill you."

"I seem to rub a lot of people the wrong way. Danny, last night in the alley behind the Blue Moon Cafe—someone fired a shotgun."

"One of her guys. The one you found dead."

"Who was he shooting at?"

"Me. They were careless for a moment as we were getting out of the van. I tried to make a break for the street. The shotgun was a warning to stop."

He wiped his eyes with one hand. Three of the fingers, once having been broken, were larger than they should have been and misshapen by excess bone.

"I shouldn't have stopped," he said. "I should've kept running. All they could have done was shoot me in the back. Then we wouldn't be here."

I went to him and poked the yellow lightning bolt on the front of his black T-shirt. "No more of that. You keep swimming in that direction, soon you'll find yourself drowning in self-pity. That isn't you, Danny."

Shaking his head, he said, "What a mess."

"Self-pity isn't you, and it never has been. We're a couple of tough little virgin geeks, and don't you forget it."

He couldn't suppress a smile, though it was tremulous and came with a fresh welling of tears. "I still have my Martian-brain-eating-centipede card."

"Are we sentimental fools, or what?"

"That crack about Demi Moore was funny," he said.

"I know. Listen, I'm going out there to have a look around. After I'm gone, you might think you can just tip over your chair and set off the bomb."

His evasive eyes revealed that self-sacrifice had indeed crossed his mind.

"You might think blowing yourself into pâté would get me off the hook, then I'd call Wyatt Porter for help, but you'd be way wrong," I assured him. "I'd feel more obligated than ever to get all three of them myself. I wouldn't leave this place until I did. You understand that, Danny?"

"What a mess."

"Besides, you've got to live for your dad. Don't you think so?"

He sighed, nodded. "Yeah."

"You've got to live for your dad. That's your job now."

Danny said, "He's a good man."

Picking up the flashlight, I said, "If Datura

checks on you before I get back, she'll see your arms and legs have been freed. That's all right. Just tell her I'm here."

"What're you going to do now?"

I shrugged. "You know me. I make it up as I go along."

30

STEPPING OUT OF ROOM 1242 AND PULLING the door shut behind me, I glanced left and right along the corridor. Still deserted. Silent.

Datura.

That sounded like a name not given but instead chosen. She had been born Mary or Heather, or something equally common, and she had taken *Datura* later. It was an exotic word with some meaning that she was amused to apply to herself.

I visualized my mind as a pool of dark water in moonlight, her name as a leaf. I imagined the leaf settling upon the water, floating for a moment. Saturated, the leaf sank. Currents moved it around the pool, deeper, deeper.

Datura.

In seconds, I felt drawn north toward—and beyond—the elevator alcove in which I had arrived earlier by way of the shaft ladder. If the woman waited on this floor, she was in a room distant from 1242.

Perhaps she didn't keep Danny with her because she, too, had sensed in him a potential for self-destruction that gave her second thoughts about having strapped him to a bomb that he could choose to detonate.

Although I could have allowed myself to be drawn to Datura right away, I wasn't urgently compelled to locate her. She was Medusa, with a voice—instead of eyes—that could turn men to stone, but for the moment I was content to be a man of weary, aching, and fallible flesh.

Ideally, I would find some way to disable Datura and the two men with her—and gain possession of the remote control that could trigger the explosives. When they were no longer a threat, I could call Chief Porter.

My chances of overpowering three dangerous people, especially if all of them had guns, were not much better than the odds that the dead gamblers in the burned-out casino could win their lives back with a roll of the fire-yellowed dice.

Other than ignoring my convincing premonition that calling in the police would be the certain death of Danny, the only alternative to disabling the kidnappers was to disable the bomb. I had less desire to fiddle with that complex detonator than I had to French-kiss a rattlesnake.

Nevertheless, I had to prepare for the possibility that events would lead me inevitably to precisely that fiddling. And if I freed Danny, we would still have to get out of the Panamint.

Not agile to begin with, exhausted by the trek from Pico Mundo, he would not be able to move fast. On a good day, in peak form, my brittle-boned friend was not surefooted enough to dare to rush down a flight of stairs.

To get to the ground floor of this hotel, he would be required to descend *twenty-two* flights. Then he would have to make his way through treacherous rubble-strewn public areas—while three homicidal psychopaths pursued us.

Throw in a few dumb, manipulative, scantily clad women, add a few even dumber but hunky guys, include the requirement to eat a bowl of live worms, and we pretty much had the premise for a new reality-TV show.

I quickly searched several rooms along the south end of the main corridor, looking for a place where Danny could hide in the unlikely event that I proved able to separate him from the explosives.

If I didn't have to worry about keeping him on the move with gunmen chasing us down, and if he was beyond easy discovery, I would be better able to deal with our enemies. With Danny in hiding, I might even feel that circumstances had changed sufficiently to make it safe to bring in Chief Porter.

Unfortunately, one hotel room is pretty much like another, and they don't offer any challenges to a determined searcher. Datura and her thugs would breeze through them as quickly as I did and would be aware of the same possible hiding places as those that caught my attention.

Briefly I considered artfully rearranging a jumble of quake-tossed furniture and decorative items to create a hollow in which Danny could be tucked out of sight. An unstable mound of chairs and beds and nightstands was likely to shift noisily when I tried to reconfigure it, drawing unwanted attention before I could complete the job.

In the fourth room, I glanced out a window and saw that the land had grown darker, shadowed by a warship fleet of iron clouds that had expanded their dominion to three-quarters of the sky. The landscape flickered as if with muzzle flashes, and a cannonade, still distant but closer than before, shook the day.

Remembering the eerie quality of the thunder that earlier had echoed down through the elevator shaft, I turned from the window.

The corridor was still deserted. I hurried north, passing Room 1242, and returned to the alcove.

Nine of the ten sets of stainless-steel lift doors were shut. For safety, to facilitate rescue, they would have been designed in such a way that they could be forced open manually in the event of a loss of power from both the public-utility company and the backup generators.

They had been closed for five years. Smoke had probably corroded and gummed their mechanisms.

I started on the right-hand bank. The first pair of doors were ajar. I wedged my fingers in the one-inch gap and tried to pull the doors apart. The one on the right moved a little; initially, the other resisted, but then slid aside with a raspy noise that wouldn't have traveled far.

Even in the dim gray light, I had to pry the doors apart only four inches to discern that no cab waited beyond. It was at another floor.

Sixteen stories, ten elevators: The mathematics allowed that none of them had come to a stop on the twelfth floor. All nine sets of doors might conceal empty shafts.

Perhaps, when power was lost, the elevators were programmed to descend on backup batteries to the lobby. If that was the case, my hope was that this safety mechanism had failed—just as others in the hotel had failed.

When I let go of the doors, they eased back into the position in which I had found them.

The second set were closed tighter than the first. The leading edges were bullnosed, however, to facilitate prying in an emergency. Shuddering in their tracks, they opened with a creaking that made me nervous.

No cab.

These doors remained apart when I released them. To avoid leaving evidence of my search, I pressed them shut again, eliciting more shudders, more creaking.

I had left clear images of my hands in the grime that filmed the stainless steel. From a pocket I withdrew a Kleenex and brushed lightly to obscure the prints, feather them out of existence, without leaving a too-clean patch that might raise suspicion.

The third pair of doors would not budge.

Behind the fourth set, which opened quietly, I found a waiting cab. I pushed the doors fully apart, hesitated, then stepped into the lift.

The cab didn't plunge into the abyss, as I half expected that it might. It took my weight with a faint protest and did not settle whatsoever from the alcove threshold.

Although the doors slipped shut part of the way on their own, I had to press to complete the closure. More prints, more Kleenex.

I wiped my sooty hands on my jeans. More laundry.

Although I thought I knew what I must do next, it was such a bold move that I stood in the alcove for a minute or two, considering other options. There weren't any.

This was one of those moments when I wished that I had striven harder to overcome my deep-seated aversion to guns.

On the other hand, when you shoot at people who also have guns, they tend to shoot back. This invariably complicates matters.

If you don't shoot first and aim well, maybe it's better not to have firearms. In an ugly situation like this, people who have heavy weaponry tend to feel superior to people who don't; they feel smug, and when they're smug, they underestimate their opponents. An unarmed man, of necessity, will be quicker of wit—more aware, more feral and more ferocious—than the gunman who relies on his weapon to think for him. Therefore, being unarmed can be an advantage.

In retrospect, that line of reasoning is patently absurd. Even at the time, I knew it was stupid, but I pursued it anyway, because I needed to talk myself out of that alcove and into action.

Datura.

The leaf in the moonlit water, sharing its essence with the pool, sinking deep and carried on a lazy current that pulls, pulls, pulls . . .

I stepped out of the alcove, into the corridor. I turned left, proceeded north.

Some tough, violent phone-sex babe, crazy as a mad cow, gets it in her addled head that she's got to kidnap Danny so she can use him to force me to reveal my closely guarded secrets. But why does Dr. Jessup have to die, and in such a brutal fashion? Just because he was *there*?

This phone-sex babe, this nut case, has three

guys—now two—who apparently are willing to commit any crime necessary to help her get what she wants. There's no bank to be robbed, no armored car to be held up, no illegal drugs to be sold. She's not after money; she's after true ghost stories, icy fingers up and down her spine, so there's no loot for the other members of her gang to share. Their reason for putting their lives and freedom on the line for her at first seems puzzling if not mysterious.

Of course even nonhomicidal guys often think with the little head instead of with the big head that has a brain in it. And the annals of crime are replete with cases in which dim-bulb men in the thrall of bad women did the most vicious and idiotic things solely for sex.

If Datura looked as sultry as she sounded on the phone, she would find it easy to manipulate certain men. Her kind of guy would have more testosterone than white blood cells in his veins, would lack a sense of right and wrong, would have a taste for excitement, would savor every cruelty he performed, and would have no capacity to think about tomorrow.

Putting together her entourage, she would not have encountered a shortage of candidates. The news seemed to be full of such cold-blooded men these days.

Dr. Wilbur Jessup had died not just because he was in the way, but also because killing him had been *fun* to these people, a release, a lark. Rebellion in its purest form.

In the elevator alcove, I had found it hard to believe that she could have put such a crew together. While walking a mere hundred feet of hotel corridor, I had come to find them inevitable.

Dealing with these kinds of people, I would need every advantage that my gift could provide.

Door after door, whether open or closed, failed to entice me, until I stopped finally at 1203, which stood ajar.

31

MOST OF THE FURNITURE HAD BEEN REMOVED from Room 1203. Only a pair of nightstands, a round wood table, and four captain's chairs remained.

Some cleaning had occurred. Although the space was far from immaculate, it looked more accommodating than any place I'd seen previously in the ruined hotel.

The pending storm had dimmed the day, but fat candles in red and amber glass containers provided light. Six were arranged precisely on the floor in each corner of the room. Six more stood on the table.

The pulse and flicker of candlelight might have been cheerful in other circumstances. Here it seemed cheerless. Menacing. Occult.

Scented, the candles produced a fragrance that masked the bitter malodor of long-settled smoke. The air smelled sweet rather than flowery. I had never breathed anything quite like it before.

White sheets had been tucked and pinned to the upholstery of the captain's chairs, to provide clean seating.

The nightstands flanked the big view window. On each stood a large black vase, and in each vase were two or three dozen red roses that either had no scent or could not compete with the candles.

She enjoyed drama and glamour, and she carried her creature comforts with her even into the wilds. Like a European princess visiting Africa in the century of colonialism, having a picnic on a Persian carpet unrolled on the veldt.

Gazing out the window, her back to me as I entered the room, stood a woman in tight black toreador pants and a black blouse. Five feet five. Thick, glossy blonde hair so pale it looked almost white, cut short but not in a manly style.

I said, "I'm almost three hours ahead of sundown."

She neither twitched with surprise nor turned to me. Continuing to stare at the gathering storm, she said, "So you're not a complete disappointment after all."

In person, her voice was no less bewitching, no less erotic than it had been on the phone.

"Odd Thomas, do you know who was the greatest conjurer in history, who summoned spirits and used them better than anyone ever?"

I took a guess: "You?"

"Moses," she said. "He knew the secret names of God, with which he could conquer Pharaoh and divide the sea."

"Moses the conjurer. That must have been a freaky Sunday school you went to."

"Red candles in red glasses," she said.

"You camp out in style," I acknowledged.

"What do they achieve—red candles in red glasses?"

I said, "Light?"

"Victory," she corrected. "Yellow candles in yellow glasses—what do they achieve?"

"It's got to be the right answer this time. Light?"

"Money."

By keeping her back to me, she meant to draw me to the window by the power of her mystery and will.

Determined not to play her game, I said, "Victory and money. Well, there's my problem. I always burn white candles."

She said, "White candles in clear glasses achieve peace. I never use them."

Although I had no intention of bending to her will and joining her at the window, I did move toward the table, which stood between us. In addition to the candles, several objects lay there, one of which appeared to be a remote control.

"Always, I sleep with salt between my mattress

and my sheet," she said, "and over my bed hangs a spray of five-finger grass."

"I don't sleep much these days," I said, "but then I've heard that's true of everyone when they get old."

Finally she turned from the window to look at me.

Stunning. In myth, the succubus is a demon in exquisite female form, and has sex with men to steal their souls. Datura had the face and body ideal for such a demon's purpose.

Her posture and attitude were those of a woman confident that her looks transfixed.

I could admire her as I might admire a perfectly proportioned bronze statue of any subject—woman or wolf, or whidding horse—but a bronze lacking the ineffable quality that fires passions in the heart. In sculpture, that quality is the difference between craft and art. In a woman, it is the difference between mere erotic power and beauty that enchants a man, that humbles him.

Beauty that steals the heart is often imperfect, suggests grace and kindness, and inspires tenderness more than it incites lust.

Her blue stare, by its directness and intensity, was meant to promise ecstasy and utter satiation, but it was too sharp to excite, less like a metaphoric arrow through the heart than like a whittling knife testing the hardness of the material to be carved.

"The candles smell nice," I said, to prove that

I was neither dry-mouthed nor stiffened into speechlessness.

"They're Cleo-May."

"Who's she?"

"Are you really so ignorant of these things, Odd Thomas, or are you so much more than the simple soul you appear to be?"

"Ignorant," I assured her. "Not just of five-finger grass and Cleo-May. I'm ignorant of lots of things, entire broad areas of human knowledge. I'm not proud of it, but it's true."

She was holding a glass of red wine. As she raised it to her full lips and took a slow sip, savored the taste, and swallowed, she stared at me across the table.

"The candles are scented with Cleo-May," she said. "The scent of Cleo-May compels men to love and obey she who lights the candles." She indicated a bottle of wine and another glass on the table. "Will you join me in a drink?"

"That's hospitable of you. But I better keep a clear head."

If the *Mona Lisa*'s smile had been the same as Datura's, no one would ever have heard of that painting. "Yes, I think you better."

"Is that the remote control to trigger the explosives?"

Only her frozen smile revealed her surprise. "Did you and Danny have a nice reunion?"

"It's got two buttons. The remote."

"The black one detonates. The white one disarms the bomb."

The device lay closer to her than to me. If I rushed to the table, she would seize the remote first.

I'm not the kind of guy who punches women. I might have made an exception in her case.

I was restrained by the suspicion that she would slide a knife in my guts even as I cocked my fist to throw the punch.

Also, I feared that, in a flush of perversity, she would press the black button.

"Did Danny tell you much about me?" she asked.

Deciding to play to her vanity, I said, "How does a woman who has so much going for her wind up selling phone sex?"

"I made some porn films," she said. "Good money. But they use up women fast in that racket. So I met this guy who owned an on-line porn store and a phone-sex operation that're like faucets you open and cash pours out. I married him. He died. I own the business now."

"You married him, he died, you're rich."

"Things happen for me. They always have."

"You own the business, but you still take calls?"

This time her smile seemed more genuine. "They're such pathetic little boys. It's fun, turning them inside out with words. They don't even realize how completely they're being humiliated—

and they pay you to make fools of them."

Behind her, still without a toothy edge, storm light fluttered like veils of radiance cast off by luminous wings. But the subsequent thunder cracked hard and rumbled rough, the voice not of angels but of a beast.

"Someone must have killed a blacksnake," she said, "and hung it in a tree."

Considering her frequent inscrutable statements, I thought that I had been holding my own pretty well in our conversation, but this defeated me. "Blacksnake? Tree?"

She indicated the darkening sky. "Isn't the hanging of a dead blacksnake certain to bring the rain?"

"Could be, I guess. I don't know. It's news to me."

"Liar." She sipped the wine. "Anyway, I've had money for a few years. It gives me the freedom to pursue spiritual matters."

"No offense, but it's difficult to picture you on a prayer retreat."

"Psychic magnetism is new to me."

I shrugged. "It's just my fancy term for intuition."

"It's more than that. Danny told me. And you've given me a convincing demonstration. You can conjure spirits."

"No. Not me. You need Moses for that."

"You see spirits."

I decided that playing dumb with her would accomplish nothing except to anger her. "I don't summon them. They come to me. I'd rather they didn't."

"This place must have its ghosts."

"They're here," I admitted.

"I want to see them."

"You can't."

"Then I'll kill Danny."

"I swear to you, I can't conjure."

"I want to see them," she repeated in a colder voice.

"I'm not a medium."

"Liar."

"They don't wrap themselves in ectoplasm that other people can see. Only I can see them."

"You're so special, huh?"

"Unfortunately, yes."

"I want to talk to them."

"The dead don't talk."

She picked up the remote. "I'll waste the little shit. I really will."

Taking a calculated risk, I said, "I'm sure you will. Whether I do what you want or not. You won't risk going to prison for Dr. Jessup's murder."

She put down the remote. She leaned against the window sill: one hip cocked, breasts thrust forward, posing. "Do you think I intend to kill you, too?"

"Of course."

"Then why are you here?"

"To buy some time."

"I warned you to come alone."

"There's no posse on the way," I assured her.

"Then—buy time for what?"

"For fate to take an unexpected turn. For an advantage I can seize."

She had the sense of humor of a rock, but this amused her. "You think I'm ever careless?"

"Killing Dr. Jessup wasn't smart."

"Don't be thick. The boys need their sport," she said, as though there was a logical necessity to the radiologist's murder that should be obvious to me. "That's part of the deal."

As if on cue, the "boys" arrived. Hearing them, I turned.

The first looked like a laboratory-manufactured hybrid, half man and half machine, with a locomotive somewhere in his heritage. Big, solid, the kind of specimen who seemed muscle-bound and slow but who could probably chase you down faster than a runaway train.

Heavy brutish features. A stare as direct as Datura's, but not as readable as hers.

They were not merely guarded eyes, but deeply enigmatic as none others I had ever seen. I had the weird feeling that behind those eyes lay a mind with a landscape so different from that of the ordinary human mind that it might as well have belonged to an entity born on another world.

Given his physical power, the shotgun seemed superfluous. He carried it to the window and held it in both hands as he stared at the desert afternoon.

The second man was beefy but not as pumped as the first. Though young, he had a dissolute look, the puffy eyes and ruddy cheeks of a barroom brawler who would be content to spend his life drinking and fighting, both of which he no doubt did well.

He met my eyes, but not boldly as had the human locomotive. His gaze slid away from me, as if I made him uneasy, though that seemed unlikely. A charging bull probably wouldn't make him uneasy.

Although he carried no weapon that I could see, he might have had a handgun holstered under his summer-weight cotton sports coat.

He pulled a chair out from the table, sat, and poured some of the wine that I had declined.

Like the woman, both men dressed in black. I suspected that their outfits matched not by happenstance, that Datura liked black and that they dressed to her instructions.

They must have been guarding the staircases. She had not called them on a phone or sent them a text message, yet somehow they had known that I had gotten past them and was with her.

"This," she told me, indicating the brute at the window, "is Cheval Andre."

He didn't glance at me. He didn't say *Pleased to meet you.*

As the brawler drank a third of a glass of wine in one swallow, Datura said, "This is Cheval Robert."

Robert glowered at the candles on the table.

"Andre and Robert Cheval," I said. "Brothers?"

"Cheval is not their last name," she said, "as you well know. *Cheval* means 'horse.' As you well know."

"Horse Andre and Horse Robert," I said. "Lady, I have to tell you, even considering the strange life I lead, all this is getting too weird for me."

"If you show me spirits, and everything I want to see, I might not have them kill you, after all. Wouldn't you like to be my Cheval Odd?"

"Gee, I suppose it's an offer most young men might envy, but I don't know what my duties would be as a horse, what the pay is, if there's health insurance—"

"Andre and Robert's duty is to do what I tell them, anything I tell them, as you well know. As compensation, I give them what they need, anytime they need it. And once in a while, as with Dr. Jessup, I give them what they *want.*"

The two men looked at her with a hunger that seemed only in part to be lust. I sensed in them another need that had nothing to do with sex, a need that only she could satisfy, a need so grotesque that I hoped never to learn its nature.

She smiled. "They are such needy boys."

Lightning with a dragon's worth of teeth flashed across the black clouds, sharp and bright, and flashed again. Thunder crashed. The sky convulsed and shook off a million silvery scales of rain, and then millions more.

32

THE HEAVY DOWNPOUR SEEMED TO WASH out of the air some of the light that managed to penetrate the storm clouds, and the afternoon grew both murky and dismal, as if the rain were not only weather but also a moral judgment on the land.

With less light from the window, the glow of the candles swelled. Red and orange chimeras prowled the walls and shook their manes across the ceiling.

Cheval Andre put down his shotgun on the floor and faced the tempest, placing both enormous hands flat against the window glass, as if drawing power from the storm.

Cheval Robert remained at the table, gazing at the candles. An ever-shifting tattoo of victory and money played across his broad face.

When Datura pulled another chair out from the table and told me to sit, I saw no reason to defy her. As I had said, my intention was to buy time and wait for fate to take a turn in my favor. As if I were already a good horse, I sat without objection.

She stalked the room, drank wine, stopped again and again to smell the roses, frequently stretched like a cat, ripe and lithe and acutely aware of how she looked.

Whether moving or standing in place, head tipped back and gazing at the nimbuses of candlelight pulsing on the ceiling, she talked and taunted.

"There's a woman in San Francisco who levitates when she chants. Only the select are invited to observe her on the solstices or All Saints' Eve. But I'm sure you've been there, and know her name."

"We've never met," I assured her.

"There's a fine house in Savannah, inherited by a special young woman, willed to her by an uncle, who also left to her a diary in which he described murdering nineteen children and burying them in his basement. He knew that she would understand and not disclose his crimes to the authorities even though he was dead. You've no doubt visited more than once."

"I don't travel," I said.

"I've been invited several times. If the planets are properly aligned and the guests are of the right caliber, you can hear the voices of the dead speaking from their graves in the floor and walls.

Lost children pleading for their lives, as if they don't know they're dead, crying for release. It's a riveting experience, as you well know."

Andre stood and Robert sat, eyes on the storm in the first case, on the candles in the second, perhaps mesmerized by Datura's singular voice. Neither had yet spoken a word. They were unusually silent men, and uncannily still.

She came to my chair, leaned toward me, and extracted a pendant from her ample cleavage: a teardrop stone, red, perhaps a ruby, as large as a peach pit.

"I have captured thirty in this," she said.

"You told me on the phone. Thirty . . . thirty something in an amulet."

"You know what I said. Thirty *ti bon ange.*"

"I imagine that took a while, collecting thirty."

"You can see them in there," she said, holding the stone close to my eyes. "Others can't, but I'm sure you can."

"They're cute little things," I said.

"Your pretense of ignorance would be convincing to most people, but you don't fool me. With thirty, I am invincible."

"You said before. I'm sure being invincible is comforting."

"I need one more *ti bon ange,* and this one must be special. It must be yours."

"I'm flattered."

"As you know, there are two ways I can collect

it," she said, tucking the stone between her breasts again. She poured more wine. "I can take it from you through a water ritual. That is the painless method of extraction."

"I'm glad to hear it."

"Or Andre and Robert can force you to swallow the stone. Then I can gut you like a fish and take it from your steaming stomach as you die."

If her two horses had heard what she proposed, they were not surprised by it. They remained as still as coiled snakes.

Picking up the glass of wine, moving toward the roses, she said, "If you show me ghosts, I'll take your *ti bon ange* the painless way. But if you insist on playing ignorant, this is going to be a very bad day for you. You're going to know agony of a degree that few men ever experience."

33

THE WORLD HAS GONE MAD. YOU MIGHT HAVE argued against that contention twenty years ago, but if you argue it in our time, you only prove that you, too, live in delusion.

In an asylum world, the likes of Datura rise to the top, the crème de la crème of the insane. They rise not by merit but by the force of their will.

When social forces press for the rejection of age-old Truth, then those who reject it will seek meaning in their own truth. These truths will rarely be Truth at all; they will be only collections of personal preferences and prejudices.

The less depth a belief system has, the greater the fervency with which its adherents embrace it. The most vociferous, the most fanatical are those whose cobbled faith is founded on the shakiest grounds.

I would humbly suggest that collecting someone's *ti bon ange*—whatever that might be—

by forcing him to swallow a gemstone, then eviscerating him and collecting the stone from his stomach, is proof that you are fanatical, mentally unsteady, no longer operating within classic Western philosophy, and not suitable to be a contestant in the Miss America Pageant.

Of course, because it was *my* stomach threatened by the sexy eviscerator, you might feel that I am biased in this analysis. It's always easy to charge prejudice when it's the other guy who's being disemboweled.

Datura had found her truth in a mishmash of occultisms. Her beauty, her fierce will to power, and her ruthlessness drew to her others, like Andre and Robert, whose secondary truth was her weird system of magical thinking and whose primary truth was Datura herself.

As I watched the woman restlessly circle the room, I wondered how many of the employees in her business operations—the on-line porn store, the phone-sex operation—had gradually been replaced with true believers. Other employees, with empty hearts, might have been converted.

I wondered how many men like these two she could call upon to murder in her name. I suspected that although they were strange, they were not unique.

What must the women be like who were their gender's equivalents of Andre and Robert? You wouldn't want to leave your children with them if they ran a day-care center.

If an opportunity arose for me to escape, disarm the package of explosives, get Danny out of this place, and finger Datura for the police, I would be hated by the fanatics devoted to her. If that circle proved to be small, it might quickly fragment. They would find other belief systems or settle back into their natural nihilism, and soon I would mean nothing to them.

If on the other hand her cash-gushing enterprises served as the fountainhead of a cult, I would have to take more precautions than just relocating to a new apartment and changing my name to Odd Smith.

As if energized by the swords of lightning ripping through the sky, Datura pulled a fistful of long-stemmed red roses from one of the vases and gestured with them, lashing the air, as she shared her supernatural experiences.

"In Paris, in the *sous-sol* of a building that occupying Germans used as a police headquarters after the fall of France, a Gestapo officer named Gessel raped many young women in the process of his interrogations, whipped them, too, and killed some for pleasure."

Crimson petals flew from the roses as she emphasized Gessel's brutality.

"One of his most desperate victims fought back—bit his throat, tore open his carotid artery.

Gessel died there in his own abattoir, which he haunts to this day."

An entire tattered bloom broke from its stem and landed in my lap. Startled, I brushed it to the floor as though it had been a tarantula.

"At the invitation of the current owner of that building," said Datura, "I've visited that *sous-sol,* which is actually a sub-basement two floors below the street. If a woman disrobes there and offers herself . . . I felt Gessel's hands all over me—eager, bold, demanding. He entered me. But I couldn't see him. I had been promised I would see him, a full-blown apparition."

In sudden anger, she threw down the roses and ground one of the blooms under her heel.

"I wanted to *see* Gessel. I could feel him. Powerful. Demanding. His everlasting rage. But I couldn't *see* him. That last best proof, *seeing*, eludes me."

Drawing quick shallow breaths, face flushed, not because the violent gestures taxed her but because her anger excited her, she approached Robert, who sat across the table from me, and held out her right hand to him.

He brought her palm to his mouth. For a moment I thought that he was kissing her hand, a strangely gentle moment for a pair of savages like them.

His subtle sucking sounds belied his tender manner.

At the window, Andre turned from the storm that thus far had entranced him. Dancing candlelight brightened his face but did not soften its hard features.

Like a mountain moving, he came to the table. He stood beside Robert's chair.

When Datura had gripped the three long-stemmed roses in her fist, thorns had punctured her palm. She revealed no pain when she had lashed the air, but now she bled.

Robert might have contented himself at her wounds until no taste remained. From him issued a murmur of deep satisfaction.

As disturbing as this was, I doubted it was the "need" of which she had spoken. That would be a worse thing than this.

With an expression of perverse noblesse oblige, the would-be goddess denied Robert further favor and offered communion to Andre.

I tried to focus on the window and the spectacle of the storm, but I could not keep my gaze averted from the chilling tableau across the table.

The giant lowered his mouth into the cup of her hand. He lapped like a kitten, not seeking sustenance, surely, but craving something more than blood, something unknown and unholy.

As Cheval Andre accepted his mistress's grace, Cheval Robert watched intently. Yearning tortured his face.

More than once since I'd entered Room 1203,

the scent of Cleo-May had grown so sweet that it became repellent. Now it thickened to such a degree that it began to sicken me.

As I strove to repress my nausea, I had an impression that I don't mean should be taken literally, that was metaphoric but no less disturbing:

During this blood-sharing ritual, Datura no longer seemed to be a woman, no longer a sexually distinct creature of either gender, but a member of some monoclinous species that harbored both sexes in the same individual, and almost *insectile*. I expected that if lightning backlighted her, I would see her body as a mimicry of human form within which quivered a many-legged entity.

She withdrew her hand from Andre, and he relinquished it with reluctance. When she turned her back on him, however, he returned obediently to the window, once more placed his hands flat upon the glass, and gazed into the storm.

Robert's attention focused again on the table candles. His face settled into placidity, but his eyes were lively with reflections of the flames.

Datura redirected her attention to me. For a moment she stared as if she did not remember who I was. Then she smiled.

She picked up her wineglass and came to me.

If I had realized that she intended to sit in my lap, I would have exploded to my feet as she rounded the table. By the time her intention became clear, she had already settled.

Feathering against my face, her warm breath smelled of wine.

"Have you seen an advantage yet that you can seize?"

"Not yet."

"I want you to drink with me," she said, holding the wineglass to my lips.

34

SHE HELD THE WINE IN THE HAND THAT HAD been pricked by thorns, the hand upon which the two men had suckled.

A new wave of nausea washed through me, and I pulled my head back from the coolness of the glass rim against my lips.

"Drink with me," she repeated, her smoky voice alluring under even these circumstances.

"I don't want any," I told her.

"You do want it, baby. You just don't know you want it. You don't yet understand yourself."

She pressed the glass to my lips again, and I turned my head away from it.

"Poor Odd Thomas," she said, "so fearful of corruption. Do you think I'm a dirty thing?"

Offending her too openly might be bad for Danny. Now that she had lured me here, she had little if any further use for him. She could punish me for any insult by pushing the black button on the remote.

Lamely, I said, "I just catch cold easily, that's all."

"But I don't have a cold."

"Well, you never know. You might have one but not be showing symptoms yet."

"I take echinacea. You should, too. You'll never have a cold again."

"I'm not much into herbal remedies," I said.

She slid her left arm around my neck. "You've been brainwashed by the big drug companies, baby."

"You're right. I probably have been."

"Big drugs, big oil, big tobacco, big media—they've gotten inside everyone's head. They're poisoning us. You don't need man-made chemicals. Nature has a cure for everything."

"Brugmansia is really effective," I said. "I could use some brugmansia leaf right now. Or flower. Or root."

"I'm not familiar with that one."

Under the bouquet of Cabernet Sauvignon, her breath carried another scent, an astringent odor, almost bitter, that I could not identify.

I remembered reading that the sweat and breath of certifiable psychopaths have a subtle but distinctive chemical odor because of certain physiological conditions accompanying that mental disorder. Maybe her breath smelled of craziness.

"A spoonful of white mustard seed," she said, "protects against all harm."

"I wish I had a spoonful."

"Eating wonder-world root will make you rich."

"Sounds better than hard work."

She pressed the glass against my lips again, and when I tried to pull my head back, she resisted my effort with the arm that she had slipped around my neck.

When I turned my head to the side, she took the glass away and surprised me by giggling. "I know you're a *mundunugu,* but you're so good at pretending to be a church mouse."

A sudden shift of wind threw shatters of rain against the windows.

She wriggled her bottom against my lap, smiled, and kissed my forehead.

"It's stupid not to use herbal remedies, Odd Thomas. You don't eat meat, do you?"

"I'm a fry cook."

"I know you cook it," she said, "but *please* tell me you don't eat it."

"Even cheeseburgers with bacon."

"That's *so* self-destructive."

"And French fries," I added.

"Suicidal."

She sucked a mouthful of wine from the glass and spat it in my face. "Now what did resistance get you, baby? Datura always has her way. I can break you."

Not if my mother couldn't, I thought as I wiped my face with my left hand.

"Andre and Robert can hold you," she said, "while I pinch your nose shut. When you open your mouth to breathe, I pour the wine down your throat. Then I bust the glass against your teeth, and you can chew the pieces. Is that what you'd prefer?"

Before she could press the wineglass to my lips again, I said, "Do you want to see the dead?"

No doubt some men saw an exciting blue fire in her eyes, but they mistook appetite for passion; her gaze was that of a cool and ravenous crocodile.

Searching my eyes, she said, "You told me no one but you could see them."

"I guard my secrets."

"So you can conjure, after all."

"Yes," I lied.

"I knew you could. I knew."

"The dead are here, just like you thought."

She looked around. The shimmering candlelight shivered the shadows.

"They aren't in this room," I said.

"Then where?"

"Downstairs. I saw several earlier, in the casino."

She rose from my lap. "Conjure them here."

"They choose where they haunt."

"You have the power to summon."

"It doesn't work that way. There are exceptions, but for the most part, they cling to the very place where they died . . . or where they were happiest in life."

Putting her wineglass on the table, she said, "What trick do you have up your sleeve?"

"I'm wearing a T-shirt."

Her eyes narrowed. "What does that mean?"

Rising from the chair, I said, "Gessel, the Gestapo agent—does he ever manifest anywhere but in the basement of that building in Paris? Anywhere but the very place where he died?"

She thought about that. "All right. We'll go to the casino."

35

TO FACILITATE THE EXPLORATION OF THE abandoned hotel, they had brought Coleman lanterns, which operated on canned fuel. These lamps would press back the darkness more effectively than flashlights.

Andre left the shotgun on the floor near the window of Room 1203, which convinced me that both he and Robert carried pistols under their black jackets.

The remote control remained on the table. If my conjuring act in the casino failed to please Datura, at least she wouldn't be able to waste Danny at once. She would have to return here to retrieve the device that could trigger the blast.

As we were about to leave the room, she realized that she had not eaten a banana since the previous day. This oversight clearly concerned her.

Picnic coolers packed with food and drink were

in the adjacent bathroom. She returned from there with one of Chiquita's finest.

As she peeled the fruit, she explained that the banana tree—"as you know, Odd Thomas"—was the tree of forbidden fruit in the Garden of Eden.

"I thought it was an apple tree."

"Play dumb if you want," she said.

Although certain that I was aware of it, she also told me that the Serpent (with a capital *S*) lives forever because he eats twice daily of the fruit of the banana tree. And every serpent (with a small *s*) will live for a thousand years by following this simple dietary requirement.

"But you're not a serpent," I said.

"When I was nineteen," she revealed, "I made a *wanga* to charm the spirit of a snake from its body into mine. As I'm sure you can see, it's twined among my ribs, where it'll live forever."

"Well, for a thousand years, anyway."

Her patchwork theology—obviously stitched together in part from voodoo, but God alone knew from what else—made the ravings of Jim Jones in Guyana, David Koresh in Waco, and the leader of the comet cult that committed mass suicide near San Diego sound like rational men of faith.

Although I expected Datura to make the eating of the banana an erotic performance, she consumed the fruit with a kind of dogged determination. She chewed without apparent pleasure, and more than once grimaced when she swallowed.

I guessed that she was twenty-five or twenty-six years old. She might have been on this two-bananas-per-day regimen for as long as seven years.

Having by now eaten in excess of five thousand bananas, she might understandably have lost her taste for them—particularly if she had done the math relating to her remaining obligation. With 974 years to live (as a serpent, small *s*), she had approximately 710,000 more bananas in her future.

I find it so much easier being a Catholic. Especially one who doesn't get to church every week.

So much about Datura was foolish, even pitiable, but her fatuity and ignorance made her no less dangerous. Throughout history, fools and their followers, willfully ignorant but in love with themselves and with power, have murdered millions.

When she had consumed the banana and calmed the spirit of the snake entwined through her ribs, we were ready to visit the casino.

A squirming against my groin startled me, and I thrust my hand into my pocket before realizing that I felt only Terri Stambaugh's satellite phone.

Having seen, Datura said, "What have you got there?"

I had no choice but to reveal it. "Just my phone. I had it set to vibrate instead of ring. It surprised me."

"Is it vibrating still?"

"Yes." I held it in the palm of my hand, and we stared at it for a moment, until the caller hung up. "It stopped."

"I'd forgotten your phone," she said. "I don't think we should leave it with you."

I had no choice but to give it to her.

She took it into the bathroom and slammed it into a hard countertop. Slammed it again.

When she returned, she smiled and said, "We were at the movies once, and this dork took two phone calls during the film. Later we followed him, and Andre broke both his legs with a baseball bat."

This proved that even the most evil people could occasionally have a socially responsible impulse.

"Let's go," she said.

I had entered Room 1203 with a flashlight. I left with it, too—switched off, clipped to my belt—and no one objected.

Carrying a Coleman lantern, Robert led the way to the nearest stairs and descended at the front of our procession. Andre came last with the second lantern.

Between those big somber men, Datura and I followed the wide stairs, not one behind the other, single file, but side by side at her insistence.

Down the first flight to the landing at the eleventh floor, I heard a steady menacing hiss. I half convinced myself that this must be the voice of the serpent spirit that she claimed to carry within her. Then I realized it was the sound of the burning gas in the saclike wicks of the lamps.

On the second flight, she took my hand. I might have pulled free of her grip in revulsion if I hadn't thought her capable of ordering Andre to lop my hand off at the wrist as punishment for the insult.

More than fear, however, encouraged me to accept her touch. She did not seize my hand boldly, but took it hesitantly, almost shyly, and then held it firmly as a child might in anticipation of a spooky adventure.

I would not have bet on the proposition that this demented and corrupted woman harbored within her any wisp of the innocent child that she once must have been. Yet the quality of submissive trust with which she inserted her hand in mine and the shiver that passed through her at the prospect of what lay ahead suggested child-like vulnerability.

In the eldritch light, which cast about her an aura that seemed almost supernatural, she looked at me, her eyes adance with wonder. This was not the usual Medusa stare; it lacked her characteristic cold hunger and calculation.

Likewise, her grin was without mockery or

menace, but expressed a natural and wholesome delight in conspiratorial feats of daring.

I warned myself against the danger of compassion in this case. How easy it would be to imagine the traumas of childhood that might have deformed her into the moral monster she had become, and then to convince myself that those traumas could be balanced—and their effects reversed—by sufficient acts of kindness.

She might not have been formed by trauma. She might have been born this way, without an empathy gene and other essentials. In that case, she would interpret any kindness as weakness. Among predatory beasts, any display of weakness is an invitation to attack.

Besides, even if trauma shaped her, that didn't excuse what had been done to Dr. Jessup.

I remembered a naturalist who, having come to despise humanity and to despair of it, set out to make a documentary about the moral superiority of animals, particularly of bears. He saw in them not only a harmonious relationship with nature that humankind could not achieve, but also a playfulness beyond human capacity, a dignity, a compassion for other animals, and even a mystical quality that he found moving, humbling. A bear ate him.

Long before I could precipitate a fog of self-delusion equal to that of the devoured naturalist, in fact by the time we had descended only three flights of stairs, Datura herself brought me sharply to my senses by launching into another of her charming anecdotes. She liked the sound of her own voice so much that she could not allow the good impression, made by her smile and silence, to stand for long.

"In Port-au-Prince, if you are invited under the protection of a respected juju adept, it's possible to attend a ceremony of one of the forbidden secret societies shunned by most voodooists. In my case, it was the Couchon Gris, the "Gray Pigs." Everyone on the island lives in terror of them, and in the more rural areas, they rule the night."

I suspected that the Gray Pigs would prove to have little in common with, say, the Salvation Army.

"From time to time, the Couchon Gris perform a human sacrifice—and sample the flesh. Visitors may only observe. The sacrifice is made on a massive black stone hanging on two thick chains suspended from a great iron bar embedded in the walls near the ceiling."

Her hand tightened in mine as she recalled this horror.

"The person being sacrificed is killed with a knife through the heart, and in that instant, the chains begin to sing. The *gros bon ange* flies at once from this world, but the *ti bon ange,* restrained by the ceremony, can only travel up and down the chains."

My hand grew damp and chill.

I knew she must feel the change.

The faint, disturbing scent that I had smelled earlier, when I'd considered climbing these stairs, arose again. Musky, mushroomy, and strangely suggestive of raw meat.

As before, I flashed back to the dead face of the man whom I had hauled out of the water in the storm drain.

"When you listen closely to the singing chains," Datura continued, "you realize it isn't just the sound of twisting links grinding against one another. There's a voice expressing in the chains, a wail of fear and despair, a wordless urgent pleading."

Wordlessly, urgently, I pleaded with her to shut up.

"This anguished voice continues as long as the Couchon Gris continue to sample the flesh on the altar, usually half an hour. When they're done, the chains immediately stop singing because the *ti bon ange* dissipates, to be absorbed in equal measure by all those who tasted the sacrifice."

We were three flights from the ground floor, and I wanted to hear no more of this. Yet it seemed to me that if this story was true—and I believed that it was—the victim deserved the dignity of an identity, and should not be spoken of as if he or she were but a fattened calf.

"Who?" I asked, my voice thin.

"Who what?"

"The sacrifice. Who was it that night?"

"A Haitian girl. About eighteen. Not all that pretty. A homely thing. Someone said she had been a seamstress."

My right hand grew too weak to maintain a grip, and I let go of Datura with relief.

She smiled at me, amused, this woman who was physical perfection by almost any standard, whose beauty—icy or not—would turn heads wherever she went.

And I thought of a line from Shakespeare: *O, what may man within him hide, though angel on the outward side!*

Little Ozzie, my literary mentor, who despairs that I am not more well read in the classics, would have been proud to hear that a line from the immortal bard had come to me, in fully accurate quotation and appropriate to the moment.

He would also have lectured me on the stupidity of my continued aversion to firearms in light of the fact that I had chosen to put myself in the company of people whose idea of holiday fun was to book tickets not to a Broadway play but to a human sacrifice.

As we descended the final flight, Datura said: "The experience was fascinating. The voice in those chains had the identical tonal qualities of the voice of the little seamstress when she lay not yet dead on that black stone."

"Did she have a name?"

"Who?"

"The seamstress."

"Why?"

"Did she have a name?" I repeated.

"I'm sure she did. One of those funny Haitian names. I never heard it. The thing is, her *ti bon ange* didn't materialize in any way. I want to *see*. But there was nothing to *see*. That part was disappointing. I want to *see*."

Each time that she said *I want to see*, she sounded like a pouting child.

"You won't disappoint me, will you, Odd Thomas?"

"No."

We reached the ground floor, and Robert continued to lead the way, holding his lantern higher than he had on the stairs.

En route to the casino, I remained alert to the topography of the rubble and the burned-out spaces, committing them to memory as best I could.

36

IN THE WINDOWLESS CASINO, THE PLEASANT-looking man with receding hair sat at one of the two remaining blackjack tables, where I had first seen him, where for five years he had been waiting to be dealt another hand.

He smiled at me and nodded—but regarded Datura and her boys with a frown.

At my request, Andre and Robert put the Coleman lanterns on the floor, about twenty feet apart. I asked for a couple of adjustments—bring that one a foot this way, move the other one six inches to the left—as if the precise placement of the lamps was essential to some ritual that I intended to perform. This was all for Datura's benefit, to help convince her that there was a *process* about which she needed to be patient.

The farther reaches of the vast chamber remained dark, but the center had enough light for my purpose.

"Sixty-four died in the casino," Datura told me. "The heat was so intense in some areas that even bones burned."

The patient blackjack player remained the only spirit in sight. The others would come eventually, as many as lingered this side of death.

"Baby, look at those melted slot machines. Casinos, they're always advertising they have hot slots, but this time they weren't bullshitting."

Of the eight spirits who had been here previously, only one might serve my purpose.

"They found the remains of this old lady. The quake tipped over a bank of slot machines, trapped her under them."

I didn't want to hear Datura's grisly details. By now, I knew there was no way that I could dissuade her from providing them, and vividly.

"Her remains were so twisted up with melted metal and plastic, the coroner couldn't completely extract them."

Under the time-mellowed rankness of char and sulfur and myriad toxic residues, I detected the half-fungal, half-fleshy odor from the stairwell. Elusive but not imagined, it swelled and faded breath by breath.

"The coroner thought the old bitch should be cremated, since the job was already half done, and since that was the only way to separate her from the melted machine."

Out of shadows came the elderly lady with the

long face and the vacant eyes. Perhaps she had been the one trapped under the bank of one-armed bandits.

"But her family—they didn't want cremation, they wanted a traditional burial."

From the corner of my eye, I detected movement, turned, and discovered the cocktail waitress in the Indian-princess uniform. I was saddened to see her. I had thought—and hoped—that she might have moved on at last.

"So the casket contained part of the slot machine that the hag had been fused with. Is that nuts or what?"

Here came the uniformed guard, walking a little bit like John Wayne, one hand on the gun at his hip.

"Are any of them here?" Datura asked.

"Yeah. Four."

"I don't see anything."

"Right now they're only manifesting to me."

"So show me."

"There should be one more. I have to wait until they're all gathered."

"Why?"

"That's just the way it is."

"Don't screw with me," she warned.

"You'll get what you want," I assured her.

Although Datura's customary self-possession had given way to an evident excitement, to a twitchy anticipation, Andre and Robert exhibited all the enthusiasm of a pair of boulders. Each stood by his lantern, waiting.

Andre stared off into the gloom beyond the lamplight. He did not seem to be looking at anything in this universe. His features were slack. His eyes seldom blinked. The only emotion that he'd exhibited thus far had been when he had suckled at her thorn-pricked hand, and even then he had not revealed an ability to emote any greater than that of the average oak stump.

While Andre seemed perpetually anchored in placid waters, Robert occasionally revealed, by a fleeting expression or a furtive glance, that he rode a marginally more active inner sea. Now his hands had his complete attention as he used the fingernails of his left to clean under the fingernails of his right, slowly, meticulously, as though he would be content to spend hours at the task.

At first I had decided that both were on the stupid side of dumb, but I had begun to rethink that judgment. I couldn't believe that their interior lives were rich in intellectual pursuit and philosophical contemplation, but I did suspect that they were more formidable, mentally, than they appeared to be.

Perhaps they had been with Datura for enough years and through enough ghost hunts that the prospect of supernatural experiences no longer interested them. Even the most exotic excursions can become tedious through repetition.

And after years of listening to her all but constant chatter, they could be excused for taking refuge in silence, for creating redoubts of inner quietude to which they could retreat, letting her ceaseless crazy talk wash over them.

"All right, you're waiting for a fifth spirit," she said, plucking at my T-shirt. "But tell me about those that are here already. Where are they? Who are they?"

To placate her and to avoid worrying that the dead man I most needed to see might not put in an appearance, I described the player at the blackjack table, his kind face, full mouth and dimpled chin.

"So he's manifesting the way that he was before the fire?" she asked.

"Yes."

"When you conjure him for me, I want to see him both ways—as he was in life, and what the fire did to him."

"All right," I agreed, because she would never be persuaded that I lacked the power to compel such revelations.

"All of them, I want to see what it did to them. Their wounds, their suffering."

"All right."

"Who else?" she asked.

One by one, I pointed to where they stood: the elderly woman, the guard, the cocktail waitress.

Datura found only the waitress intriguing. "You

said she was a brunette. Is that right—or is her hair black?"

Peering more closely at the apparition, which moved toward me in response to my interest, I said, "Black. Raven hair."

"Gray eyes?"

"Yes."

"I know about her. There's a story about her," Datura said with an avidness that made me uneasy.

Now focusing on Datura, the young waitress came closer still, to within a few feet of us.

Squinting, trying to see the spirit, but staring to one side of it, Datura asked, "Why does she linger?"

"I don't know. The dead don't talk to me. When I command them to be visible to you, maybe you'll be able to get them to speak."

I scanned the casino shadows, searching for the lurking form of the tall, broad man with buzz-cut hair. Still no sign of him, and he was my only hope.

Speaking of the cocktail waitress, Datura said, "Ask if her name was . . . Maryann Morris."

Surprised, the waitress moved closer and put a hand on Datura's arm, a contact that went unnoticed, for only I can feel the touch of the dead.

"It must be Maryann," I said. "She reacted to the name."

"Where is she?"

"Directly in front of you, within arm's reach."

In the manner of a domesticated creature reverting to a wilder state, Datura's delicate nostrils flared, her eyes shone with feral excitement, and her lips pulled back from her white-white teeth as if in anticipation of blood sport.

"I know why Maryann can't move on," Datura said. "There was a story about her in the news accounts. She had two sisters. Both of them worked here."

"She's nodding," I told Datura, and at once wished that I had not facilitated this encounter.

"I'll bet Maryann doesn't know what happened to her sisters, whether they lived or died. She doesn't want to move on until she knows what happened to them."

The apprehensive expression on the spirit's face, which was not entirely without a fragile hope, revealed that Datura had intuited the reason Maryann lingered. Reluctant to encourage her, I didn't confirm the accuracy of her insight.

She needed no encouragement from me. "One sister was a waitress working the ballroom that night."

The Lady Luck Ballroom. The collapsed ceiling. The crushing, skewering weight of the massive chandelier.

"The other sister worked as a hostess in the main restaurant," Datura said. "Maryann had used her contacts to get jobs for them."

If that was true, the cocktail waitress might feel responsible for her sisters having been in the Panamint when the quake struck. Hearing that they had survived, she would most likely feel free to shake off the chains that bound her to this world, these ruins.

Even if her sisters had died, the sad truth was likely to release her from her self-imposed purgatory. Although her sense of guilt might increase, that would be trumped by her hope of a reunion with her loved ones in the next world.

Seeing not the usual cold calculation in Datura's eyes, nor the childlike wonder that had briefly brightened them as we had descended the stairs from the twelfth floor, seeing instead a bitterness and a meanness that emphasized the new feral quality in her face, I felt no less nauseated than when, with blood-smeared hand, she had pressed the wineglass to my lips.

"The lingering dead are vulnerable," I warned her. "We owe them the truth, only the truth, but we have to be careful to comfort them and encourage them onward by what we say and how we say it."

Listening to myself, I realized the futility of urging Datura to act with compassion.

Directly addressing the spirit whom she could not see, Datura said, "Your sister Bonnie is alive."

Hope brightened the late Maryann Morris's face, and I could see that she readied herself for joy.

Datura continued: "Her spine was snapped when a ton-and-a-half ballroom chandelier fell on her. Crushed the shit out of her. Her eyes were punctured, ruined—"

"What're you doing? Don't do this," I pleaded.

"Now Bonnie's paralyzed from the neck down, and blind. She lives on the government dole in a cheap nursing home where she'll probably die from neglected bedsores."

I wanted to shut her up even if I had to hit her, and maybe half the reason I wanted to shut her up was because it would *give me an excuse* to hit her.

As though attuned to my desire, Andre and Robert stared at me, tense with the expectation of action.

Although the chance to knock her flat would have been worth the beating the thugs would have administered to me, I reminded myself that I had come here for Danny. The cocktail waitress was dead, but my friend with brittle bones had a chance to live. His survival must be my focus.

Addressing the spirit she could not see, Datura said, "Your other sister, Nora, was burned over eighty percent of her body, but she survived. Three fingers on her left hand were burned completely away. So were her hair and many of her facial features, Maryann. One ear. Her lips. Her nose. Seared away, gone."

Grief so tortured the cocktail waitress that I

could not bear to look at her, because I could do nothing to comfort her in the face of this vicious assault.

Breathing rapidly, shallowly, Datura had allowed the wolf in her bones to rise into her heart. Words were her teeth and cruelty her claws.

"Your Nora has had thirty-six operations with more to come—skin grafts, facial reconstruction, painful and tedious. And still she's hideous."

"You're making this up," I interrupted.

"Like hell I am. She's *hideous*. She rarely goes out, and when she does, she wears a hat and ties a scarf across her sickening face to avoid frightening children."

Such aggressive gleefulness in the administration of emotional pain, such inexplicable bitterness revealed Datura's perfect face to be not just a contrast to her nature but in fact a mask. The longer she assailed the cocktail waitress, the less opaque the mask became, and you could begin to see the suggestion of an underlying malignancy so ugly that, were the mask to be stripped suddenly away, a face would be revealed that would make Lon Chaney's Phantom of the Opera look lamb-sweet, lamb-gentle.

"You, Maryann, *you* got away easy by comparison. Your pain is over. You can go on from here any damn time you choose. But because your sisters were where they were, when they were, their suffering is going to continue for years and years, for all the rest of their miserable lives."

The intensity of misbegotten guilt that Datura strove to foster would keep this tortured spirit chained to these burned-out ruins, to this bleak plot of land, for another decade, or century. And for no purpose but to attempt to agitate the poor soul into a visible manifestation.

"Do I piss you off, Maryann? Do you hate me for revealing the helpless, broken *things* your sisters have become?"

To Datura, I said, "This is disgusting, despicable, and it won't work. It's all for nothing."

"I know what I'm doing, baby. I always know *exactly* what I'm doing."

"She isn't like you," I persisted. "She doesn't hate, so you can't enrage her."

"*Everyone* hates," she said, and warned me off with a murderous look that dropped the temperature of my blood. "Hate makes the world go 'round. Especially for girls like Maryann. They're the best of all haters."

"What would you know about girls like her?" I asked scornfully, angrily. And answered my question: "Nothing. You know nothing about women like her."

Andre took one step away from his lantern, and Robert glowered at me.

Relentless, Datura said, "I've seen your picture in newspapers, Maryann. Oh, yes, I did my research before I came here. I know the faces of so many who died in this place, because if I meet *them—when* I meet them through my new boyfriend here, my little odd one—I want the encounters to be *memorable.*"

The tall broad brick of a man with buzz-cut hair and deep-set bile-green eyes had appeared, but I'd been so distracted by Datura's unconscionable badgering of the cocktail waitress that I had not been aware of this spirit's belated arrival. I saw him now as he abruptly loomed closer to us.

"I've seen your picture, Maryann," Datura repeated. "You were a pretty girl but not a beauty. Just pretty enough for men to use you, but not pretty enough to be able to use *them* to get what you wanted."

No more than ten feet from us, the eighth spirit of the casino appeared to be as angry as he had been when I had seen him earlier. Jaws clenched. Hands fisted.

"Just pretty isn't good enough," Datura continued. "Prettiness fades quickly. If you had lived, your life would have been nothing but cocktail waitressing and disappointment."

Buzz-cut came closer, now three feet behind the stricken spirit of Maryann Morris.

"You had high hopes when you came to this job," Datura said, "but it was a dead end, and soon you knew you were already a failure. Women like you turn to their sisters, to their friends, and make a life that way. But you . . . *you* even failed your sisters, didn't you?"

One of the Coleman lanterns brightened markedly, dimmed, and brightened again, causing shadows to fly away, leap close, and fly away once more.

Andre and Robert somberly considered the lamp, looked at each other, and then surveyed the room, puzzled.

37

"FAILED YOUR SISTERS," DATURA REPEATED, "your paralyzed, blind, disfigured sisters. And if that isn't true, if I'm full of crap, then let me *see* you, Maryann. Show yourself, confront me, let me *see* you the way the fire ruined you. Show me, and scare me off."

Although I would never have been able to conjure these spirits into a sufficiently material state for Datura to have seen them, I had hoped that Buzz-cut, with his high poltergeist potential, would provide a spectacle that would not only entertain my captors but also distract them so completely that I might get away.

The problem had been how to fuel his already simmering anger into the fiery rage needed to power poltergeist phenomena. Now it seemed that Datura would solve that problem for me.

"You weren't there for your sisters," she taunted. "Not before the quake, not during, not after, not ever."

Although the cocktail waitress only buried her face in her hands and endured the poisonous accusations, Buzz-cut glared at Datura, his expression heating from a simmering to a boiling anger.

He and Maryann Morris were bonded by untimely death as well as by their inability to move on, but I can't know that his mood grew darker because he took offense on behalf of the cocktail waitress. I don't believe these stranded spirits feel any sense of community. They see one another, but each is fundamentally alone.

More likely, Datura's viciousness resonated with this man, excited him, and amplified his existing anger.

"The fifth spirit has arrived," I told her. "Conditions are perfect now."

"Then *do* it," she said sharply. "Conjure them right here, right now. Let me *see*."

God forgive me, to save myself and Danny, I said, "What you're doing is helpful. It's . . . I don't know . . . it's emotionalizing them or something."

"I told you I always know exactly what I'm doing. Don't ever doubt me, baby."

"Just keep hammering at her, and with my help, in a few minutes, you'll not just see Maryann but all of them."

She hurled more abuse at the cocktail waitress, in language far more vile than she'd used thus far, and both of the Coleman lanterns pulsed, pulsed, as though in sympathy with the lightning that might at the same moment have been ripping through the sky outside.

Stalking, turning, stalking, circling, as if caged, as though frustrated beyond tolerance by his confinement, Buzz-cut banged his fists together hard enough to fracture knuckle against knuckle if he had been a material presence, but not even making a sound in his spirit form.

He could have swung those fists at me, but they would have had no effect. No spirit can harm a living person by direct touch. This world belongs to us, not to them.

If an earthbound soul is sufficiently debased, however, if the anger and envy and spite and stubborn rebellion that characterized him in life should ripen into blackest spiritual malignancy during the days when he lingers between worlds, he will be able to vent the power of his demonic rage on inanimate objects.

To the cocktail waitress whom she couldn't see and never would, Datura said with pitiless persistence, "You know what I think, what I'd bet, Maryann? In that shabby nursing home at night, some scummy guy on the staff sneaks in your sister's room, Bonnie's room, and rapes her."

Past rage, approaching fury, Buzz-cut threw back his head and screamed, but the sound was trapped with him in the realm between here and Elsewhere.

"She's helpless," Datura said, her voice as

venomous as the contents of a rattlesnake's poison sacs. "Bonnie would be afraid to tell anyone because the rapist never talks, and she doesn't know his name, and she can't see, so she's afraid they won't believe her."

Buzz-cut tore at the air with his hands, as though trying to claw his way back through the veil that separated him from the world of the living.

"So Bonnie has to endure anything he does to her, but when she's enduring, she thinks of you, thinks because of you, she was where she was when the quake destroyed her life, and she thinks about how you, her sister, aren't there for her now, and never were."

Listening to herself, her own most appreciative audience, Datura thrived on her viciousness. After each hateful rant, she seemed to thrill to the discovery of a deeper vileness in herself.

The malignant mass beneath the mask of beauty now rose all but fully into view. Her flushed and twisted features were no longer the stuff of adolescent boys' dreams, but of madhouses and of prisons for the criminally insane.

I tensed, sensing that a forceful demonstration of the spirit's fury was almost upon us.

Inspired by Datura, energized, Buzz-cut thrashed spastically, as if he were lashed by a hundred whips or tormented by jolt after jolt of electricity. He threw his arms out, palms spread, like an enraptured preacher of an expressive sect, exhorting a congregation to be penitent.

From his big hands pulsed concentric rings of power. They were visible to me, but only by their effects would they be visible to my hostess and her men.

Rattles, clicks, creaks, and pings arose from the piles of ruined slot machines, and the two black-jack-table stools began to dance in place. Here and there across the casino, small funnels of whirling ashes spun up from the floor.

"What's happening?" Datura asked.

"They're about to appear," I told her, though every spirit other than Buzz-cut had disappeared. "All of them. At last, you'll *see*."

Poltergeists are as impersonal as hurricanes. They cannot aim themselves or cause precise effects. They are blind, thrashing power, and can harm human beings only by indirection. If furiously flung debris brains you, however, the effect is no less devastating than a well-swung club to the head.

Broken slabs of plaster ceiling ornamentation levitated out of the craps table into which they had fallen during the earthquake, and exploded at us.

I dodged, Datura ducked, and the missiles flew past us, over us, crashing into columns and walls behind us.

Buzz-cut flung bolts of power from his hands,

and when he let out another silent scream, concentric circles of energy poured from his open mouth.

More and larger funnels of gray ashes and soot and scraps of charred wood spun up from the floor, while chips and clods of plaster shook down from the ceiling, while lashing down from above as well were loose wires and electrical conduits, while a battered blackjack table tumbled across the room as if blown by a wind that otherwise we could not feel, while a fire-scorched wheel of fortune spun by in a blur of losing numbers, while a pair of metal crutches stilted past as if in search of the dead gambler who had once needed them, and while an eerie screeching came out of the gloom and rapidly swelled both in volume and in pitch.

In this furiously escalating chaos, a chunk of plaster weighing perhaps fifteen pounds struck Robert in the chest, knocking him backward and off his feet.

As the thug went down, the mysterious screaming thing appeared out of the darker reaches of the casino, proving to be a half-melted life-size bronze statue of an Indian chief on a horse, spinning with alarming rotational velocity, the base shrieking against the concrete floor, from which nearly all carpeting had been burned, scouring away debris, striking sprays of white and orange sparks.

With Robert still falling, with Datura and Andre riveted by the approaching, whirling, shrieking bronze, I seized the moment, stepped to the nearest Coleman lantern, snared it, and threw it at the second lamp.

In spite of my lack of practice at bowling, I scored a strike. Lantern met lantern with a crash and a brief bloom of light, and then we were in darkness relieved only by the sparks showering from the spinning horse and rider.

38

ONCE A POLTERGEIST AS POWERFUL AS BUZZ-cut has committed itself to a violent release of pent-up fury, it will with rare exception rage out of control until it exhausts itself—much like the usual incoherent-rap-star-going-postal at the annual Vibe Awards. In this case, the storming spirit might give me another minute of cover, as long as two or three.

In the dark, in the rattle-clatter-bang-shriek, I stayed low, scuttling, anxious to avoid being knocked unconscious or decapitated by flying debris. I squinted, too, because enough chips and splinters of this and that were spinning through the air to make me wish that I'd brought an ophthalmologist with me.

As well as I could in such blinding dark, I tried to follow a straight line. My goal: a gallery of demolished shops beyond the casino, through which we had passed on our way here from the north stairs of the hotel.

Encountering piles of rubble, I went around some, over others, keeping on the move. I felt my way with both hands, but cautiously lest I clamber across debris bristling with nails and sharp metal edges.

I spat ashes, spat unidentifiable bits of debris, plucked away fuzzy twirls of fluffy stuff that tickled my ears. I sneezed without worrying that I could be tracked by sound through the poltergeist cacophony.

Too soon, I grew concerned that I had strayed off course, that it was not possible to remain oriented in pitch blackness. I quickly became convinced that I would bump into a voluptuous form in the dark, and that it would say *Why, if it isn't my new boyfriend, my little odd one.*

That stopped me.

I unclipped the flashlight from my belt. But I hesitated to use it, even just long enough to sweep my surroundings and reorient myself.

Datura and her needy boys probably had not relied solely on the Coleman lanterns. Most likely they would have a flashlight or even three. If not, then Andre would let her set his hair on fire and use him as a walking torch.

When Buzz-cut ran out of steam, when the merry band of three could stop hugging the floor and dared to raise their heads, they would expect to find me in their immediate area. With flashlights, in this gloom, they would need a minute or two, maybe longer, to realize that I was neither dead nor alive in the mess of poltergeist-tossed trash.

If I used my light now, they might see the sweep of it and know that I was already escaping. I didn't want to draw their notice sooner than necessary. I needed every precious minute of lead time that I could get.

A hand touched my face.

I screamed like a little girl but couldn't make a sound, and thus avoided humiliating myself.

Fingers pressed gently to my lips, as if to warn me against the cry that I had tried and failed to make. A delicate hand, that of a woman.

Only three women had been in the casino this time. Two of them were five years dead.

The would-be goddess, even if invincible by virtue of having thirty thingumadoodles in an amulet, even if destined to live one thousand years by virtue of playing host to a banana-loving serpent, could not see in the dark. She had no sixth sense. She could not have found me without a flashlight.

The hand slipped from my lips to my chin, my cheek. Then she touched my left shoulder, traced the line of my arm, and took my hand.

Perhaps because I want the dead to feel warm, they are that way to me, and this hand in mine also felt indescribably cleaner than had the well-manicured hand of the phone-sex heiress. Clean and honest, strong but gentle. I wanted to believe that this was Maryann Morris, the cocktail waitress.

Giving her my trust, after having paused no longer than ten seconds in the drowning dark, I allowed her to be my pilot fish.

With Buzz-cut noisily working off his frustrations in the gloom behind us, we hurried forward much faster than I had been able to progress on my own, bypassing obstacles instead of clambering over them, never hesitating in fear of falling. The ghost could see as well without light as with.

In less than a minute, following a few turns that felt right, she brought me to a stop. She let go of my left hand and touched my right, in which I held the flashlight.

Switching it on, I saw that we had gone through the gallery of shops and that we were at the end of a hallway, at the door to the north stairs. My guide, indeed, was Maryann, appropriately dressed as an Indian princess.

Seconds were important, but I could not leave her without an attempt to right Datura's wrongs.

"The darkness loose in this world damaged your sisters. The fault isn't yours. Eventually when they leave here, don't you want to be there for them on . . . the other side?"

She met my gaze. Her gray eyes were lovely.

"Go home, Maryann Morris. There's love waiting for you, if only you'll go to it."

She glanced back the way that we had come, then looked at me worriedly.

"When you get there, ask for my Stormy. You won't be sorry you did. If Stormy's right and the next life is service, there's nobody better to have great adventures with than her."

She backed away from me.

"Go home," I whispered.

She turned and walked away.

"Let go. Go home. Leave life—and live."

As she faded, she looked over her shoulder, and smiled, and then she was not in the hallway anymore.

This time, I believe, she passed through the veil.

I tore open the staircase door, plunged through, and climbed like a sonofabitch.

39

CLEO-MAY CANDLES, COMPELLING ME TO love and obey the charming young woman who consorted with Gestapo ghosts, splashed the walls red, splashed them yellow.

Nevertheless, in the storm-swallowed day, Room 1203 swarmed with as much darkness as light. A draft with the disposition of a nervous little dog had gotten in from somewhere, chasing its tail this way and that, so each ripple of radiance spawned an undulant shadow; a dark billow chased each tremulous bright wave.

The shotgun lay on the floor by the window, where Andre had left it. The weapon was heavier than I expected. As soon as I picked it up, I almost put it down.

This was not one of the long shotguns you might use for hunting wild turkeys or wildebeest, or whatever you hunt with long shotguns.

This was a short-barreled, pistol-grip model good for home defense or for holding up a liquor store.

Police use weapons like this, as well. Two years ago, Wyatt Porter and I had been in a tight situation involving three operators of an illegal crystal-meth lab and their pet crocodile, during which I might have wound up with one less leg, and possibly no testicles, if the chief hadn't made good use of a pistol-grip 12-gauge pretty much like this one.

Although I had never fired such a gun—in fact had only once previously in my life used any kind of firearm at all—I had seen the chief use one. Of course this is no different from saying that watching all of Clint Eastwood's Dirty Harry movies will make you a master marksman and an expert in ethical police procedure.

If I left the gun here, the needy boys would use it on me. If I was backed into a corner by those behemoths and didn't at least *try* to use the shotgun on them, I would be committing suicide, considering that what they ate for breakfast probably weighed more than I did.

So I burst into the room, ran to the shotgun, snatched it off the floor, grimaced at the lethal feel of it, warned myself that I was too young for adult diapers, and stood by the window, quickly examining it in the twitchy dazzle of a series of lightning bolts. Pump action. Three-round magazine tube. Another round in the breech. Yes, it had a trigger.

I felt I could use it in a crisis, though I must admit much of my confidence came from the fact that I had recently paid my health-insurance premium.

I scanned the floor, the table, the window sill, but didn't see any additional ammunition.

From the table, I grabbed the remote control, careful not to press the black button.

Figuring that the Buzz-cut brouhaha might be winding down about now, I had just a few minutes before Datura and her boys got through the post-poltergeist confusion and back on their game.

I blew precious seconds stepping into the bathroom to see if she had done a thorough job on Terri's satellite phone. I found it dented but not in pieces, so I shoved it in a pocket.

Beside the sink was a box of shotgun ammo. I jammed four shells into my pockets.

Out of the room, into the hall, I glanced in the direction of the north stairs, then sprinted the other way, to Room 1242.

Probably because Datura didn't want Danny to have any victory or money, she hadn't provided him with any candles in red and yellow glass holders. Now that armies of black clouds had stormed the entire sky, his room was a sooty-smelling pit brightened only fitfully by nature's war light, filled with a rapid patter that brought to mind an image of a horde of running rats.

"Odd," he whispered when I came through the door, "thank God. I was sure you were dead."

Switching on the flashlight, handing it to him to hold, matching his whisper, I said, "Why didn't you *tell* me what a lunatic she is."

"Do you ever listen to me? I told you she was crazier than a syphilitic suicide bomber with mad-cow disease!"

"Yeah. Which is as much of an understatement as saying Hitler was a painter who dabbled in politics."

The running-rat patter proved to be rain slanting into the room through one of the three window panes that were broken, rattling against a jumble of furniture.

I leaned the shotgun against the wall and showed him the remote control, which he recognized.

"Is she dead?" he asked.

"I wouldn't count on it."

"What about Doom and Gloom?"

I didn't have to ask who they might be. "One of them took a hit, but I don't think it did him serious damage."

"So they'll be coming?"

"As sure as taxes."

"We gotta split."

"Splitting," I assured him, and almost pressed the white button on the remote.

At the penultimate instant, thumb poised, I asked myself who had told me that the black button would detonate thc explosives and the white would disarm them.

Datura.

40

DATURA, WHO HOBNOBBED WITH THE GRAY Pigs of Haiti and observed seamstresses being sacrificed and cannibalized, had told me that the black button detonated, that the white disarmed.

In my experience, she had not proved herself to be a reliable source of dependable fact and unvarnished truth.

More to the point, the ever-helpful madwoman had *volunteered* this information when I had asked if the remote on the table might be the one that controlled the bomb. I couldn't think of any reason why she would have done so.

Wait. Correction. I could after all think of one reason, which was Machiavellian and cruel.

If by some wild chance I ever got my hands on the remote, she wanted to program me to blow up Danny instead of save him.

"What?" he asked.

"Gimme the flashlight."

I went around behind his chair, crouched, and studied the bomb. In the time since I had first seen this device, my subconscious had been able to mull over the tangle of colorful wiring—and had come up with zip.

This does not necessarily reflect badly on my subconscious. At the same time, it had been presented with other important tasks—such as listing all the diseases I might have contracted when Datura spat wine in my face.

As previously, I tried to jump-start my sixth sense by tracing the wires with one fingertip. After 3.75 seconds I admitted this was a desperation tactic with no hope of getting me anything but killed.

"Odd?"

"Still here. Hey, Danny, let's play a word-association game."

"Now?"

"We could be dead later, then when would we play it? Humor me. It'll help me think this through. I'll say something, and you tell me the first thing that comes into your mind."

"This is nuts."

"Here we go: black and white."

"Piano keys."

"Try again. Black and white."

"Night and day."

"Black and white."

"Salt and pepper."

"Black and white."

"Good and evil."

I said, "Good."

"Thank you."

"No. That's the next word for association: *good.*"

"Grief."

"Good," I repeated.

"Bye."

"Good."

"God."

I said, "Evil."

"Datura," he said at once.

"Truth."

"Good."

I sprang "Datura" on him again.

At once he said, "Liar."

"Our intuition brings us to the same conclusion," I told him.

"What conclusion?"

"White detonates," I said, putting my thumb lightly on the black button.

Being Odd Thomas is frequently interesting but nowhere near as much fun as being Harry Potter. If I were Harry, with a pinch of this and a smidgin of that and a muttered incantation, I would have tossed together a don't-explode-in-my-face charm, and everything would have turned out just fine.

Instead, I pushed the black button, and everything *seemed* to turn out just fine.

"What happened?" Danny asked.

"Didn't you hear the boom? Listen close—you still might."

I hooked my fingers through the wires, tightened my hand into a fist, and ripped that colorful mare's-nest out of the device.

The small version of a carpenter's level tipped on its side, and the bubble slipped into the blast zone.

"I'm not dead," Danny said.

"Me neither."

I went to the furniture that had been stacked haphazardly by the earthquake and retrieved my backpack from the crevice in which I had tucked it less than an hour ago.

From the backpack, I withdrew the fishing knife and cut the last of the duct tape that bound Danny to the chair.

The kilo of explosives fell to the floor with a thud no louder than would have been produced by a brick of modeling clay. Boomplastic can be detonated only by an electrical charge.

As Danny got up from the chair, I dropped the knife into the backpack. I switched off the flashlight and clipped it to my belt once more.

Freed of the obligation to puzzle out the meaning of the bomb wires, my subconscious was counting off the elapsing seconds since I had fled the casino, and being a total nag about the situation: *Hurry, hurry, hurry.*

41

AS THOUGH WAR HAD BROKEN OUT BETWEEN Heaven and Earth, another extended barrage of lightning blasted the desert, making pools of glass in the sand somewhere. Thunder cracked so hard that my teeth vibrated as if I were absorbing chords from the massive speakers at a death-metal concert, and bustling rat battalions of rain blew in through the broken window.

Looking at the tempest, Danny blurted, "Holy crap."

I said, "Some irresponsible bastard killed a blacksnake and hung it in a tree."

"Blacksnake?"

After handing my backpack to him and grabbing the shotgun, I stepped onto the threshold of the open door and checked the corridor. The furies had not yet arrived.

Close behind me, Danny said, "My legs are on fire after the walk out from Pico Mundo, and my hip's like full of knives. I don't know how long I'll hold up."

"We aren't going far. Once we get across the rope bridge and through the room of a thousand spears, it's a piece of cake. Just be as fast as you can."

He couldn't be fast. His usual rolling gait was emphasized as his right leg repeatedly buckled under him, and though he had never been a complainer, he hissed in pain with nearly every step.

Had I planned to take him directly out of the Panamint, we would not have gotten far before the harpy and the ogres caught up with us and dragged us down.

I led him north along the hall to the elevator alcove and was relieved when we ducked out of sight into it.

Although I hated to put down the shotgun, though I wished I'd had time to have it biologically attached to my right arm and wired directly into my central nervous system, I leaned it against the wall.

As I began to pry at the lift doors that I had scoped out earlier, Danny whispered, "What—you're going to pitch me down a shaft so it looks like an accident, then my Martian-brain-eating-centipede card will be all yours?"

Doors open, I risked a quick sweep of the flashlight to show him the empty cab. "No light, heat, or running water, but no Datura, either."

"We're going to hide here?"

"*You* are going to hide here," I said. "I'm going to distract and mislead."

"They'll find me in twelve seconds."

"No, they won't stop to think that the doors could've been pried open. And they won't expect us to try to hide this close to where they were keeping you."

"Because it's stupid."

"That's right."

"And they won't expect us to be stupid."

"Bingo."

"Why don't we both hide in there?"

"Because that *would* be stupid."

"Both eggs in one basket."

I said, "You're getting a feel for this, compadre."

In my backpack were three additional half-liter bottles of water. I kept one and passed the others to him.

Squinting in the dim light, he said, "Evian."

"If you'd like to think so."

I gave both of the coconut-raisin power bars to him. "You could last three or four days if you had to."

"You'll be back before then."

"If I can elude them for a few hours, they'll think the plan is to buy you time to get away at your pace. They'll start to sweat that you're bringing the cops, and they'll blow this place."

He accepted from me several foil-wrapped packets. "What are these?"

"Moist towelettes. If I don't come back, I'm dead. Wait two days to be sure it's safe. Then pry open the doors and get yourself out to the interstate."

He entered the elevator, gingerly tested its stability. "What about—how do I pee?"

"In the empty water bottles."

"You think of everything."

"Yeah, but then I won't reuse them. Be dead quiet, Danny. Because if you're not quiet, you're dead."

"You've saved my life, Odd."

"Not yet."

I gave him one of my two flashlights and advised him not to use it in the elevator. Light might leak out. He needed to save it for the stairwells in the event that he had to leave by himself.

As I pushed shut the doors, closing him in, Danny said, "I've decided I don't wish I were you, after all."

"I didn't know identity theft had ever crossed your mind."

"I'm so sorry," he whispered through the narrowing gap. "I'm so damn sorry."

"Friends forever," I told him, which was a thing we said for a while when we were ten or eleven. "Friends forever."

42

PAST ROOM 1242 WITH ITS UNEXPLODED bomb, from the main corridor to the secondary, wearing the backpack, toting the shotgun, I schemed to survive. The desire to ensure that Datura rotted in prison had given me a stronger will to live than I'd had in six months.

I expected that they would split up and return to the twelfth floor by the north *and* south staircases, to cut me off before I could shepherd Danny out. If I could descend just two or three stories, to the tenth or ninth level, and let them pass by me, I might be able to slip back onto the stairs behind them and race all the way down, out, and away—to return in but an hour or two with the police.

When I had first walked into Room 1203 and had spoken to Datura as she'd stood at the window, she had known without having to ask that I must have gotten around the staircases by using an elevator shaft. No other route could have brought me to the twelfth floor.

Consequently, although they would know that I couldn't get Danny down by that route, they would at least listen at the shafts now and then for sounds of movement. I couldn't use that trick again.

Arriving at the entry to the south stairs, I found the door half open. I eased through, onto the landing.

Not a sound rose from lower flights. I crept down step to step—four, five—and paused to listen. The silence held.

The alien smell, musk-mushrooms-meat, eddied no thicker here than it had earlier, perhaps thinner, but no less off-putting.

The flesh on the nape of my neck did the crawly thing that it does so well. Some people say this is God's warning that the devil is near, but I've noticed I also experience it when someone serves me Brussels sprouts.

Whatever the precise source of the odor, it must have arisen from the toxic stew left over from the fire, which was why I'd never encountered it prior to the Panamint. It was a product of a singular event, but it wasn't otherworldly. Any scientist could have analyzed it, tracked down its origin, and provided me with a molecular recipe.

I had never encountered a supernatural entity

that signaled its presence with this smell. People smell, not ghosts. Yet the nape of my neck continued to do its thing even in the absence of Brussels sprouts.

Impatiently counseling myself that nothing threatening crouched in the stairwell, I quickly went down another step in the dark, and another, loath to use my flashlight and thereby reveal my presence in case Datura or one of her horses was somewhere below me.

I reached the midfloor landing, descended two more steps—and saw a pale glow blossom on the wall at the eleventh level.

Someone coming up. He could be only a floor or two below me, because light didn't travel well around 180-degree turns.

I considered racing ahead in the hope that I could reach the eleventh floor and spring rabbit-quick out of the stairwell before the climber turned onto a new flight and saw me. But that door might be corroded shut and incapable of being opened. Or might shriek like a banshee on rusted hinges.

The blot of light on the wall brightened, grew larger. He was ascending fast. I heard footsteps.

I had the shotgun. In a confined space like the stairwell, even I couldn't fail to score a solid hit.

Necessity had driven me to take the weapon, but I wasn't keen to use it. The gun would be a last resort, not a first option.

Besides, the moment I pulled the trigger, they would know that I had not left the hotel. Then the hunt would be on with even greater intensity.

As quietly as possible, I backtracked. At the twelfth-floor landing, I kept ascending in the dark, intending to proceed to the thirteenth, but within three steps, I discovered a riser littered with rubble.

Unsure what lay above, afraid of stumbling and making too much noise if treacherous mounds of trash lay underfoot, worried that the way might be blocked altogether, I retreated three steps to the twelfth floor.

The light on the landing wall below swelled bright, the beam directly upon it. He must be only a flight and a half below; and he would see me when he made the turn.

I dodged through the half-open door, returning to the twelfth floor.

In the gray light, I saw that at the first two rooms, to my left and right, the doors were closed. I did not dare waste time trying them, in case they proved to be locked.

The second room on my right stood open. I slipped out of the hallway and took refuge behind the door.

I seemed to be in a suite. To both sides of this room, drowned daylight seeped through open connecting doors.

Directly across from the entrance that I had just used, two sliding glass doors provided access to a balcony. Silvery skeins of rain raveled past the high-rise, and wind softly rattled the doors in their tracks.

Out in the hallway, the climber—Andre or Robert—shoved the stairwell door all the way open as he came through. It banged against the stop.

Standing with my back pressed to the wall, holding my breath, I heard him pass my room. A moment later, the stair door rebounded from the stop and fell shut.

He would be heading for the main corridor and 1242, hoping to nail me there before I pressed the white button to free Danny—and instead blew both of us to bits.

I intended to give him ten seconds, fifteen, long enough to be sure he had left the secondary corridor. Then I would make a break for the stairwell.

Now that he was past me, I no longer needed to fear that anyone might be ascending. I could use the flashlight, plunge down two steps at a time, and be on the ground floor before he could return to the stairwell and hear me.

Two seconds later, from the main corridor, Datura shrieked a curse that would have brought a blush to the whore of Babylon.

She must have come up by the north stairs

with her other best fella. Having arrived at Room 1242, she had discovered that Danny Jessup was neither strapped to the bomb nor splattered across the walls.

43

IN THE CASINO, DURING DATURA'S VERBAL assault on Maryann Morris, she had proved that her silky voice could be twisted into a garrote as cruel as any strangler's cord.

Now, hiding behind the entry door, just inside the three-room suite, I listened to her curse me at alarming volume, sometimes using words that I had never realized could apply to a *guy,* and with each passing second, I felt less confident about my chances of escaping.

Mad-cow crazy she might be, and syphilitic, for all I knew, but Datura was also more than prettily packaged lunacy, more and worse than a homicidal porn merchant whose narcissism exceeded that of Narcissus himself. She seemed to be an elemental force, of no less power than earth, water, wind, and fire.

Into my mind sprang the name *Kali,* the Hindu goddess of death, dark side of the mother goddess, the only of their many gods who had conquered time. Four-armed, violent, insatiable, Kali devours all beings, and in temples where she's worshipped, the usual idols present her with a necklace of human skulls, dancing on a corpse.

This metaphoric mental image, the dark gaunt form of savage Kali embodied in the lush blonde Datura, instantly felt so right, so true, that my sense of reality seemed to shift, to deepen. Every detail of the shadowy hotel room, of the wreckage around me, of the strafing storm beyond the balcony doors came into sharper focus, and I felt that I might momentarily see even deeper than the molecular structure of it all.

Yet simultaneous with this new clarity, in everything within my view, I detected a transcendental mystery that I had never before perceived, a transforming revelation waiting to be accepted. A chill of a character not easily conveyed worked through me, an awe that felt more like reverence than like dread, although dread was a part of it.

You might think that I'm struggling to describe the heightened perception that frequently accompanies mortal jeopardy. I've been in mortal jeopardy often enough to know what *that* feels like, too, but this metaphysical incident was not the same.

Like all mystical experiences, I suppose, when the ineffable seems about to be made clear, the moment passes, no less ephemeral than a dream.

But after passing, this one left me electrified, as if I had been zapped by a different kind of Taser, one designed to energize the mind and force it to confront a difficult truth.

The nasty truth before me was that Datura, for all her lunacy and ignorance and laughable eccentricities, was a more formidable adversary than I had acknowledged. When it came to committing extreme violence, she had as many eager hands as Kali, and my two hands were reluctant.

My plan had been either to bolt from the hotel and get help or, failing that, to elude this woman and her two enforcers long enough to convince them that I had in fact escaped and that they themselves ought to flee before I sent back the authorities. This was not a plan of action as much as it was a plan of avoidance.

Listening to Datura rant, apparently somewhere near the junction of the corridors—much too near for comfort—I realized that while rage might be an impediment to clear thinking in most people, for her it sharpened her cunning and her senses. Likewise, hatred.

Her talent for evil, especially for the vicious brand of it that once went by the name *wickedness,* was so great that she seemed to be possessed of uncanny gifts to rival my own. I might be persuaded that Datura could smell the blood of her enemy while it remained in his veins, and follow the scent to spill it.

Upon her arrival, I had put on hold my plan to make a break for the north stairs. Making a move while she lingered in the vicinity seemed suicidal.

Avoidance most likely would not be possible. Yet I wasn't eager to hasten a confrontation.

In the light of my new and more fearsome perception of this disturbed woman, I began to steel myself for what survival might require of me.

I recalled another grim fact about the four-armed Hindu goddess that inspired me not to underestimate Datura. Kali entertained a thirst for horror so unquenchable that she had once decapitated herself in order to be able to drink her own blood as it spouted from her neck.

Being a goddess only in her own mind, Datura would not survive decapitation. But when I recalled her vile stories of the cries of murdered children in a Savannah basement and the sacrifice of a seamstress in Port-au-Prince, which had seemed so delectable to her in the telling, I couldn't pretend that she was any less bloodthirsty than Kali.

And so I remained behind the door, in shadows that were often relieved by storm light, listening to her curse, then rant. Soon her voice softened to the degree that I could make out no words at all, but there was no mistaking the urgency of it, the insistent frenzied cadences of rage and hate and dark desire.

If Andre and Robert spoke—or dared to try—I didn't hear their deeper voices. Only hers. In the degree of their obedience and self-effacement, I read the souls of two true believers, as ready to drink the poisoned Kool-Aid as any cultists had ever been.

When she fell silent, I suppose I should have been relieved, but instead I got that Brussels-sprouts feeling. Intensely.

I had slumped wearily against the wall. I stood straighter.

In my two-hand grip, the shotgun, which had come to seem like nothing more than a tool, suddenly felt alive, slumbering but alive and aware, as guns had always felt to me before. As in the past, I worried that I would not be in control of the weapon when the crisis arrived.

Thank you, Mom.

When Datura ceased talking, I expected to hear movement, perhaps doors opening and closing, indications that they had begun a search. Only quiet followed.

The muffled hiss of rain spending itself against the balcony and the occasional grumble of thunder had been mere background noise. But as I listened intently for activity in the hallway, I resented the storm, as if it were Datura's willing conspirator.

I tried to imagine what I would do in her circumstances, but the only rational answer seemed to be *Get out.* With Danny freed and both of us missing, she should want to strip her bank accounts bare and head at high speed for the border.

An ordinary psychopath bails when the going gets rough—but not Kali, eater of the dead.

They must have parked a vehicle or two at the hotel. After snatching Danny, they had returned here on foot, by a circuitous route, to test my psychic magnetism, but they had no reason to walk out, rather than ride, when the fun was over.

Maybe she had grown worried that if Danny and I reached the ground floor and got out of the Panamint, we would find their car, hot-wire it, and leave them stranded. If so, Andre or Robert—or Datura herself—might have gone down to disable the vehicle or to stand guard over it.

Rain. The ceaseless susurration of rain.

A faint mewl of wind, pleading at the balcony doors.

No sound alerted me. Instead, the threat revealed itself by that musky, mushroomy, cold-meat smell.

44

I GRIMACED AT THAT UNIQUE SUBTLE SMELL, which was not conducive to a healthy appetite. Then he must have taken a step or shifted his weight, because I heard the feeble but crisp crunch of a small bit of debris crushed underfoot.

Two-thirds open, the door afforded me a wedge of space in which to stand concealed between it and the wall. If my stalker pushed it wider, the door would rebound from me and reveal my presence.

The construction of many other buildings would have allowed the space between the back edge of the open door and the jamb to provide a narrow view of someone standing on the threshold. This casing was deeper than standard code required and the stop molding so thick that it occluded the gap.

Looking on the bright side, as I desperately needed to do at that point: If I could not see him, he could not see me.

Having encountered this disquieting smell only at various times in the staircases and on the second visit to the casino, I had not associated it with Andre and Robert. Now I realized that I could not have detected it within the candlelit walls of Room 1203, where I had also enjoyed their company, because the cloying fragrance of Cleo-May had effectively masked it.

Framed by the big sliding doors, to the north, an inverted tree of lightning caught fire, its trunk in the heavens and its branches shaking at the earth. A second tree overlaid the first, and a third overlaid the second: a brief-lived bright forest that burnt out even as it grew.

He stood in the doorway so long that I began to suspect that he knew not only of my presence but also of my exact position, and that he was toying with me.

Second by second, my nerves wound tighter than the rubber band on the propeller of a child's balsa-wood airplane. I warned myself not to fly into rash action.

He might, after all, just go away. The fates are not always in a snotty mood. Sometimes a hurricane roars toward a vulnerable coast, then veers away from land.

No sooner had I been buoyed by that hopeful thought than he stepped off the threshold and ventured into the room, movement that I as much sensed as heard.

A pistol-grip shotgun is not, by definition, one that you fire with the stock butted against your shoulder. You hold it forward, but to the side.

Initially, the door still screened the searcher from me. When he moved farther into the space, I would need my cloak of invisibility, which I did not have with me because, unfortunately, I still wasn't Harry Potter.

When Chief Porter had used a pistol-grip shotgun to save me from the loss of a leg and from emasculation-by-crocodile, the weapon had appeared to have a mean kick. The chief had stood with his feet wide apart, the left somewhat in front of the right, knees slightly bent, to absorb the recoil, and he had been visibly jolted by it.

Moving far enough into the room to reveal himself, Robert was not aware of me. By the time he stepped forward into my line of sight, I was well out of his.

Even if he turned his head to look sideways, his peripheral vision might not pick me up behind him. Should instinct warn him, however, the shadows in which I stood weren't deep enough to blind him to me if he turned around.

The gloom didn't reveal enough of his features to allow me to identify him by looks alone. He was big rather than massive, which ruled out Andre.

In the thrashing garden of the storm, more

lightning put out roots, and the jarring crash of thunder was the sound of an entire forest felled.

He continued across the room, looking neither left nor right. I began to think that he had entered here not in search of me, but for some other reason.

Judging by his behavior, even more somnambulant than usual, he had been drawn by the call of the storm. He stopped in front of the balcony doors.

I dared to think that if this current escalation of the storm's pyrotechnics continued for as much as a minute, distracting Robert and covering what sounds I made, I might be able to come out from hiding, slip quickly into the hall without alerting him, avoid this confrontation, and make that break for the stairs, after all.

As I eased forward, intending to peer around the entry door to be sure that Datura and Andre were searching elsewhere and that the hall was safe, an effect of the next barrage of thunderbolts stunned and arrested me. Each flare bounced off Robert and cast his ghostly reflection in the glass of the balcony doors. His face shone as pale as a Kabuki mask, but his eyes were even whiter, bright white with the reflected lightning.

I thought at once of the snaky man, fished from the flood tunnel, his eyes rolled far back in his head.

Three more flares repeatedly revealed a reflection with white eyes, and I stood immobilized by a marrow-freezing chill, even as Robert turned toward me.

45

DELIBERATELY, NOT WITH THE QUICK REFLEXES of violent intent, Robert turned toward me.

The inscrutable semaphore of the storm no longer brightened his face, but silhouetted him. The sky, one great galleon with a thousand black sails, signaled, signaled, as if to regain his attention, and thunder boomed.

Averted from the lightning, his eyes no longer shone a moonish white. Nevertheless . . . though his features were deeply shadowed, his gaze still seemed vaguely phosphorescent, as milky as that of a man blinded by cataracts.

Although I could not see him well enough to be certain, I felt that his eyes were turned back in his head, no color revealed. This might have been a shiver of imagination born of the chill that had seized me.

Having assumed the stance that I recalled Chief Porter taking, I brought the shotgun to bear on him, aiming low because the kick might pull the muzzle higher.

Regardless of the condition of Robert's eyes, whether they were as white as hard-boiled eggs or the sullen bloodshot beryl-blue they had been earlier, I felt sure that he was not merely aware of my presence but that he could see me.

Yet his demeanor and his slump-shouldered posture suggested that the sight of me failed to shift him into psycho-killer gear. If not confused, he appeared to be at least distracted, and weary.

I began to think that he had not come in search of me, but had wandered in here either for another purpose or without any purpose. Having found me inadvertently, he stood as if in resentment of the need to resolve the confrontation.

Curiouser and curiouser: He let out a long sigh of exhaustion, with a thin plaintive edge that seemed to express a sense of being harassed.

As far as I could recall, these were the first sounds that I had heard issue from his lips: a sigh, a plaint.

His inexplicable malaise and my disinclination to use the shotgun in the absence of a clear threat to my life had brought us to a bizarre impasse that, just two minutes ago, I could never have imagined.

A sudden sweat greased my brow. The situation was not tenable. Something had to give.

His arms hung at his sides. Lambent storm light

licked the shape of a pistol or a revolver in his right hand.

When he first turned from the window, Robert could have whipped toward me, squeezing off shots, dropping and rolling as he fired to avoid the 12-gauge. I had no doubt that he was a practiced killer who knew the right moves. His chances of killing me would have been much better than my odds of wounding him.

The gun hung like an anchor at the end of his arm as he took two steps toward me, not in a threatening manner, but almost as though he wished to beseech me for something. These were heavy draft-horse steps that comported with the title, *cheval,* that Datura had given him.

I worried that Andre would come through the door next, with all the irresistible power of the locomotive of which he had initially reminded me.

Robert might then shake off his indecision—or whatever mood caused his inaction. The two could cut me down in a cross fire.

But I was not capable of blasting away at a man who didn't at this moment seem inclined to shoot me.

Although he'd drawn closer, I could see his dissolute face no more clearly than before. Still I had the unnerving impression that his eyes were frosted panes.

From him came another sound, which at first

I thought must be a mumbled question. But when it came again, it seemed more like a stifled cough.

At last the hand with the gun came up from his side.

My impression was that he raised the weapon not with lethal purpose, but unconsciously, almost as though he had forgotten that he held it. Given what I knew of him—his devotion to Datura, his taste for blood, his evident participation in the brutal murder of Dr. Jessup—I couldn't wait for a clearer indication of his intent.

The recoil rocked me. He took the buckshot like the truck he was, and did not drop his handgun, and I pumped a round into the chamber and fired again, and the glass doors behind him dissolved because I must have pulled high or wide, so I pumped and fired a third time, and he staggered backward through the gap where the sliding doors had been.

Although he had still not dropped his weapon, he had not used it, either, and I doubted that a fourth shot was necessary. At least two of the first three rounds had hit him square and hard.

But I rushed toward him, hot to be done with this, almost as if the gun controlled me and wanted to be fully spent. The fourth round blew him off the balcony.

Only as I stepped to the shattered doors did I see what rain and perspective had previously concealed from me. The outermost third of the balcony must have broken away in the earthquake five years ago, taking with it the railing.

If any life had remained in him after three hits out of four rounds, a twelve-story fall would have taken it.

46

KILLING ROBERT LEFT ME WEAK IN THE knees and light in the head, but it did not nauseate me as I had half expected that it would. He was, after all, Cheval Robert, not a good husband or a kind father, or a pillar of his community.

Furthermore, I had the feeling that he had wanted me to do what I had done. He seemed to have embraced death as if it was a mercy.

As I backed away from the balcony doors and a sudden squall of rain that burst through them, I heard Datura screaming from some distant point of the twelfth floor. Her voice swelled like a siren as she approached at a run.

If I sprinted for the stairs, I would surely be caught in the hall before I reached them. She and Andre would be armed; and it defied reason to suppose that they would be afflicted with Robert's indecision.

I traded the living room of the suite for the

bedroom to the right of the entry door. This place was darker than the previous room because the windows were smaller and because the rotting draperies had not fallen off their rods.

I didn't expect to find a hiding place. I just needed to buy time to reload.

Mindful of the shotgun fire that had drawn their attention, they would enter the living room cautiously. Most likely they would first lay down a volley of suppressing fire.

By the time one of them dared to explore this adjoining room, I would be ready for them. Or as ready as I would ever be. I had only four more shells, not an arsenal.

If luck was on my side, they didn't know where Robert's part of the search had led him—if he had been searching. They couldn't pinpoint, by the sound alone, precisely from where the shots had come.

Should they decide to search all the rooms along the secondary hallway, an opportunity might yet arise for me to get off the twelfth floor.

Much closer now, but not from within the suite, perhaps from the intersection of corridors, Datura shouted my name. She wasn't calling me out for a milkshake at the local soda fountain, but she sounded more excited than pissed.

The shotgun barrel, breech, and receiver were warm from the recent firing.

Leaning against a wall, shuddering as I remembered Robert plunging backward off the balcony, I plucked the first of the spare rounds from a pocket of my jeans. I fumbled in the shadows, clumsy at the unfamiliar task, trying to insert the shell into the breech.

"Can you hear me, Odd Thomas?" Datura shouted. "Can you hear me, boyfriend?"

The breech continued to defeat me, would not take the shell, and my hands began to shake, making the task more difficult.

"Was that shit what it seemed to be?" she shouted. "Was that a poltergeist, boyfriend?"

The standoff with Robert had prickled my face with sweat. The sound of Datura's voice turned the sweat to ice.

"That was so *wild,* that really totally *kicked*!" she declared, still out in the hallway somewhere.

Deciding to load the breech last, I tried to insert the shell through what I believed to be the loading gate of the three-round magazine.

My fingers were sweaty, trembling. The shell slipped out of my grasp. I felt it bounce off my right shoe.

"Did you trick me, Odd Thomas?" she asked. "Did you get me to crank up old Maryann until she blew?"

She didn't know about Buzz-cut. There was some justice in letting her think that the spirit of a merely pretty-but-not-pretty-enough cocktail waitress had gotten the best of her.

Squatting in the dark, feeling the floor around me, I feared that the shell had rolled beyond discovery and that I would have to use the flashlight to locate it. I needed all four rounds. When I found it in mere seconds, I almost let out a groan of relief.

"I want a repeat performance!" she shouted.

Remaining in a squat, the shotgun propped across my thighs, I tried again to load the magazine, turning the shell first one way, then the other, but the loading gate, if it *was* the loading gate, wouldn't receive the round.

The task seemed simple, a lot easier than flipping eggs over-easy without breaking the yolks, but evidently it wasn't so simple that someone unfamiliar with the weapon could load it in the dark. I needed light.

"Let's crank up the dumb dead bitch again!"

At the window, I eased aside the rotting drapery.

"But this time, I'm keeping you on a leash, boyfriend."

An hour or two of light remained in the afternoon, but the filter of the storm cast false twilight across the drenched desert. I could still see well enough to examine the gun.

I fished another shell from another pocket. Tried it. No good.

I put it on the window sill, tried a third. In the grip of absolute denial, I tried a fourth.

"You and Danny the Geek aren't getting out of here. You hear me? *There is no way out.*"

The ammunition I had found on the bathroom counter, beside the sink, had evidently been for another weapon.

For all intents and purposes, this couldn't be considered a shotgun anymore. It had become just a fancy club.

I was up the famous creek not only without a paddle but also without a boat.

47

I USED TO THINK THAT I MIGHT ONE DAY LIKE to work in the retail tire business. I spent some time hanging around Tire World, out near the Green Moon Mall, on Green Moon Road, and everyone there seemed to be relaxed and happy.

In the tire life, at the end of the work day, you don't have to wonder if you've accomplished anything meaningful. You've taken in people with bad rubber, and you've sent them rolling away on fine new wheels.

Americans thrive on mobility and feel shrunken in spirit when they do not have it. Providing tires is not only good commerce but also soothes troubled souls.

Although selling tires does not involve a lot of hard bargaining, as do real-estate transactions and deals brokered with international arms merchants, I am concerned that I might find the sales end of the business too emotionally draining.

If the supernatural aspect of my life involved nothing more stressful than daily interaction with Elvis, tire sales would make sense, but as you've seen, the favorite son of Memphis isn't the half of it.

Before I went to the Panamint, I figured that eventually I would return to work for Terri Stambaugh. If the griddle proved too taxing on my nerves, on top of everything else that was perpetually cooking with me, I might succumb to the lure of the tire life, working not sales but installation.

That stormy day in the desert, however, much changed for me. We must have our goals, our dreams, and we must strive for them. We are not gods, however; we do not have the power to shape every aspect of the future. And the road the world makes for us is one that teaches humility if we are willing to learn.

Standing in a moldering room in a ruined hotel, contemplating a useless shotgun, listening to a murderous madwoman assure me that my fate was hers to decide, having given away both my coconut-raisin power bars, I felt humbled, all right. Maybe not as humbled as Wile E. Coyote when he finds himself flattened under the same boulder with which he intended to crush the Road Runner, but pretty humble.

She shouted, "You know why there's no way out, boyfriend?"

I didn't inquire, confident that she would tell me.

"Because I know about you. I know all about you. I know that it works both ways."

This statement made no immediate sense to me, but it was no more mystifying than a hundred other things she'd said, so I didn't devote much effort to translation.

I wondered when she would stop squawking and come looking. Maybe Andre already had crept into the suite, searching, and her shouting in the corridor was intended to mislead me into thinking the ax was not already on the downswing.

As if she had read my mind, she said, "I don't have to come searching for you, do I, Odd Thomas?"

After putting the shotgun on the floor, I wiped my face with my hands, blotted my hands on my jeans. I felt six-days dirty, with no hope of a Sunday bath.

I had always expected to die clean. In my dream, when I open that paneled white door and get the pike through the throat, I'm wearing a clean T-shirt, pressed jeans, and fresh underwear.

"No way I have to risk getting my head shot off looking for you," she shouted.

Considering all the messes I get into, I don't know *why* I had always expected to die clean. Now that I thought about it, this seemed self-delusional.

Freud would have had a grand time analyzing my have-to-die-clean complex. But then Freud was an ass.

"Psychic magnetism!" she shouted, getting more of my attention than I had recently been giving her. "Psychic magnetism works both ways, boyfriend."

My spirits had not been high by virtually any measure, but at her words, they fell a little.

When I have a specific target in mind, I can cruise at random, and my psychic magnetism will often lead me to him, but sometimes, when I am thinking a lot about another person yet am not actively seeking him, the same mechanism operates, and he is casually drawn to me, all unaware.

When psychic magnetism works in reverse, without my conscious intent, I am without control . . . and vulnerable to nasty surprises. Of all the things about me that Danny could have told Datura, this might have been the most dangerous for her to know.

Previously, whenever a bad guy has found himself wandering into my presence by virtue of reverse psychic magnetism, he has been as surprised by this development as I have been. Which at least puts us on equal footing.

Instead of searching urgently room to room, floor to floor, Datura intended to remain alert but calm, to make herself receptive to the pull of my aura, or whatever the hell it is that exerts this paranormal attraction. She and Andre could cover the two staircases, periodically check the elevator shafts for noise, and wait until she found herself at my side—or at my back—drawn to me by virtue of the fact that, as in the Willie Nelson song, she was *always on my mind.*

No matter how clever I was about finding a way out of the hotel, before I got to freedom, I was likely to encounter her. It was a little like destiny.

If you've had a beer too many and are in an argumentative mood, you might say *Don't be an idiot, Odd. All you have to do is not think about her.*

Imagine yourself running barefoot on a summer day, as carefree as a child, and your foot comes down on an old board, and a six-inch spike spears your metatarsal arch, penetrating all the way through your instep. No need to cancel your plans and seek out a doctor. You'll be fine if you just don't think about that big sharp rusty spike sticking through your foot.

You're playing eighteen holes of golf, and your ball goes into the woods. Retrieving it, you're bitten on the hand by a rattlesnake. Don't bother calling 911 on your cell phone. You can finish the round with aplomb if you simply concentrate on the game and forget all about the annoying snake.

No matter how many beers you have consumed, I trust that you get my point. Datura was a spike through my foot, a snake with fangs sunk into my hand. Trying not to think about that woman, under these circumstances, was like being in a room with an angry naked sumo wrestler and trying not to think about *him*.

At least she had revealed her intentions. Now *I* knew that *she* knew about reverse psychic magnetism. She might fall upon me when I least expected it, but I would no longer be entirely surprised when she decapitated me and drank my blood.

She had stopped shouting.

I waited tensely, unnerved by the silence.

Not thinking about her had been easier when she was yammering than when she shut up.

A rattle and blur of rain on the window. Thunder. A threnody of wind.

Ozzie Boone, mentor and man of letters, would like that word. *Threnody:* a dirge, a lamentation, a song for the dead.

While I played hide-and-seek with a madwoman in a burned-out hotel, Ozzie was probably sitting in his cozy study, sipping thick hot cocoa, nibbling pecan cookies, already writing the first novel in his new series about a detective who is also a pet communicator. Maybe he would title it *Threnody for a Hamster.*

This threnody, of course, would be for Robert: full of lead shot and broken, twelve stories below.

After a while, I checked the luminous face of

my wristwatch. I consulted it every few minutes until a quarter of an hour had passed.

I wasn't enthusiastic about returning to the corridor. On the other hand, I didn't have any enthusiasm about staying where I was, either.

In addition to Kleenex, a bottle of water, and a few other items of no value for a man in my fix, my backpack held the fishing knife. The sharpest blade wasn't a match for a shotgun, assuming she had one, but it was better than attacking her with a packet of Kleenex.

I couldn't carve anyone, not even Datura. Using a firearm is daunting, but it allows you to kill at some distance. Any gun is less intimate than a knife. Killing her intimately, up close and personal, her blood pouring back along the handle of the knife: That required a different Odd Thomas from a parallel dimension, one who was crueler than I and less worried about cleanliness.

Armed with only my bare hands and attitude, I finally returned to the living room of the suite.

No Datura.

The corridor—where she had recently prowled, shouting—was deserted.

The shotgun blasts had brought her at a run from the north end of the building. Most likely she had been monitoring those stairs, and had now returned to them.

I glanced at the south stairs, but if Andre waited anywhere, he waited there. I might have attitude, but Andre had gravitas. And for sure, in a fist-fight, he would leave me in the condition of a pack of saltines after he had crushed them to put in his soup.

She hadn't known where I was when she had stood here shouting, had not known with certainty that I could hear her. But she had told me the truth about her plan: no search, just patience, counting on a chilling kind of kismet.

48

WITH THE STAIRS AND ELEVATOR SHAFT OFF-limits, I had only those resources that the twelfth floor offered.

I thought of the kilo of gelignite, or whatever they called it these days. A quantity of explosives that could reduce a large house to matchsticks ought to be of some use to a young fellow as desperate as I was.

Although I'd received no training in the handling of explosives, I had the benefit of paranormal insight. Yes, my gift had gotten me into this mess; but if it didn't get me in deeper, it might get me out.

I also had that can-do American spirit, which should never be underestimated.

According to the history I've learned from movies, Alexander Graham Bell, fiddling around with some cans and wire, invented the telephone, with the help of his assistant Watson, who was also an associate of Sherlock Holmes, and achieved great success after enduring the scorn and naysaying of lesser men for ninety minutes.

Weathering the scorn and naysaying of a remarkably similar set of lesser men, Thomas Edison, another great American, invented the electric lightbulb, the phonograph, the first sound movie camera, and the alkaline battery, among a slew of other things, also in ninety minutes, and looked like Spencer Tracy.

When he was my age, Tom Edison looked like Mickey Rooney, had invented a number of clever devices, and already exhibited the self-confidence to ignore the negativism of the naysayers. Edison, Mickey Rooney, and I were all Americans, so there was reason to believe that by studying the components of the now dismantled bomb, I might tinker together a useful weapon.

Besides, I didn't see any other prospects.

After slinking along the main corridor and slipping into Room 1242, where Danny had been held captive, I switched on my flashlight and discovered that Datura had taken away the package of explosives. Maybe she didn't want it to fall into my hands or maybe she had a use for it, or perhaps she just wanted it for sentimental reasons.

I didn't see any healthy purpose in dwelling on what use she might have for a bomb, so I switched off my light and moved to the window.

By the pallid lamp of the fading day, I examined Terri's phone, which Datura had hammered against the bathroom counter.

When I flipped the phone open, the screen brightened. I would have been heartened if it had presented a logo, a recognizable image, or data of some kind. Instead, there was only a meaningless blue-and-yellow mottle.

I keyed in seven digits, Chief Porter's mobile number, but they did not appear on the screen. I pressed SEND and listened. Nothing.

Had I lived a century earlier, I might have fiddled with scraps of this and that until, in the can-do spirit, I jury-rigged a nifty communications device, but things were more complicated these days. Even Edison could not have, on the spot, tinkered up a new microchip brain board.

Disappointed by Room 1242, I returned to the corridor. Much less daylight penetrated from the rooms with open doors than had been the case even half an hour earlier. The hallways would go dark at least an hour before dusk actually arrived.

Although plagued by the creepy feeling of being watched, though visibility was so poor that I couldn't dismiss these heebie-jeebies as groundless, I avoided using the flashlight while in the corridor. Andre and Datura had guns; the light would make of me an easy target.

Inside each room that I explored, once I closed

the door behind me, I felt safe enough to resort to the flashlight. I had searched some of these spaces previously, when I'd been looking for a hidey-hole in which to stash Danny. I had not found in them what I wanted then; and I didn't find what I needed now.

Deep down, in that coziest corner of the heart, where a belief in miracles abides even in the darkest hours, I expected to stumble upon some long-dead hotel guest's suitcase in which would be packed a loaded pistol. Although a handgun would have been acceptable, I preferred to discover a freight elevator isolated from the bank of public lifts, or a roomy dumbwaiter leading to the kitchen on the ground floor.

Eventually I discovered a service closet about ten feet deep and fourteen wide. Cleaning supplies, bars of guest soap, and spare lightbulbs stocked the shelves. Vacuum sweepers, buckets, and mops were tumbled on the floor.

The sprinkler system that had failed elsewhere appeared to have overperformed here, or perhaps a water line had burst. Part of the ceiling had collapsed; and swags of Sheetrock, obviously once waterlogged, drooped into the room around the edges of the void.

I quickly inventoried the items on the shelves. Bleach, ammonia, and other common household products can be combined in ways that produce explosives, anesthetics, blistering agents, smoke bombs, and poison gases. Unfortunately, I didn't know any of those formulas.

Considering that I frequently find myself in a patch of trouble and that I'm not by nature a walking machine of death, I should be more diligent about educating myself in the arts of destruction and assassination. The Internet provides a wealth of such information for the earnest autodidact. And these days, serious universities offer courses if not entire programs in the philosophy of anarchy and its practical application.

When it comes to this kind of self-improvement, I admit to being a slacker. I'd rather perfect my pancake batter than commit to memory recipes for sixteen varieties of nerve gas. I'd rather read an Ozzie Boone novel than spend hours practicing one-thrust heart punctures with a dagger and a CPR dummy. I never claimed to be perfect.

A trapdoor caught my attention in that portion of the service-room ceiling that had not collapsed from water damage. When I yanked on a dangling rope handle, the heavy-duty spring closure creaked, groaned, but opened, and a segmented ladder unfolded from the back of the door.

When I climbed to the top, the flashlight revealed a four-to-five-foot-high crawlspace between the twelfth and thirteenth floors. Here lay a maze of copper and PVC pipes, electrical conduits, duct work, and equipment related to heating, ventilation, and air conditioning.

I could explore that space or go back down the ladder and drink a bleach-and-ammonia cocktail.

Because I didn't have any slices of fresh lime, I climbed into the crawlspace, pulled up the ladder, and closed the trap behind me.

49

LEGEND CLAIMS THAT ALL AFRICAN ELEPHANTS, as they realize they are dying, proceed to the same burial ground, still undiscovered by man, deep in a primeval jungle, where lies a mountain of bones and ivory.

Between the twelfth and thirteenth floors of the Panamint Resort and Spa, I discovered a graveyard equivalent to the elephant burial ground—for rats. I didn't encounter one live specimen, but I found at least a hundred that had left this world for eternal cheese.

They had died mostly in clusters of three and four, although I found one pile of perhaps twenty. I suspected they had suffocated in the smoke that had filled this space on the night of the catastrophe. After five years, nothing remained of them but skulls, bones, a few scraps of fur, and an occasional fossilized tail.

Until this discovery, I would never have

imagined that I had within me the sensitivity to find something melancholy about piles of rat carcasses. The abrupt termination of their busy scurrying lives, the collapse of all their whisker-twitching dreams of room-service leftovers, the premature end to their cozy mutual grooming sessions and warm nights of frantic copulation were sad considerations. This rat graveyard, no less than an elephant burial ground, spoke to the transitory nature of all things.

I mean, I didn't weep over their fate. I didn't even get a lump in my throat. Having most of my life been a fan of Mr. Mickey Mouse, however, I was understandably affected by this ratty apocalypse.

Smoke residue filmed most surfaces, though I saw little evidence of direct fire damage. Flames had leapfrogged stories, traveling by way of improperly constructed mechanical chases, and had spared this crawlspace as they had spared the twelfth floor.

At four and a half feet, this between-floor realm didn't force me to crawl. I wandered through it in a crouch, at first not certain what I hoped to find, but eventually arriving at the realization that vertical chases, which allowed fire to ascend through the structure, might also allow me to descend.

The quantity of equipment amazed me. Because the thermostat in every hotel room can be set independently of that in every other, each room is heated and cooled by its own fan-coil unit. Each fan-coil is connected to branch lines from the four-pipe system that circulates superchilled and superheated water throughout the building. These units, served by pumps and humidifiers and drain-overflow basins, created a geometric labyrinth that reminded me of the machinery-encrusted surfaces of one of those massive spaceships in *Star Wars,* through the canyons of which starfighters do battle with one another.

Instead of starfighters, I saw spiders and vast webs as complex as the spiral patterns of galaxies, an occasional empty soda can left behind by repairmen, here and there a fast-food sandwich container licked clean long ago, and more rats, before at last I located one of the chases that might be my way out of the Panamint.

The five-foot-square shaft, lined with metal-skinned fireboard, continued four stories above my position. Below, it dwindled into darkness that my flashlight could not fully probe.

Such a roomy chimney would have been a vertical superhighway, easily accommodating me, if not for all the pipes and conduits that lined three and a half of its walls. Bolted to the one otherwise clear section of wall, a ladder offered not just rungs, but four-inch-wide treads that provided surer footing.

This chute did not lie near the elevator shafts.

If Datura or Andre listened at that location, they would not hear me as I made my way down this vertical chase.

Additional handholds and steel rings to receive the snap links of safety tethers bristled from among the pipes and conduits on the other three walls.

Fixed at the top of the building, a half-inch-diameter nylon line, of the type employed by mountain climbers, hung loose down the center of the shaft. Massive knots, spaced at one-foot intervals, could serve as handholds. This appeared to have been replaced after the fire, perhaps by rescue workers.

I deduced, perhaps incorrectly, that if in spite of the generous steps of the ladder and the ubiquitous anchor points for tethers, you took a plunge, the plumb-bobbed rope was a lifeline to be seized in free fall.

Although I had fewer monkey genes than these conditions implied were necessary to transit the service well, I saw no alternative but to make use of it. Otherwise, I could wait for the mothership to beam me up—and one day be discovered here, all bones and jeans, in the rat graveyard.

The beam of my flashlight had dimmed. I replaced the batteries with spares from my backpack.

Using the spelunker's Velcro cuff, I fixed the light to my left forearm.

I put the folded fishing knife in one of my pockets.

I drank half of the bottle of water that I hadn't left with Danny, and I wondered how he was doing. The shotgun fire would have scared him. He probably thought I was dead.

Maybe I was, and I just didn't know it yet.

I considered whether I needed to pee. I didn't.

Unable to find any further reasons to delay, leaving my backpack behind, I went into the vertical chase.

50

ON A HIGH-NUMBER CABLE CHANNEL THAT I think is called Crap That Nobody Else Will Show TV, I once saw an ancient movie serial about these adventurers who descend to the center of the earth and discover an underground civilization. It's an evil empire, of course.

The emperor resembles Ming the Merciless from those old Flash Gordon festivals of hokum, and he intends to make war on the surface world and take it over as soon as he develops the right death ray. Or when his immense fingernails grow long enough to be appropriate for the ruler of an entire planet, whichever comes first.

This underworld is populated by the usual thugs and knaves, but also by two or three kinds of mutants, women in horned hats, and of course dinosaurs. This film masterwork was made decades before the invention of computer animation, and the dinosaurs were not even stop-motion clay models but iguanas. Rubber appliances were glued to the iguanas to make them appear scarier and more like dinosaurs, but they just looked like embarrassed iguanas.

Descending the vertical chase, careful step by careful step, I reran the plot of that old serial in my mind, striving to focus on the absurd mustache of the emperor, on the particular race of mutants that looked suspiciously like dwarfs outfitted with rubber-snake headgear and leather pantaloons, on remembered bits of the hero's dialogue marked by a wit that crackled like cream cheese, and on those campily amusing iguana-saurs.

My mind kept drifting to Datura, that dependable spike through the foot: to Datura, to reverse psychic magnetism, to how unpleasant it would be when she disemboweled me and fished her amulet out of my stomach. Not good.

The air in the service well proved not to be as savory as the soot-scented, toxin-laced air in the rest of the hotel. Stale, dank, alternately sulfurous and mildewy, it gathered substance as I went down into the hotel, until it seemed thick enough to drink.

From time to time, horizontal chases entered the well, and in some instances, drafts flowed from them. These cool currents smelled different from but no better than the shaft air.

Twice I began to gag. Both times I had to pause to repress the urge to heave.

The stink, the claustrophobic dimensions of this chimney, the trace chemicals and mold spores in the air combined to make me feel light-headed by the time I had descended only four floors.

Although I knew that my imagination was running away with me, I wondered if a couple of dead bodies—human, not rat—might lie at the bottom of the shaft, undiscovered by the rescue crews and post-fire search teams, reposing in a slime of decomposition.

The deeper I went, the more determined I became *not* to direct the flashlight downward, for fear of what I would see at the bottom: not just the tumbled dead, but a grinning figure standing atop them.

Representations of Kali always show her naked, brazen. In that particular idol called a *jagrata,* she is gaunt and very tall. From her open mouth protrudes a long tongue, and she bares two fangs. She radiates a terrible beauty, perversely appealing.

Every two floors, I passed through another crawlspace. At each of these interruptions, I could have gotten off the ladder, then on it once more; instead, I found myself switching to the rope, using the knots as grips, swinging back to the ladder when it reappeared.

Given my lightheadedness and incipient nausea, using the rope struck me as reckless. I used it anyway.

In her temple representations, Kali holds a noose in one hand, a staff topped by a skull in another. In her third, she holds a sword; in her fourth, a severed head.

I thought I heard movement below me. I paused, but then told myself that the noise had been only the echo of my breathing, and I continued down.

Painted numbers on the wall identified each floor as I went by it, even when no passable opening existed at that level. As I reached the second floor, my right foot dipped into something wet and cold.

When I dared to direct my light below, I found that the bottom of the shaft was filled with stagnant black water and debris. I could go no farther by this route.

I climbed to the crawlspace between the second and third floors and exited the vertical chase.

If rats had perished at this level, they died not by suffocation but by hungry mouths of fire that spat out not even charred bones. The flames had been so intense, they left behind an absolute black soot that absorbed the beam of the flashlight and gave back no reflection.

Twisted, buckled, melted, mercurial metal shapes, which had once been heating-and-cooling equipment, formed a bewildering landscape that no mere drinking binge or jalapeno pizza could have inspired in a nightmare. The soot that coated everything—here a film, there an inch deep—was not powdery, not dry, but greasy.

Weaving around and climbing over these amorphous and slippery obstacles proved treacherous. In places, the floor felt as if it had bowed, suggesting that the heat at the height of the blaze had been so terrible that rebar embedded inside the concrete had begun to melt and had almost failed.

The air here was more foul than in the shaft, bitter, almost rancid, yet seemed thin, as if I were at some great altitude. The singular texture of the soot gave me intolerable ideas about the source of it, and I tried to think instead about the iguanasaurs, but saw Datura in my mind's eye, Datura with a necklace of human skulls.

I crawled on hands and knees, slithered on my belly, squeezed through a heat-smoothed sphincter of metal in a blast-blown bulkhead of rubble, and thought of Orpheus in Hell.

In the Greek myth, Orpheus goes to Hell to seek Eurydice, his wife, who has gone there upon her death. He charms Hades and wins permission to take her out of the realm of damnation.

I could not be Orpheus, however, because Stormy Llewellyn, my Eurydice, had not gone to Hell, but to a far better place, which she so well deserved. If this was Hell and if I had come here on a rescue mission, the soul that I struggled to save must be my own.

As I began to conclude that the trapdoor between this crawlspace and the second level of the hotel must have been plated over with twisted and melted metal, I almost fell through a hole in the floor. Beyond that hole, my light played across the skeletal walls of what might have once been a supply room.

The trapdoor and ladder were gone, reduced to ashes. Relieved, I dropped into the space below, landed on my feet, stumbled, but kept my balance.

I stepped between the twisted steel studs of a missing wall, into the main corridor. Only one floor above ground level, I should be able to escape the hotel without resorting to the guarded stairs.

The first thing my flashlight fell upon were tracks that looked like those I had seen when I first entered the Panamint. They had made me think *sabertooth.*

The second thing the light revealed were human footprints, which led within a few steps to Datura, who switched on her flashlight the moment that mine found her.

51

WHAT A BITCH. AND I MEAN THAT IN EVERY sense of the phrase.

"Hey, boyfriend," Datura said.

In addition to a flashlight, she held a pistol.

She said, "I was at the bottom of the north stairs, having some wine, staying loose, waiting to feel the power, you know, your power, drawing me, the way Danny the Geek said it could."

"Don't talk," I pleaded. "Just shoot me."

Ignoring my interruption, she continued: "I got bored. I get bored easy. Earlier, I noticed these big cat prints in the ashes at the foot of the stairs. They're on the stairs, too. So I decided to follow them."

The fire had raged with special ferocity in this part of the hotel. Most of the inner walls had burned away, leaving a vast and gloomy space, the ceiling supported by red-steel columns encased in concrete. Over the years, ashes and dust had continued to settle, laying a smooth, lush carpet, over which my saber-toothed tiger had recently been wandering this way and that.

"The beast has been all over this place," she said. "I got so interested in the way it went in circles and meandered back on itself, I completely forgot about you. Completely forgot. And that's *just when* I heard you coming and switched off my flashlight. Mondo cool, boyfriend. I thought I was following the cat, but I was being drawn to you when I least expected. You are one strange dude, you know that?"

"I know that," I admitted.

"Is there really a cat, or were the prints made by a phantom you conjured up to lead me here?"

"There's really a cat," I assured her.

I was very tired. And dirty. I wanted to be done with this, go home, and take a bath.

Approximately twelve feet separated us. If we had been a few feet closer, I might have tried to rush her, duck in under her arm and take the gun away from her.

If I could keep her talking, an opportunity to turn the tables might arise. Fortunately, keeping her talking would require no more effort on my part than would breathing.

"I knew this prince from Nigeria," Datura said, "he claimed to be an *isangoma,* said he could change into a panther after midnight."

"Why not at ten o'clock?"

"I don't think he really could. I think he was lying because he wanted to screw me."

"You don't have to worry about that with mc," I said.

"This must be a phantom cat, some sort of eidolon. Why would a real cat be prowling around in this smelly dump?"

I said, "Close to the western summit of Kilimanjaro, around nineteen thousand feet, there's the dried, frozen carcass of a leopard."

"The mountain in Africa?"

I quoted, "'No one has explained what the leopard was seeking at that altitude.'"

She frowned. "I don't get it. What's the mystery? He's a mean damn leopard, he can go anywhere he wants."

"It's a line from 'The Snows of Kilimanjaro.'"

Gesturing with the gun, she expressed her impatience.

I explained: "That's a short story by Ernest Hemingway."

"The guy with the line of furniture? What's Hemingway got to do with this?"

I shrugged. "I have a friend who's always thrilled when I make a literary allusion. He thinks I could be a writer."

"Are the two of you gay or something?" she asked.

"No. He's hugely fat, and I'm supernaturally gifted, that's all."

"Boyfriend, sometimes you don't make a lot of sense. Did you kill Robert?"

Except for our two swords of light, shining past each other, the second floor receded into unrelieved darkness. While I had been in the crawlspaces and the vertical chase, the last light had washed out of the winter day.

I didn't mind dying, but this cavernous fire-blackened pit was an ugly place to do it.

"Did you kill Robert?" she repeated.

"He fell off a balcony."

"Yeah, after you shot him." She didn't sound upset. In fact she regarded me with the calculation of a black widow spider deciding whether to take a mate. "You play clueless pretty well, but you're for sure a *mundunugu*."

"Something was wrong with Robert."

She frowned. "I don't know what it is. My needy boys don't always stay with me as long as I'd like."

"They don't?"

"Except Andre. He's a real bull, Andre is."

"I thought he was a horse. Cheval Andre."

"A total stallion," she said. "Where's Danny the Geek? I want him back. He's a funny little monkey."

"I cut his throat and pitched him down a shaft."

My claim electrified her. Her nostrils flared, and a hard pulse appeared in her slender throat.

"If he didn't die in the fall," I told her, "he's

bled to death by now. Or drowned. The shaft's got twenty or thirty feet of water at the bottom."

"Why would you have done that?"

"He betrayed me. He told you my secrets."

Datura licked her lips as though she had just finished eating a tasty dessert. "You've got as many layers as an onion, boyfriend."

I had decided to play the we're-two-of-a-kind-why-don't-we-join-forces game, but another opportunity arose.

She said, "The Nigerian prince was full of shit, but I might believe *you* can become a panther after midnight."

"It's not a panther," I said.

"Yeah? So what is it you become?"

"It's not a saber-toothed tiger, either."

"Do you become a leopard, like on Kilimanjaro?" she asked.

"It's a mountain lion."

The California mountain lion, one of the world's most formidable predators, prefers to live in rugged mountains and forests, but it adapts well to rolling hills and low scrub.

Mountain lions thrive in the dense, almost lush scrub in the hills and canyons around Pico Mundo, and often they venture into adjoining territory that would be classified as true desert. A male mountain lion will claim as much as a hundred square miles as his hunting range, and he likes to roam.

In the mountains, he'll feed on mule deer and bighorn sheep. In territory as barren as the Mojave, he will chase down coyotes, foxes, raccoons, rabbits, and rodents, and he will enjoy the variety.

"Males of the species average between one hundred thirty and one hundred fifty pounds," I told her. "They prefer the cover of night for hunting."

That look of wide-eyed girlish wonder—which I had first seen on our way to the casino with Doom and Gloom, and which was the only appealing and guileless expression that she possessed—overcame her again. "Are you gonna show me?"

I said, "Even in the daytime, if a mountain lion is on the move instead of resting, people rarely see it because it's so quiet. It passes without detection."

As excited as ever she had been at a human sacrifice, she said, "These paw prints—they're *yours,* aren't they?"

"Mountain lions are solitary and secretive."

"Solitary and secretive, but you're going to show *me.*" She had demanded miracles, fabulous impossible things, icy fingers up and down her spine. Now she thought that I would at last deliver. "You didn't conjure these tracks to lead me here. You *transformed* . . . and made these tracks yourself."

If Datura's and my positions had been reversed, I would have been standing with my back to the mountain lion, oblivious as it stalked me.

As *wrong* as nature is—with its poisonous plants, predatory animals, earthquakes, and floods—sometimes it gets things right.

52

IMMENSE, THE PAWS, WITH WELL-DEFINED toes . . . Lowered so slowly, planted so gently that the carpet of ashes, as powdery as talcum, did not plume under them . . .

Beautiful coloration. Tawny, deepening to dark brown at the tip of the long tail. Also dark brown on the backs of the ears and on the sides of the nose.

If our positions had been reversed, Datura would have watched the approach of the mountain lion with cold-eyed amusement, darkly delighted by my cluelessness.

Although I tried to remain focused on the woman, my attention kept drifting to the cat, and I was not amused, but grimly fascinated and overcome by a growing sense of horror.

My life was hers to take or spare, and the only future I could count on was but a fraction of a second long, whatever time a bullet would take to travel from the muzzle of the pistol to me. Yet at the same time, her life lay in my hands, and it seemed that my silence in the matter of the stalking lion could not be entirely justified by the fact that I was literally under the gun.

If we rely upon the tao with which we're born, we always know what is the right thing to do in any situation, the good thing not for our bank accounts or for ourselves, but for our souls. We are tempted from the tao by self-interest, by base emotions and passions.

I believe that I can honestly say I did not hate Datura, though I had reason to, but certainly I *detested* her. I found her repugnant in part because she emblematized the willful ignorance and narcissism that characterize our troubled times.

She deserved to be imprisoned. In my opinion, she had earned execution; and in extreme jeopardy, to save myself or Danny, I had the right—the obligation—to kill her.

Perhaps no one, however, deserves as hideous a death as being mauled and eaten alive by a wild beast.

Regardless of the circumstances, perhaps it is indefensible to allow such a fate to unfold to the point of inevitability when the potential victim, armed with a gun, could save herself if warned.

Every day we make our way through a moral forest, along pathways ever branching. Often we get lost.

When the array of paths before us is so perplexing that we can't make a choice, or won't, we can hope that we will be given a sign to guide us. A reliance on signs, however, can lead to the evasion of all moral obligations, and thus earn a terrible judgment.

If a leopard in the highest snows of Kilimanjaro, where nature would never have taken it, is understood by everyone as a *sign,* then the timely appearance of a hungry mountain lion in a burned-out casino-hotel should be as easy to understand as would be a holy voice from a burning bush.

This world is mysterious. Sometimes we perceive the mystery, and retreat in doubt, in fear. Sometimes we go with it.

I went with it.

Waiting for me to transform from my human state, an instant before discovering she was not after all invincible, Datura realized that something at her back enthralled me. She looked to see what it might be.

By turning, she invited the pounce, the jaws that bite, the claws that catch.

She screamed, and the ferocious impact of the lion knocked the pistol from her hand before she was able to aim or to squeeze the trigger.

In the spirit of mystery that defined the moment, the gun arced high toward me, and reaching up, I received it from the air with a casual grace.

Perhaps she was mortally torn already, beyond rescue, but the unavoidable truth is that I held the gun, equivalent to a vorpal blade, yet did not slay the Jabberwock, and cannot claim to be a beamish boy. Ashes plumed around my feet as I sprinted toward the north end of the building, and the stairs.

Although I never saw her blood drawn nor the lion at its feast, I'll never be able to purge her screams from my memory.

Perhaps the seamstress, under the knife of the Gray Pigs, had sounded like this, or the walled-up children in the basement of that house in Savannah.

Another voice roared—not that of the lion—half in anguish and half in rage.

Glancing back, I saw Datura's flashlight, knocked this way and that by thrashing cat and prey.

Farther away, from the south end of the building, beyond black columns that might have marked the peristyle of Hell, another light approached, in the possession of a hulking shadowy shape. Andre.

Datura's screaming stopped.

Andre's flashlight swept across her and found the timely lion. If he had a gun, he didn't use it.

Respectfully cutting a wide berth around the cat and its kill, Andre kept coming. I suspected he would never stop coming. Runaway locomotives have gravity on their side.

My trembling light drew the giant more certainly than psychic magnetism could have done, but if I switched it off, I would be all but blinded.

Although he was still at some distance and though I was not the master marksman of my age, I squeezed off a shot, then another and a third.

He had a gun. He returned my fire.

As would have been anyone's, his aim was better than mine. One slug ricocheted off a column to my left, and another round whistled past my head so close that I could hear it cutting the air separate from the boom and echo of the shot itself.

Trading fire, I would get my candle snuffed, so I ran, crouching and weaving.

The stairwell door was missing. I plunged through, raced down.

Past the landing, on the second flight, I realized that he would expect me to exit at the ground floor and that in those hallways and spaces, all familiar to him, he would catch me, for he was strong and fast and not as stupid as he looked.

Hearing him enter the stairwell, realizing that he had closed the gap between us even faster than I had feared he might, I kicked open the door at the ground floor but didn't go through it. Instead, I swept the light across the next set of downbound stairs to be sure they weren't obstructed, then switched it off and descended in the dark.

Having been kicked open, the ground-floor door rebounded shut with a crash. As I reached the lower landing, sliding my hand along the railing for guidance, and continued blindly into territory that I had not scouted, I heard Andre slam out of the stairwell, into the ground floor.

I kept moving. I'd bought some time, but he wouldn't be fooled for long.

53

RISKING LIGHT WHEN I REACHED THE BASEment level, I found more stairs but hesitated to follow them. A *sub*-basement would be likely to present me with a dead end.

Shuddering, I remembered her story of the lingering spirit of the Gestapo torturer haunting that *sous-sol* in Paris. Datura's silken voice: *I felt Gessel's hands all over me—eager, bold, demanding. He entered me.*

Choosing the basement, I expected to find a parking garage or loading docks at which deliveries had been made. In either case, there would be exits.

I'd had enough of the Panamint. I preferred to take my chances in the open, in the storm.

Doors lined both sides of a long concrete-walled corridor with a vinyl-tile floor. Neither fire nor smoke had touched this area.

Because the doors were white but not paneled,

I checked out a few of the rooms as I passed them. They were empty. Either offices or storerooms, they had been cleaned out after the disaster because what they contained evidently had not been damaged either by fire or water.

The acrid stink of the fire's aftermath had not penetrated here. I had been breathing that miasma for so many hours that clean air felt astringent in my nostrils, in my lungs, almost abrasive in its comparative purity.

An intersection of corridors presented me with three choices. After the briefest hesitation, I hurried to the right, hoping that the door at the farther end would lead to the elusive parking garage.

Just as I reached the termination of this passage, I heard Andre crash through the steel door from the north stairs, back in the first hallway.

At once, I doused my flashlight. I opened the door in front of me, stepped across the threshold, and closed myself into this unknown space.

My light revealed a set of metal service stairs with rubberized treads. They led only down.

The door had no lock.

Andre might conduct a thorough search of this area. Instead he might follow his instinct elsewhere.

I could wait to see what he did, hope to shoot him before he shot me if he yanked open this door. Or I could follow the stairs.

Glad that I had snared the pistol from midair, but not daring to take it as a sign that my destiny was survival, I hurried down into the sub-basement, which such a short time ago I had tried to avoid.

Two landings and three quick flights brought me 360 degrees around to a vestibule and a formidable-looking door. Emblazoned on that barrier were several warnings; the most prominent promised HIGH VOLTAGE in big red letters. A stern admonition restricted access to authorized personnel.

I authorized myself to enter, opened the door, and from the threshold explored with my flashlight. Eight concrete steps led down five feet, into a sunken electrical vault, a thick-walled concrete bunker approximately fifteen by twenty feet.

On a raised pad in the center, as on an island, stood a tower of equipment. Perhaps some of these things were transformers, perhaps a time machine for all I knew.

At the far end of the chamber, a three-foot-diameter tunnel, at floor level, bored away into darkness. Evidently, the vault needed to be a subterranean bunker in the event that equipment exploded, as transformers sometimes did. But in case of a plumbing break or other sudden flood, the drain would be able to carry away a high volume of water.

Having avoided the main stairs into the

sub-basement, I had taken these, which served only the vault. Now I had come to the dead end that I had feared.

From the instant the lion attacked, I'd weighed options at each turn in my flight, calculating probabilities. In my panic, I had not listened to the still, small voice that is my sixth sense.

Nothing is more dangerous for me than to forget that I am a man both of reason *and* supernatural perception. When I function in only one mode or the other, I am denying half myself, half my potential.

To a lesser extent with other people than with me, this is true of everyone.

Dead end.

Nevertheless, I went through the vault door and eased it shut. I checked for a lock, doubting there would be one, and had my doubt confirmed.

I hurried down the concrete stairs, all the way into the pit, and around the tower of equipment.

Probing with the flashlight, I saw that the tunnel sloped and gradually curved away to the left, out of sight. The walls were dry and clean enough. I wouldn't leave a trail.

If Andre entered this chamber, he would surely peer into the drain. But if I managed to get out of sight, beyond the curve, he would not press the search that far. He would think that I had given him the slip farther back.

Three feet of diameter did not allow me to

proceed in a stoop. I had to crawl into the drain.

I tucked Datura's pistol under my belt, in the small of my back, and got moving.

The shielding curve lay about twenty feet from the entrance. With no need for the flashlight, I switched it off, inserted it in the spelunker's cuff, and crawled on my hands and knees into the darkness.

Half a minute later, near the bend in the tunnel, I stretched out full length and turned on my side. I directed the flashlight back the way that I had come, studying the floor.

A few smudges of soot on the concrete marked my progress, but from such spoor alone no one would be able to deduce that I had passed this way. Those traces could have been there for years. Water stains patterned the concrete, too, and they helped to camouflage the soot.

In the dark again, returning to my hands and knees, I finished rounding the gradual turn. When I should have been out of sight of the vault, I continued another ten feet, fifteen, just to be sure before stopping.

I sat crosswise to the tunnel, my back against the curve, and waited.

After a minute, I remembered that old movie serial about the secret civilization under the surface of the earth. Maybe somewhere along this route lay a subterranean city with women in horned hats, an evil emperor, and mutants. Fine. None of that could be as bad as what I'd left behind in the Panamint.

Suddenly creeping through my memory of the movie came Kali, who didn't belong in that scenario; Kali, lips painted with blood, tongue lolling. She wasn't carrying the noose, the skull-topped staff, the sword, or the severed head. Her hands were empty, the better to touch me, to fondle me, to pull my face forcefully toward her for a kiss.

Alone, without either a campfire or marsh-mallows, I was telling ghost stories to myself. You might think that my life inoculates me against being scared by mere ghost stories, but you would be wrong.

Living every day with proof that the afterlife is real, I can't take refuge in unleavened reason, can't say *But ghosts don't really exist.* Not knowing the full nature of what comes after this world, but knowing for certain that *something* does, my imagination spins into vortexes darker than any yours has ever visited.

Don't get me wrong. I'm sure you've got a fabulously dark, twisted, and perhaps even deeply sick imagination. I'm not trying to devalue the dementedness of your imagination and do not mean to diminish your pride in it.

Sitting in that tunnel, spooking myself, I banished Kali not only from the role that she had given herself in that movie serial, but banished her entirely from my mind. I concentrated on the iguanas tricked up to pass for dinosaurs and on the dwarfs in leather chaps or whatever they had been wearing.

Instead of Kali, within seconds Datura crept into my thoughts, torn by the lion but nonetheless amorous. She was crawling toward me along the tunnel *right now.*

I couldn't hear her breathing, of course, because the dead do not breathe.

She wanted to sit in my lap and wriggle her bottom and share her blood with me.

The dead don't talk. But it was easy to believe that Datura might be the sole exception to the rule. Surely even death could not silence that garrulous goddess. She would heave herself upon me, sit on my lap, wriggle her bottom, press her dripping hand to my lips, and say *Want to taste me, boyfriend?*

Very little of *that* mind movie was enough to make me want to switch on the flashlight.

If Andre had intended to check out the electrical vault, he would have done so by this time. He had gone elsewhere. With both his mistress and Robert dead, the giant would blow this place in the car that they had stashed on the property.

In a few hours, I could dare to venture back into the hotel and from there to the interstate.

As I touched my thumb to the flashlight switch, before I pressed it, light bloomed beyond the curve that I had recently transited, and I heard Andre at the mouth of the tunnel.

54

ONE GOOD THING ABOUT REVERSE PSYCHIC magnetism is that I can never be lost. Drop me into the middle of a jungle, without a map or a compass, and I'll draw my searchers to me. You'll never find my face on a milk carton: *Have you seen this boy?* If I live long enough to develop Alzheimer's and wander away from my care facility, pretty soon all the nurses and patients will be wandering after me, compelled in my wake.

Watching the light play around the first length of the tunnel, past the curve, I warned myself that I was indulging in another ghost story, spooking myself for no good reason. I should not assume that Andre sensed where I had gone.

If I sat tight, he would decide there were more likely places that I might have taken refuge, and he would go away to search them. He hadn't entered the drain. He was a big man; he would make a lot of noise, crawling in that cramped tunnel.

He surprised me by firing a shot.

In that confined space, the concussion seemed bad enough to make my ears bleed. The report—a loud bang but also like the hard toll of an immense bell—rang with such vibrato, I swore that I could feel sympathetic tremors racing through the haversian canals of my bones. The bang and the toll chased each other through the drain, and the echoes that followed were higher pitched, like the terrifying shrieks of incoming rockets.

The noise so disoriented me that the tiny chips of concrete, peppering my left cheek and neck, mystified me for a moment. Then I understood: *ricochet.*

I rolled flat, facedown, minimizing my exposure, and frantically wriggled deeper into the tunnel, scissoring my legs like a lizard and pulling myself forward with my arms, because if I rose onto my hands and knees, I would for sure take a round in the buttocks or the back of the head.

I could live with one butt cheek—just sit at a slant for the rest of my life, not worry about how baggy the seat of my blue jeans looked, get used to the nickname *Halfass*—but I couldn't live with my brains blown out. Ozzie would say that I often made such poor use of the brain I had that, if worse came to worst, I might in fact be able to get along without it, but I didn't want to try.

Andre fired another shot.

My head was still ringing from the first blast, so this one didn't seem as loud, though my ears ached as if sound of this volume had substance and, passing through them, strained their dimensions.

In the instant required for the initial crash of the shot to be followed by the shrieking echo, the slug would have ricocheted past me. As scary as the noise might be, it signified that my luck held. If a bullet found me, the shock of impact would effectively deafen me to the gunfire.

Skittering like a salamander, away from his light, I knew that darkness offered no protection. He couldn't see his target, anyway, and relied on luck to wound me. In these circumstances, with curved concrete walls conducive to multiple ricochets of the same slug, his odds of nailing me were better than his chances would have been at any game in the casino.

He squeezed off a third shot. What pity I'd once had for him— and I think there might have been a little—was *so over.*

I couldn't guess how often a bullet would have to glance off a wall until its wounding power had been sapped. Salamandering proved exhausting, and I had no confidence that I would be able to reach a safe distance before my luck changed.

A draft suddenly sucked at me from the darkness to my left, and I instinctively scrambled toward it. Another storm drain. This one, a feeder line to the first, also about three feet in diameter, sloped slightly upward.

A fourth shot slammed through the tunnel I had departed. All but certainly beyond the reach of ricochet, I returned to my hands and knees and crawled forward.

Soon the angle of incline increased, then increased again, and ascent became more difficult minute by minute. I grew frustrated that my pace should slow so much with the rising grade, but finally I accepted the cruel fact of my diminished capacity and counseled myself not to push my body to collapse. I wasn't twenty anymore.

Numerous shots rang out, but I did not keep count of them after my buttocks were no longer at risk. In time I realized that he had ceased firing.

At the top of its slope, the branch I traveled opened into a twelve-foot-square chamber that I explored with my flashlight. It appeared to be a catch basin.

Water poured in from three smaller pipes at the top of the room. Any driftwood or trash carried by these streams sank to the bottom of the space, to be cleaned out by maintenance crews from time to time.

Three exit drains, including the one by which I had arrived, were set at different levels in different walls, none near the floor where the flotsam would be allowed to accumulate. Water already was flowing out of the catch basin through the lowest of these.

With the storm raging, the level within the chamber would rise inexorably toward my observation post, which was in the middle of the three outflow lines. I needed to transfer to the highest of the exit drains and continue my journey by that route.

A series of ledges encircling the chamber would make it possible for me to stay out of the debris in the catch basin and get across to the farther side. I would just need to take my time and be careful.

The tunnels I had thus far traveled had been claustrophobic for a man my size. Given his bulk, Andre would find them intolerable. He would rely on a ricochet having wounded or killed me. He would not follow.

I squirmed out of the drain, into the catch basin, onto a ledge. When I looked down the slope I had just mastered, I saw a light in the distance. He grunted as he doggedly ascended.

55

I LIKED THE IDEA OF WITHDRAWING DATURA'S pistol from under my belt and firing down on Andre as he crawled toward me in the tunnel. Payback.

The only thing better would have been a shotgun, or maybe a flamethrower, like the one with which Sigourney Weaver torched the bugs in *Aliens*. A vat of boiling oil, bigger than the one Charles Laughton, as the hunchback, poured down on the Parisian rabble from the heights of Notre Dame would have been cool, too.

Datura and her acolytes had left me less willing than usual to turn the other cheek. They had lowered my threshold of anger and raised my tolerance for violence.

Here was a perfect illustration of why you must always choose carefully the people with whom you hang out.

Poised on a six-inch ledge, my back to the

murky pool, holding with one hand to the lip of the drain, I could not have a taste of revenge without putting myself at too much risk. If I tried to fire Datura's pistol at Andre, the recoil would surely upset my precarious balance, and I would fall backward into the catch basin.

I did not know how deep the water might be, but more to the point, I didn't know what junk lay just below the surface. The way my luck had been waxing and waning lately, mostly waning, I would fall onto the broken hardwood handle of a shovel, splintered and sharp enough to put an end to Dracula, or the rusted tines of a pitchfork, or a couple of spear-point iron fence staves, or maybe a collection of Japanese samurai swords.

Unharmed by the single shot that I had gotten off, Andre would reach the top of the drain and see me impaled in the catch basin. I would discover that, brutish as he appeared to be, he possessed a jolly laugh. As I died, he would speak his first word, in Datura's voice: *Loser*.

So I left the gun at the small of my back and made my way around the ledge to the farther side of the room, where the highest of the exit drains lay an inch or two above my head, four feet higher than the one from which I had just extracted myself.

The dirty water cascading out of the high inflow pipes kicked up spray when it met the pool, splashing my jeans to mid thigh. But I couldn't get any filthier or hardly any more miserable.

As soon as that thought crossed my mind, I tried to reel it back because it seemed like a challenge to the universe. No doubt inside of ten minutes, I would be *astonishingly* filthier and *immensely* more miserable than I was at that moment.

I reached overhead, got a two-hand grip on the lip of the new drain, toed the wall, muscled myself up and in.

Ensconced in this new warren, I considered waiting until Andre appeared at the mouth of the tunnel that I had left, and shooting him from my elevated position. For a guy who had been so reluctant even to handle firearms earlier this same day, I had developed an unseemly eagerness to pump my enemies full of lead.

The flaw in my plan immediately became clear to me. Andre had a gun of his own. He would be cautious about leaving that lower tunnel, and when I fired at him, he would fire back.

All of these concrete walls, more ricochets, more earsplitting noise . . .

I didn't have sufficient ammunition to keep him pinned down until the water rose into his drain and forced him to retreat. The best thing I could do was keep moving.

The tunnel into which I had climbed would be the last of the three outflow drains to take water. In an ordinary storm, it would probably remain dry, but not in this deluge. The level of the pool below rose visibly, minute by minute.

Happily, this new tunnel was of greater diameter than the previous one, perhaps four feet. I would not have to crawl. I could proceed at a stoop and make good time.

I didn't know where that progress would take me, but I was game for a change of scenery.

As I gathered myself off the floor and into the aforementioned stoop, a shrill twittering arose in the chamber behind me. Andre didn't strike me as a guy who would twitter, and at once I knew the source of the cries: bats.

56

HAIL IN THE DESERT IS A RARITY, BUT ONCE in a while, a Mojave storm can deliver an icy pelting to the land.

If hail had fallen outside, then as soon as I felt boils forming on my neck and face, I could be certain that God had chosen to amuse Himself by restaging the ten plagues of Egypt upon my beleaguered person.

I don't think that bats were one of the Biblical plagues, though they should have been. If memory serves me, instead of bats, frogs terrorized Egypt.

Large numbers of angry frogs won't get your blood pumping half as fast as will a horde of incensed flying rodents. This truth calls into question the deity's skill as a dramatist.

When the frogs died, they bred lice, which was the third plague. This from the same Creator who painted the sky blood-red over Sodom and Gomorrah, rained fire and brimstone on the cities, overthrew every habitation in which their people tried to hide, and broke every building stone as though it were an egg.

Circling the catch basin on the ledge and levering myself into the highest tunnel, I had not pointed the light directly overhead. Evidently a multitude of leathery-winged sleepers had depended from the ceiling, quietly dreaming.

I don't know what I did to disturb them, if anything. Night had fallen not long ago. Perhaps this was the usual time at which they woke, stretched their wings, and flew off to snare themselves in little girls' hair.

As one, they raised their shrill voices. In that instant, even as I finished rising into a stoop, I dropped flat, and folded my arms over my head.

They departed their man-made cave by the highest of the out-flow drains. This route would never entirely fill with water and would always offer at least a partially unobstructed exit.

If I'd been asked to estimate the size of their community as they passed over me, I would have said "thousands." To the same question an hour later, I would have replied "hundreds." In truth, they numbered fewer than one hundred, perhaps only fifty or sixty.

Reflected off the curved concrete walls, the rustle of their wings sounded like crackling cellophane, the way movie sound-effects specialists used to rumple the stuff to imitate all-devouring fire. They didn't stir up much of a breeze, hardly an eddy, but brought an ammonial odor, which they carried away with them.

A few fluttered against my arms, with which I protected my head and face, brushed like feathers across the backs of my hands, which should have made it easy to imagine that they were only birds, but which instead brought to mind swarming insects—cockroaches, centipedes, locusts—so I had bats for real and bugs in the mind. Locusts had been the eighth of Egypt's ten plagues.

Rabies.

Having read somewhere that a quarter of any colony of bats is infected with the virus, I waited to be bitten viciously, repeatedly. I didn't sustain a single nip.

Although none of them bit me, a couple crapped on me in passing, sort of like a casual insult. The universe had heard and accepted my challenge: I was now filthier and more miserable than I had been ten minutes previously.

I rose into a stoop again and followed the descending drain away from the catch basin. Somewhere ahead, and not too far, I would find a manhole or another kind of exit from the system. Two hundred yards, I assured myself, three hundred at most.

Between here and there, of course, would be the Minotaur. The Minotaur fed on human flesh. "Yeah," I muttered aloud, "but only the flesh of virgins." Then I remembered that I was a virgin.

The flashlight revealed a Y in the tunnel, immediately ahead. The branch to the left continued to descend. The passage to the right fed the one I'd been following from the catch basin, and because it rose, I figured it would lead me closer to the surface and to a way out.

I had gone only twenty or thirty yards when, of course, I heard the bats returning. They had soared out into the night, discovered a tempest raging, and had fled at once back to their cozy subterranean haven.

Because I doubted that I would escape a second confrontation unbitten, I reversed directions with an agility born of panic and ran, hunched like a troll. Returning to the down-bound tunnel, I went to the right, away from the catch basin, and hoped the bats would remember their address.

When their frenzied flapping crescendoed and then diminished behind me, I came to a halt and, gasping, leaned against the wall.

Maybe Andre would be on the ledge, crossing from the lowest drain to the highest, when the bats returned. Maybe they would frighten him, and he would fall into the catch basin, skewering himself on those samurai swords.

That fantasy brought a brief glow to my heart, but only brief because I couldn't believe that Andre would be afraid of bats. Or afraid of anything.

An ominous sound arose that I had not heard before, a rough rumbling, as if an enormous slab of granite was being dragged across another slab. It seemed to be coming from between me and the catch basin.

Usually this meant that a secret door in a solid-stone wall would roll open, allowing the evil emperor to make a grand entrance in knee-high boots and a cape.

Hesitantly, I moved back toward the Y, cocking my head one way, then the other, trying to determine the source of the sound.

The rumble grew louder. Now I perceived it as less like stone sliding over stone than like friction between iron and rock.

When I pressed a hand to the wall of the tunnel, I could feel vibrations passing through the concrete.

I ruled out an earthquake, which would have produced jolts and lurches instead of this prolonged grinding sound and consistent level of shaking.

The rumbling stopped.

Under my hand, vibrations were no longer coursing through the concrete.

A rushing sound. A sudden draft as something pushed air out of the nearby ascending branch, stirring my hair.

Somewhere a sluice gate had opened.

The air had been displaced by a surge of water. A torrent exploded out of the ascending branch, knocked me off my feet, and swept me down into the dark bowels of the flood-control system.

57

TOSSED, TURNED, TUMBLED, SPUN, I SPIRALED along the tunnel like a bullet along a rifle barrel.

At first the flashlight, strapped to my left arm, revealed the undulant gray tide, lent glitter to the spray, brightened the dirty foam. But the spelunker's cuff failed, peeled away from my arm, and took the light with it.

Down through the blackness, bulleting, I wrapped my arms around myself, tried to keep my legs together. With limbs flailing, I'd be more likely to break a wrist, an ankle, an elbow, by knocking against the wall.

I tried to stay on my back, face up, rocketing along with the fatalism of an Olympic bobsledder whistling down a luge chute, but the torrent repeatedly, insistently rolled me, pushing my face under the flow. I fought for breath, jackknifing my body to reorient it, gasping when I got my head above the flux.

I swallowed water, broke through the surface, gagged and coughed and desperately inhaled the wet air. Considering my helplessness in its embrace, this modest flow might as well have been Niagara sweeping me toward its killing cataracts.

How long the aquatic torture continued, I can't say, but having been physically taxed before entering this flume ride, I grew tired. Very tired. My limbs became heavy, and my neck stiffened from the strain of the constant struggle to keep my head above water. My back ached, I seemed to have wrenched my left shoulder, and with each effort to find air, my reserves of strength diminished until I was perilously close to complete exhaustion.

Light.

The surging sluice spat me out of the four-foot drain into one of the immense flood-control tunnels that I had speculated might double, in the Last War, as an underground highway for the transport of intercontinental ballistic missiles out of Fort Kraken to farther points of the Maravilla Valley.

I wondered if the tunnel had remained lighted ever since I'd thrown the switch after coming down from the service shed near the Blue Moon Cafe. I felt as if weeks had passed since then, not mere hours.

Here, the velocity of the flood was not as

breakneck as it had been in the smaller and far more steeply sloped drain. I could tread the moving water and stay afloat as I was flushed into the middle of the passage and borne along.

A little experimentation quickly proved, however, that I could not swim crosswise to the swift current. I wouldn't be able to reach the elevated walkway that I had followed eastward in pursuit of Danny and his captors.

Then I realized that the walkway had vanished below the water when the previous stream had swelled into this mighty Mississippi. Were I able to reach the side of the tunnel by heroic effort and the grace of a miracle, I would not be able to escape the river.

If ultimately the flood-control system delivered the storm run-off to a vast subterranean lake, I would be washed onto those shores. Robinson Crusoe without sunshine and coconuts.

Such a lake might lack shores. It might be embraced instead by sheer stone walls so smoothed by eons of trickling condensation that they could not be climbed.

And if a shore existed, it would not be hospitable. With no possible source of light, I would be a blind man in a barren Hades, spared death by starvation only if I died instead by stumbling into an abyss and breaking my neck in the fall.

At that bleak moment, I thought I would die

underground. And within the hour, I did.

Treading water, keeping my head above even this less turbulent flow, was a cruel test of my stamina. I wasn't certain that I would last the miles that lay ahead before the lake. Drowning would spare me from starvation.

Meager hope unexpectedly came in the form of a depth marker situated in the center of the watercourse. I was swept straight toward the six-inch-square white post, which rose nearly to the twelve-foot-high ceiling.

As in the power of the current I began to slide past this slender refuge, I hooked one arm around the post. I snared it with one leg, as well. If I stayed on the upstream side, with the post between my legs, the insistent current at my back would help to keep me in place.

Earlier in the day, when I had towed the snaky man's corpse away from this post or another like it, to the elevated walkway, the depth of the flow had been inches shy of two feet. Now it lapped north of the five-foot mark.

Thus safely anchored, I leaned my forehead against the post for a while, catching my breath. I listened to my heart and marveled that I was alive.

After several minutes, when I closed my eyes, that mental turning, that slow dizzy sweep signifying a pending swoon into sleep, alarmed me, and my lids snapped open. If I fell asleep, I would lose my grip and be swept away once more.

I would be in this fix for a while. With the service walkway underwater, no maintenance crew would venture here. No one would see me clinging to the pole and mount a rescue.

If I held fast, however, the water level would fall when the storm passed. Eventually the service walkway would reappear out of the tide. The stream would become shallow enough to ford, as it had been before.

Perseverance.

To keep my mind occupied, I maintained a mental inventory of the flotsam that bobbed past. A palm frond. A blue tennis ball. A bicycle tire.

For a little while I thought about working at Tire World, about being part of the tire life, working around the fine smell of rubber, and that made me happy.

A yellow lawn-chair cushion. The green lid of a picnic cooler. A length of two-by-six with a rusty spike bristling from it. A dead rattlesnake.

The dead snake alerted me to the possibility of a live snake in the flood. For that matter, if a sizable chunk of lumber, like that two-by-six, propelled by the brisk current, knocked hard against my spine, it might do some damage.

I began glancing over my shoulder from time

to time, surveying the oncoming debris. Maybe the snake had been a warning sign. Because of it, I spotted Andre upstream, before he was on top of me.

58

EVIL NEVER DIES. IT JUST CHANGES FACES.

Of this face, I'd seen enough, too much, and when I spotted the giant, I thought for an instant—and fondly hoped—that only a corpse pursued me.

But he was alive, all right, and friskier than I. Too impatient for the swift current to bring him to the depth marker, he flailed, splashed, determined to swim toward me.

I had nowhere to go but up.

My muscles ached. My back throbbed. My wet hands on the wet post seemed certain to fail me.

Fortunately, the inch and foot lines that measured the depth were not merely indicated with black paint on the white background, but were also notched into the wood. These features served as grip points, toe-holds, shallow but better than nothing.

I clamped the post with my knees and pushed

myself with my thigh muscles even as I clawed upward, hand over hand. I slipped back, dug my toes in, clamped my knees, tried again, moved up an inch, another inch, two more, desperate for every one of them.

When Andre collided with the post, I felt the impact and glanced down. His features were as broad and blunt as a club. His eyes were edge weapons, sharp with homicidal fury.

With one hand, he reached for me. He had long arms. His fingers brushed the bottom of my right shoe.

I pulled my legs up. Afraid of slipping back and into his hands, measuring progress by the numbered notches, I inchwormed until my head bumped the ceiling.

When I glanced down again, I saw that even with my legs drawn up as far as they would go, so that I clamped the post fiercely with my thighs, I was only about ten inches beyond his reach.

He hooked his thick blunt fingers into the notched marks with some difficulty. He struggled to pull himself out of the water.

The top of the depth marker had a finial, like that on a newel post at the head of a staircase. With my left hand, I gripped that knob and held on as poor King Kong had held on to the dirigible-mooring mast at the top of the Empire State Building.

The analogy didn't quite work because Kong

was below me on the post. Maybe that made me Fay Wray. The big ape did seem to have an unnatural passion for me.

My legs had slipped. I felt Andre paw at my shoe. Furiously, I kicked his hand, kicked, and drew my legs up again.

Remembering Datura's pistol under my belt, at the small of my back, I reached for it with my right hand. I had lost it along the way.

While I fumbled for the missing handgun, the brute surged up the post and seized my left ankle.

I kicked and thrashed, but he held tight. In fact, he took a risk, let go of the post, and gripped my ankle with both hands.

His great weight dragged on me so pitilessly that my hip should have dislocated. I heard a shout of pain and rage, then again, but did not realize until the second time that the shout came from me.

The finial at the top of the depth marker had not been carved from the end of the post. The ornament had been made separately and applied.

It broke loose in my hand.

Together, Andre and I fell into the flood tide.

59

AS WE FELL, I SLIPPED OUT OF HIS GRASP.

I hit the water with sufficient force to go under, touch bottom. The powerful current rolled me, spun me, and I burst to the surface, coughing and sputtering.

Cheval Andre, the bull, the stallion, floated directly ahead of me, fifteen feet away, facing me. Pitted against the punishing surge, he was not able to swim to the rendezvous with death that he clearly desired.

His burning fury, his seething hatred, his lust for violence were so consuming that he would exhaust himself beyond recovery to have vengeance, and did not care that he would drown, too, after drowning me.

Aside from Datura's cheap physical appeal, I could not account for any quality in her that should elicit the absolute commitment of body, mind, and heart from any man, let alone from one who seemed to have no slightest capacity for sentimentality. Could this hard brute love beauty so much that he would die for it, even when it truly was skin deep and corrupted, even when she who possessed it had been mad, narcissistic, and manipulative?

We were pawns of the flood, which spun us, lifted us, dropped us, dunked us, and bore us along at maybe thirty miles an hour, maybe faster. Sometimes we closed to within six feet of each other. Never were we farther apart than twenty.

We passed the place at which I had entered these tunnels earlier in the day, and raced onward.

I began to worry that we would sweep out of the lighted length of the tunnel, into darkness, and I feared plunging blindly into the subterranean lake less than I feared not being able to keep Andre in sight. If I was destined to drown, let the flood itself claim me. I didn't want to die at his hands.

Ahead, flush to the circumference of the great tunnel, a pair of steel gates together formed a circle. They resembled a portcullis in that they featured both horizontal and vertical bars.

Between the crossed members of this grating, the openings were four inches square. The gate served as a final filter of the flood-borne debris.

A marked quickening of the water suggested that a falls lay not far ahead, and the lake no doubt waited below those cascades. Beyond the gates, impenetrable blackness promised an abyss.

The river brought Andre to the gate first, and I slammed against it a couple of seconds later, six feet to his right.

Upon impact, he clawed over the clog of trash at the base of the gate, and pulled himself onto it.

Stunned, I wanted only to cling there, rest, but because I knew that he would come for me, I clambered over the trash, too, and onto the gate. We hung motionless for but a moment, like a spider and its prey upon a web.

He crabbed sideways along the steel grid. He didn't appear to be breathing half as hard as I was.

I would have preferred to retreat, but I could move only two or three feet away from him before I encountered the wall.

Both feet on a vertical bar, gripping the gate with one hand, I extracted the fishing knife from my jeans. On the third try, when he had drawn within arm's length of me, I flicked the blade out of the handle.

The grievous hour had come round at last. It was him or me. Fish or cut bait.

Fearless of the knife, he crabbed closer and reached for me.

I slashed his hand.

Instead of crying out or flinching, he clutched the blade in his bleeding fist.

At some cost to him, I ripped the knife away from him.

With his wounded hand, he seized a fistful of my hair and tried to yank me off the gate.

As dirty as it was, and intimate, as terrible as it was, and necessary, I drove the knife deep into his gut and without hesitation slashed down.

Relinquishing the twist of my hair, he seized the wrist of the hand that held the knife. He let go of the gate, fell into the flood, and pulled me with him.

We rolled across the gate-held trash and plunged underwater, broke the surface, face to face, my hand in his, the knife contested, thrashing, his free hand a club battering my shoulder, battering the side of my head, then pulling me down with him, submerged, blind in the murky water, blind and suffocating, then up and into the air once more, coughing, spitting, vision blurred, and somehow he had gotten possession of the knife, the point of which felt not sharp but hot in a diagonal slash across my chest.

I have no memory from that slash until a short but inestimable time later, when I realized that I was lying across the accumulation of debris at the base of the gate, holding to a horizontal bar with both hands, afraid that I was going to slip down into the water and not be able to get my head above the surface again.

Exhausted, all power drained, strength consumed, I realized that I had lost consciousness, that I would pass out again, momentarily. I managed, barely, to pull myself up farther on the gate, to hook both arms around verticals, so if my hands relaxed and slipped loose, the crooks of my elbows might still hold me above the flood.

At my left side, he floated, snagged on the trash, faceup, dead. His eyes were rolled back in his head, as smooth and white as eggs, as white and blind as bone, as blind and terrible as Nature in her indifference.

I went away.

60

THE RATAPLAN OF NIGHT RAIN AGAINST THE windows . . . Wafting in from the kitchen, the delicious aroma of a pot roast taking its time in the oven . . .

In his living room, Little Ozzie fills his huge armchair to overflowing.

The warm light of the Tiffany lamps, the jewel tones of the Persian carpet, the art and artifacts reflect his good taste.

On the table beside his chair is a bottle of fine Cabernet, a plate of cheeses, a cup of fried walnuts, which serve as a testament to his genteel quest for self-destruction.

I sit on the sofa and watch him enjoy the book for a while before I say *You're always reading Saul Bellow and Hemingway and Joseph Conrad.*

He does not permit himself to be interrupted in the middle of a paragraph.

I bet you'd like to write something more ambitious than stories about a bulimic detective.

Ozzie sighs and samples the cheese, eyes fixed on the page.

You're so talented, I'm sure you could write whatever you want. I wonder if you've ever tried.

He sets the book aside and picks up his wine.

Oh, I say, surprised. *I see how it is.*

Ozzie savors the wine and, still holding the glass, stares into the middle distance, not at anything in this room.

Sir, I wish you could hear me say this. You were a dear friend to me. I'm so glad you made me write the story of me and Stormy and what happened to her.

After another taste of wine, he opens the book and returns to his reading.

I might have gone mad if you hadn't made me write it. And if I hadn't written it, for sure I would never have had any peace.

Terrible Chester, as glorious as ever, enters from the kitchen and stands staring at me.

If things had worked out, I'd have written about all this with Danny, too, and given you a second manuscript. You would have liked it less than the first, but maybe a little.

Chester visits with me as never he has before, sits at my feet.

Sir, when they come to tell you about me, please don't eat a whole ham in one night, don't deep-fry a block of cheese.

I reach down to stroke Terrible Chester, and he seems to like my touch.

What you could do for me, sir, is just once write a story of the kind you'd most enjoy writing. If you'll do that for me, I'll have given back the gift that you gave me, and that would make me happy.

I rise from the sofa.

Sir, you're a dear, fat, wise, fat, generous, honorable, caring, wonderfully fat man, and I wouldn't have you any other way.

TERRI STAMBAUGH SITS in her apartment kitchen above the Pico Mundo Grille, drinking strong coffee and paging slowly through an album of photographs.

Looking over her shoulder, I see snapshots of her with Kelsey, the husband she lost to cancer.

On her music system, Elvis sings "I Forgot to Remember to Forget."

I put my hands on her shoulders. She does not react, of course.

She gave me so much—encouragement, a job at sixteen, the skills of a first-rate fry cook, counsel—and all I gave her in return was my friendship, which doesn't seem enough.

I wish I could spook her with a supernatural moment. Make the hands spin on the Elvis wall clock. Send that ceramic Elvis dancing across the kitchen counter.

Later, when they came to tell her, she would know it had been me, fooling with her, saying good-bye. Then she would know I was all right, and knowing I was all right, she would be all right, too.

But I don't have the anger to be a poltergeist. Not even enough to make the face of Elvis appear in the condensation on her kitchen window.

CHIEF WYATT PORTER and his wife, Karla, are having dinner in their kitchen.

She is a good cook, and he is a good eater. He claims this is what holds their marriage together.

She says what holds their marriage together is that she feels too damn sorry for him to ask for a divorce.

What really holds their marriage together are mutual respect of an awesome depth, a shared sense of humor, faith that they were brought together by a force greater than themselves, and a love so unwavering and pure that it is sacred.

This is how I like to believe Stormy and I would have been if we could have gotten married and lived together as long as the chief and Karla: so perfect for each other that spaghetti and a salad in the kitchen on a rainy night, just the two of them, is more satisfying and more gladdening to the heart than dinner at the finest restaurant in Paris.

I sit at the table with them, uninvited. I am embarrassed to be eavesdropping on their simple yet enrapturing conversation, but this will be the only time that it ever happens. I will not linger. I will move on.

After a while, his cell phone rings.

"I hope that's Odd," he says.

She puts down her fork, wipes her hands on a napkin as she says, "If something's wrong with Oddie, I want to come."

"Hello," says the chief. "Bill Burton?"

Bill owns the Blue Moon Cafe.

The chief frowns. "Yes, Bill. Of course. Odd Thomas? What about him?"

As if with a presentiment, Karla pushes her chair away from the table and gets to her feet.

The chief says, "We'll be right there."

Rising from the table as he does, I say, *Sir, the dead do talk, after all. But the living don't listen.*

61

HERE IS THE CENTRAL MYSTERY: HOW I GOT from the portcullis-style gate in the flood tunnel to the kitchen door of the Blue Moon Cafe, a journey of which I have no slightest recollection.

I do believe that I died. The visits I paid to Ozzie, to Terri, and to the Porters in their kitchen were not figments of a dream.

Later, when I shared my story with them, my description of what each of them was doing when I visited comports perfectly with their separate recollections of their evenings.

Bill Burton says I arrived battered and bedraggled at the back door of his restaurant, asking him to call Chief Porter. By then the rain had stopped, and I was so filthy that he set a chair outside for me and fetched a bottle of beer, which in his opinion, I needed.

I don't recall that part. The first thing that I remember is being in the chair, drinking Heineken, while Bill examined the wound in my chest.

"Shallow," he said. "Hardly more than a scratch. The bleeding's stopped on its own."

"He was dying when he took that swipe at me," I said. "There wasn't any force behind it."

Maybe that was true. Or maybe it was the explanation that I needed to tell myself.

Soon a Pico Mundo Police Department cruiser came along the alley, without siren or flashing lights, and parked behind the cafe.

Chief Porter and Karla got out of the car and came to me.

"I'm sorry you didn't get to finish the spaghetti," I said.

They exchanged a puzzled look.

"Oddie," said Karla, "your ear's torn up. What's all the blood on your T-shirt? Wyatt, he needs an ambulance."

"I'm all right," I assured her. "I was dead, but someone didn't want me to be, so I'm back."

To Bill Burton, Wyatt said, "How many beers has he had?"

"That's the first one here," Bill said.

"Wyatt," Karla declared, *"he needs an ambulance."*

"I don't really," I said. "But Danny's in bad shape, and we might need a couple paramedics to carry him down all those stairs."

While Karla brought another chair out of the restaurant, put it next to mine, sat down, and fussed over me, Wyatt used the police-band radio to order an ambulance.

When he returned, I said, "Sir, you know what's wrong with humanity?"

"Plenty," he said.

"The greatest gift we were given is our free will, and we keep misusing it."

"Don't worry yourself about that now," Karla advised me.

"You know what's wrong with nature," I asked her, "with all its poison plants, predatory animals, earthquakes, and floods?"

"You're upsetting yourself, sweetie."

"When we envied, when we killed for what we envied, we fell. And when we fell, we broke the whole shebang, nature, too."

A kitchen worker whom I knew, who had worked part time at the Grille, Manuel Nuñez, arrived with a fresh beer.

"I don't think he should have that," Karla worried.

Taking the beer from him, I said, "Manuel, how're you doing?"

"Looks like better than you."

"I was just dead for a while, that's all. Manuel, do you know what's wrong with cosmic time, as we know it, which steals everything from us?"

"Isn't it 'spring forward, fall back'?" Manuel asked, thinking that we were talking about Daylight Savings Time.

"When we fell and broke," I said, "we broke nature, too, and when we broke nature, we broke time."

"Is that from *Star Trek?*" Manuel asked.

"Probably. But it's true."

"I liked that show. It helped me learn English."

"You speak it well," I told him.

"I had a brogue for a while because I got so into Scotty's character," Manuel said.

"Once, there were no predators, no prey. Only harmony. There were no quakes, no storms, everything in balance. In the beginning, time was all at once and forever—no past, present, and future, no death. We broke it all."

Chief Porter tried to take the fresh Heineken from me.

I held on to it. "Sir, do you know what sucks the worst about the human condition?"

Bill Burton said, "Taxes."

"It's even worse than that," I told him.

Manuel said, "Gasoline costs too much, and low mortgage rates are *gone.*"

"What sucks the worst is . . . this world was a gift to us, and we broke it, and part of the deal is that if we want things right, we have to fix it ourselves. But we can't. We try, but we can't."

I started to cry. The tears surprised me. I thought I was done with tears for the duration.

Manuel put a hand on my shoulder and said, "Maybe we can fix it, Odd. You know? Maybe."

I shook my head. "No. We're broken. A broken thing can't fix itself."

"Maybe it can," Karla said, putting a hand on my other shoulder.

I sat there, just a faucet. All snot and tears. Embarrassed but not enough to get my act together.

"Son," said Chief Porter, "it's not your job alone, you know."

"I know."

"So the broken world's not all on your shoulders."

"Lucky for the world."

The chief crouched beside me. "I wouldn't say that. I wouldn't say that at all."

"Or me," Karla agreed.

"I'm a mess," I apologized.

Karla said, "Me too."

"I could use a beer," Manuel said.

"You're working," Bill Burton reminded him. Then he said, "Get me one, too."

To the chief, I said, "There're two dead at the Panamint and two more in the flood-control tunnel."

"You just tell me what," he said, "and we'll handle it."

"What had to be done . . . it was so bad. Real bad. But the hard thing is . . ."

Karla gave me a wad of tissues.

The chief said, "What's the hard thing, son?"

"The hard thing is, I was dead, too, but somebody didn't want me to be, so I'm back."

"Yes. You said before."

My chest swelled. My throat thickened. I could hardly breathe. "Chief, I was *this* close to Stormy, *this* close to service."

He cupped my wet face in his hands and made me look at him. "Nothing before its time, son. Everything in its own time, to its own schedule."

"I guess so."

"You know that's true."

"This was a very hard day, sir. I had to do . . . terrible things. Things no one should have to live with."

Karla whispered, "Oh, God, Oddie. Oh, sweetie, don't." To her husband, she said plaintively, "Wyatt?"

"Son, you can't fix a broken thing by breaking another part of it. You understand me?"

I nodded. I did understand. But understanding doesn't always help.

"Giving up—that would be breaking another part of yourself."

"Perseverance," I said.

"That's right."

At the end of the block, with flashing emergency beacons but without a siren, the ambulance turned into the alley.

"I think Danny had some broken bones but was trying not to let me know," I told the chief.

"We'll get him. We'll handle him like glass, son."

"He doesn't know about his dad."

"All right."

"That's going to be so hard, sir. Telling him. Very hard."

"I'll tell him, son. Leave that to me."

"No, sir. I'd be grateful if you're there with me, but I have to tell him. He's going to think it's all his fault. He's going to be devastated. He's going to need to lean, sir."

"He can lean on you."

"I hope so, sir."

"He can lean hard on you, son. Who could he lean on any harder?"

And so we went to the Panamint, where Death had gone to gamble and had, as always, won.

62

WITH FOUR POLICE CRUISERS, ONE ambulance, a county-morgue wagon, three crime-scene specialists, two paramedics, six cops, one chief, and one Karla, I returned to the Panamint.

I felt whipped, but not exhausted to the point of collapse, as I had felt earlier. Being dead for a while had refreshed me.

When we pried open the elevator doors on the twelfth floor, Danny was glad to see us. He had eaten neither of the coconut-raisin power bars, and he insisted on returning them to me.

He had drunk the water I left with him, but not because he had been thirsty. "After all the shotgun fire," he said, "I really needed the bottles to pee in."

Karla went with Danny in the ambulance to the hospital. Later, in a room at County General, she, instead of the chief, stayed with me when I told Danny about his dad. The wives of Spartans are the secret pillars of the world.

In the dark and ashy vastness of the burned-out second floor, we found Datura's remains. The mountain lion had gone.

As I expected, her malignant spirit had not lingered. Her will was no longer hers to wield, her freedom surrendered to a demanding collector.

In the living room of the twelfth-floor suite, blood spray and buckshot proved that I'd wounded Robert. On the balcony lay a loosely tied shoe, which apparently had been pulled off his foot when he had stumbled backward across the metal track of the sliding doors.

Immediately below that balcony, in the parking lot, we found his pistol and his other shoe, as if he no longer needed the former and had taken off the latter to be able to travel with an even step.

Such a long fall onto a hard surface would have left him lying in a lake of blood. But the storm had washed the pavement clean.

The consensus was that Datura and Andre had moved the body to a dry place.

I did not share that opinion. Datura and Andre had been guarding the stairs. They would have had neither the time nor the inclination to treat their dead with dignity.

I looked up from the shoe and surveyed the Mojave night beyond the grounds of the hotel, wondering what need—or hope—and what power had compelled him.

Perhaps one day a hiker will find mummified remains dressed in black but shoeless, in the fetal position, inside a den from which foxes had been evicted to provide a refuge to a man who wished to rest in peace beyond the reach of his demanding goddess.

The disappearance of Robert prepared me for the failure of the authorities to recover the bodies of Andre and the snaky man.

Near the end of the flood-control system, the portcullis-style gates, twisted and sagging, were found open. Beyond, a falls cascaded into a cavern, the first of many caverns that formed an archipelago of subterranean seas bound all around by land, a realm that was largely unexplored and too treacherous to justify a search for bodies.

The consensus held that the water, possessed of fearsome power and prevented by a choking mass of debris from flowing easily through the gates, had torqued the steel, had bent the huge hinges, had broken the lock.

Although that scenario did not satisfy me, I had no desire to pursue an independent investigation.

In the interest of self-education, however, which Ozzie Boone is always pleased to see me undertake, I researched the meaning of some words previously unknown to me.

Mundunugu appears in similar forms in different

languages of East Africa. A *mundunugu* is a witch doctor.

Voodooists believe that the human spirit has two parts.

The first is the *gros bon ange,* the "big good angel," the life force that all beings share, that animates them. The *gros bon ange* enters the body at conception and, upon the death of the body, returns at once to God, from whom it originated.

The second is the *ti bon ange,* the "little good angel." This is the essence of the person, the portrait of the individual, the sum of his life's choices, actions, and beliefs.

At death, because sometimes it wanders and delays in its journey to its eternal home, the *ti bon ange* is vulnerable to a *bokor,* which is a voodoo priest who deals in black rather than in white magic. He can capture the *ti bon ange,* bottle it, and keep it for many uses.

They say that a skilled *bokor,* with well-cast spells, can even steal the *ti bon ange* from a living person.

To steal the *ti bon ange* of another *bokor* or of a *mundunugu* would be considered a singular accomplishment among the mad-cow set.

Cheval is French for "horse."

To a voodooist, a *cheval* is a corpse, taken always when fresh from a morgue or acquired by whatever means, into which he installs a *ti bon ange.*

The former corpse, alive again, is animated by

the *ti bon ange,* which perhaps yearns for Heaven—or even for Hell—but is under the iron control of the *bokor.*

I draw no conclusions from the meaning of these exotic words. I define them here only for *your* education.

As I said earlier, I'm a man of reason, yet I have supernatural perceptions. Daily I walk a high wire. I survive by finding the sweet spot between reason and unreason, between the rational and the irrational.

The unthinking embrace of irrationality is literally madness. But embracing rationality while denying the existence of *any* mystery to life and its meaning—that is no less a form of madness than is eager devotion to unreason.

One appeal of both the life of a fry cook and that of a tire-installation technician is that during a busy work day, you have no time to dwell on these things.

63

STORMY'S UNCLE, SEAN LLEWELLYN, IS A priest and the rector of St. Bartholomew's, in Pico Mundo.

Following the deaths of her mother and father, when Stormy was seven and a half, she had been adopted by a couple in Beverly Hills. Her adoptive father had molested her.

Lonely, confused, ashamed, she had eventually found the courage to inform a social worker.

Thereafter, choosing dignity over victimhood, courage over despair, she had lived in St. Bart's Orphanage until she graduated from high school.

Father Llewellyn is a gentle man with a gruff exterior, strong in his convictions. He looks like Thomas Edison as played by Spencer Tracy, but with brush-cut hair. Without his Roman collar, he might be mistaken for a career Marine.

Two months after the events at the Panamint, Chief Porter came with me to a consultation with

Father Llewellyn. We met in the study in St. Bart's rectory.

In a spirit of confession, requiring the priest's confidence, we told him about my gift. The chief confirmed that with my help he had solved certain crimes, and he vouched for my sanity, my truthfulness.

My primary question for Father Llewellyn was whether he knew of a monastic order that would provide room and board for a young man who would work hard in return for these provisions, but who did not think that he himself would ever wish to become a monk.

"You want to be a lay resident in a religious community," said Father Llewellyn, and by the way he put it, I knew this might be an unusual but not an unheard-of arrangement.

"Yes, sir. That's the thing."

With the rough bearish charm of a concerned Marine sergeant counseling a troubled soldier, the priest said, "Odd, you've taken some bad blows this past year. Your loss . . . my loss, too . . . has been an extraordinarily difficult thing to cope with because she was . . . such a good soul."

"Yes, sir. She was. She is."

"Grief is a healthy emotion, and it's healthy to embrace it. By accepting loss, we clarify our values and the meaning of our lives."

"I wouldn't be running away from grief, sir," I assured him.

"Or giving yourself too much to it?"

"Not that, either."

"That's what I worry about," Chief Porter told Father Llewellyn. "That's why I don't approve."

"This isn't the rest of my life," I said. "A year maybe, and then we'll see. I just need things simpler for a while."

"Have you gone back to the Grille?" the priest asked.

"No. The Grille is a busy place, Father, and Tire World's not much better. I need useful work to keep my mind occupied, but I'd like to find work where it's . . . quieter."

"Even as a lay resident, taking no instruction, you'd still have to be in harmony with the spiritual life of whatever order might have a place for you."

"I would be, sir. I would be in harmony."

"What sort of work would you expect to do?"

"Gardening. Painting. Minor repairs. Scrubbing floors, washing windows, general cleaning. I could cook for them, if they wanted."

"How long have you been thinking about this, Odd?"

"Two months."

To Chief Porter, Father Llewellyn said, "Has he talked with you about it for that long?"

"Just about," the chief acknowledged.

"Then it's not an impetuous decision."

The chief shook his head. "Odd isn't impetuous."

"I don't believe he's running from his grief, either," said Father Llewellyn. "Or to it."

I said, "I just need to simplify. To simplify and find the quiet to think."

To the chief, Father Llewellyn said, "As his friend who knows him better than I do, and as a man he obviously looks up to, do you have any other reason you don't think Odd should try this?"

Chief Porter was quiet a moment. Then he said, "I don't know what we'll do without him."

"No matter how much help Odd gives you, Chief, there will always be more crime."

"That's not what I mean," said Wyatt Porter. "I mean . . . I just don't know what we'll do without you, son."

SINCE STORMY'S DEATH, I had lived in her apartment. Those rooms meant less to me than her furnishings, small decorative objects, and personal items. I did not want to get rid of her things.

With Terri's and Karla's help, I packed Stormy's belongings, and Ozzie offered to keep everything in a spare room at his house.

On my next-to-last night in that apartment, I sat with Elvis in the lovely light of an old lamp with a beaded shade, listening to his music from the first years of his storied career.

He loved his mother more than anything in life. In death, he wants more than anything to see her.

Months before she died—you can read this in many biographies of him—she worried that fame was going to his head, that he was losing his way.

Then she died young, before he reached the peak of his success, and after that he changed. Pierced by grief for years, he nonetheless forgot his mother's advice, and year by year his life went further off the rails, the promise of his talent less than half fulfilled.

By the time he was forty—which biographies also report—Elvis had been tormented by the belief that he had not served his mother's memory well and that she would have been ashamed of his drug use and his self-indulgence.

After his death at forty-two, he lingers because he fears the very thing that he most desperately desires: to see Gladys Presley. Love of this world, which was so good to him, is not what holds him here, as I once thought. He knows his mother loves him, and will take him in her arms without a word of criticism, but he burns with shame that he became the world's biggest star—but not the man she might have hoped he would be.

In the world to come, she will be delighted to receive him, but he feels he is not worthy of her company, because he believes that she resides now in the company of saints.

I told him this theory on my next-to-last night in Stormy's apartment.

When I had finished, his eyes blurred with tears, and he closed them for a long time. When at last he looked at me again, he reached out and took one of my hands in both of his.

Indeed, that is why he lingers. My analysis, however, is not enough to convince him that his fear of a mother-and-child reunion is without merit. Sometimes he can be a stubborn old rockabilly.

My decision to leave Pico Mundo, at least for a while, has led to the solution of another mystery related to Elvis. He haunts this town not because it has any meaning for him, but because I am here. He believes that eventually I *will* be the bridge that takes him home, and to his mother.

Consequently, he wants to come with me on the next phase of my journey. I doubt that I could prevent him from accompanying me, and I've no reason to reject him.

I am amused at the thought of the King of Rock 'n' Roll haunting a monastery. The monks might be good for him, and I'm sure that he'll be good for me.

This night, as I write, will be my last night in Pico Mundo. I will spend it in a gathering of friends.

This town, in which I have slept every night of my life, will be difficult to leave. I will miss its streets, its sounds and scents, and I will remember always the quality of desert light and shadow that lend it mystery.

Far more difficult will be leaving the company of my friends. I've nothing else in life but them. And hope.

I don't know what lies ahead for me in this world. But I know Stormy waits for me in the next, and that knowledge makes this world less dark than otherwise it would be.

In spite of everything, I've chosen life. Now, on with it.

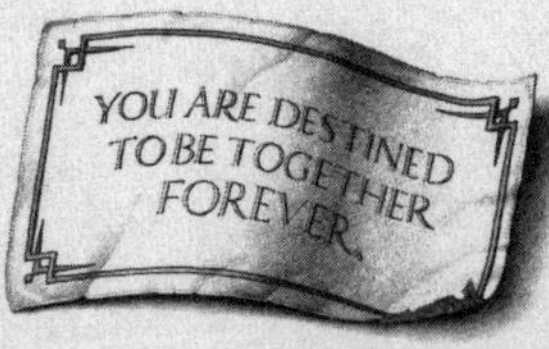
YOU ARE DESTINED
TO BE TOGETHER
FOREVER.

AUTHOR'S NOTE

The Panamint Indians of the Shoshoni–Comanche family do not operate a casino in California. If they had owned the Panamint Resort and Spa, no catastrophe would have befallen it, and I would not have had a story.

—DK

ABOUT THE AUTHOR

DEAN KOONTZ is the author of many No.1 *New York Times* bestsellers. He lives with his wife, Gerda, and their dog, Trixie, in southern California.

Correspondence for the author should be addressed to:

Dean Koontz
P.O. Box 9529
Newport Beach, California 92658,
USA